ONTARIO

ONONDAGAS

ONEIDAS

MOHAWKS

CAYUGAS

e People of the
Long-House "

SUSQUEHANNA RIVER

Marsh
Creek Hollow

The
Great Falling Waters
of the Genesee.

INDIAN CAPTIVE:
The Story of
MARY JEMISON

Mary Jemison's Journey from Marsh Creek Hollow to Fort Duquesne was taken on foot; from the Ohio River to Genishau, by canoe, on horse~back & on foot. [See Foreword]

LAKE

Fort Niagara

Buffalo Cr.

SENEC

Geni

LAKE ERIE

Genishau

The Three Falls

Presque Isle

Fort Venango

Fort Duquesne

Allegheny R.

RIVER OHIO

Seneca Town

Monongahela River

The Allegheny

Fort McCord

Mary Jemison lived also in another Ohio River Indian village one hundred miles farther south.

INDIAN CAPTIVE:
The Story of
MARY JEMISON

Written and Illustrated by
LOIS LENSKI

HarperTrophy
A Division of HarperCollinsPublishers

25577

For
R. W. G. Vail

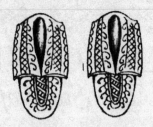

Indian Captive
The Story of Mary Jemison
Copyright 1941 by Lois Lenski
Copyright renewed 1969 by Lois Lenski Covey

LC Number 41-51956
ISBN 0-397-30072-7 —ISBN 0-397-30076-X (lib. bdg.)
ISBN 0-06-446162-9 (pbk.)
First Harper Trophy edition, 1995.

INTRODUCTION

Any work concerning the life and romance of Indian days requires a rather accurate knowledge of what these native people produced and how they lived. To weave a narrative of any consequence, the author must be familiar with the implements, utensils and the daily routine of the people. This seems self-evident but many writers have ignored this basic necessity and written purely from imagination, filling in the gaps with pre-conceived knowledge or basing it upon modern adaptations of European practices.

It is refreshing, therefore, to find an author whose initial work had gone so faithfully into the ethnology of the people of which she writes. Her detailed studies of the Indian way of looking at things and her painstaking effort to find out the exact type of implements, utensils and methods of producing them, reflect in her descriptions. This makes satisfying reading to the expert as well as to the average reader for the narrative then becomes convincing because it is based upon accurate knowledge.

The career of Mary Jemison, the White Captive of the Genesee, has been the subject of several books and many papers and addresses. Many efforts to describe her life and Indian background have lacked the very essential things which Miss Lenski has introduced. Not only did Miss Lenski make a study of the literature but visited the Indians, many of whom are descendants of the subject of her book. She carefully examined many Indian drawings and discussed with Gaoyaih, one of the skilled Indian artists, the material of which various features in his drawings and paintings were made. Her studies in the various museums containing Iroquois and especially Seneca objects culminated in a very exact understanding of how the people forming the background of her story lived.

Not only is the text interesting but her drawings are of such delightful quality that they will add a vast amount of interest to this work which she issues under title "Indian Captive." In them she has caught the spirit of ancient days. The attitudes of the individual figures and the facial expressions are characteristic and most pleasing.

—Arthur C. Parker

Director, Rochester Museum of Arts
and Sciences, Rochester, N. Y.

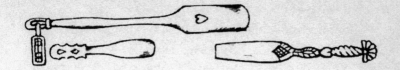

CONTENTS

FOREWORD

In the early days of the settlement of America, children were frequently captured by the Indians. Sometimes the captivity was of short duration and they were returned to their families. Some of them have left written accounts of their experiences. An interesting fact, revealed by a careful study of the subject, is that many children did not return, some by reason of their own choice. Well-known examples of children who did not return are Eunice Williams, Esther Wheelwright, Horatio Jones, Frances Slocum and Mary Jemison. The three latter lived their entire lives with the Indians, refusing various opportunities to return to the whites.

The story of Mary Jemison is one of the most interesting of all captivity stories, perhaps because we have a more complete record of it than of any other. At the age of eighty years, she told her memories of her experiences in detail to James Everett Seaver, M. D., and the book was first published at Canandaigua, N. Y., in 1824. It has been issued in some thirty editions, the last as late as 1932. Mary Jemison's story is remarkable in that it gives us a picture of Seneca Indian life from the inside, told in simplicity and sympathy.

Mary Jemison was born of Scotch-Irish parents, Thomas and Jane Erwin Jemison, on board ship during their emigration to this country, probably in the year 1743. She had two older brothers, John and Thomas, and an older sister, Betsey; also two younger brothers, Matthew and Robert, born in this country. The family landed in Philadelphia, then removed to a large tract of land on Marsh Creek in Adams County, Pennsylvania, where they lived for seven or eight years. With the exception of the two oldest boys who escaped, they were all captured by the Indians on April 5, 1758. All except Mary were massacred by the Indians the day following.

Mary Jemison, who was called the White Woman of the Genesee, *lived all her life with the Seneca tribe of the Iroquois Indians, in the western part of what is now New York State. She married two Indian husbands and had her own farm and home on Gardeau Flats, just below the Portage Falls on the Genesee River. When she died, in 1833, at the age of nearly ninety-one years, she was buried in the Seneca churchyard at South Buffalo, and later re-buried at Letchworth Park in her beloved Genesee Valley. Mary Jemison was loved, honored and respected by both red men and white and many of her descendants still live on the Indian reservations in western New York.*

My story, "Indian Captive," presents an interesting theme—the conflict between Indian and white life. Every effort has been made to present an authentic and sympathetic background of Seneca Indian life, as lived in the Genesee River Valley in the years 1758-60. It is the time of the French and Indian War, when the French and the English were competing for help from the Iroquois Indians, in order to stop the onrush of colonists westward. But the fact that the frontier was a dangerous place to live did not hold the pioneers back, and so the ground work for the Revolutionary War was rapidly laid.

The pre-Revolutionary period in Iroquois life was a transition period. The old Indian ways were being replaced by new ways for which the white man was responsible. The white traders brought iron and steel implements to replace primitive stone ones; cloth to replace deerskin; brass kettles for earthen pots; glass beads for porcupine quills; guns and powder for bows and arrows; log cabins to replace bark long houses. All these things changed the Indians' mode of living materially and marked the beginning of a new era.

For a long period the old and the new overlapped. There is no doubt that at this time and even later the Iroquois Indians still clung to many old customs and ways of working, although they were gradually adjusting themselves to the new. I have tried to suggest this transition, emphasizing at the same time those older ways which we have come to think of as typical of the Iroquois—those older ways which distinguish the Iroquois from other Indian tribes found in other parts of the United States.

My story deals only with Mary Jemison's childhood—not her later life. Certain liberties have, of necessity, been taken with Mary's own story, to adapt it to fictional use for modern young people, but the essential facts remain true to Mary's actual experiences. The chief change made has been a telescoping of events in point of time. Certain events which happened later have been moved forward to take place during the first two years of her captivity, before her early marriage. The Indian baby in my story is her Indian sister's, not her own. A few details from other captivity stories have been incorporated, to give a better-rounded picture.

Before she went to Genishau, Mary actually spent four years in southern Ohio; her winters near the mouth of the Scioto River, and her summers in two Ohio River Indian villages—the first at "Seneca Town" or Mingo Town, located about three miles below the present Steubenville, and the second, called Wiishto, at the mouth of Swan Creek, sixteen miles below the present Gallipolis.

The actual journey which Mary took from Wiishto to Genishau (which I have not described in my story) covered over 680 miles, and followed a devious route by way of the Muskingum River and its western branch to Upper Sandusky, Ohio, then by Indian trails eastward across the northern part of Ohio to French Creek, Franklin, Pa., then northward to Warren, Pa., Caneadea, N. Y. and Genishau, which was located on the Genesee River near the mouth of Little Beard's Creek, not far from the present Cuylerville.

There is some difference of opinion as to whether Mary's actual age at the time of her capture was twelve or fifteen. I have chosen to keep her twelve. She was known to be small for her age and has been described by those who saw her as "a small woman, only four and a half feet in height." Her In-

dian name was Deh-ge-wa-nus, *which meant, literally,* The-Two-Falling-Voices.

A privately printed book, dealing with reminiscences of family life in western New York State, prior to 1815, mentions the Indian captive, Molly *Jemison. In this particular family, for several generations, Mary Jemison was always called* Molly. *This would indicate that the nickname was commonly used in the vicinity where she lived and that it clung to her to the end of her life and long after her death. For this reason I have chosen to make use of the more intimate form of the name, Mary, and have called her Molly.*

The designs used on title-page and cover are typical motifs taken from Seneca embroideries. The flower design on the cover is called "the celestial tree."

Over six thousand acres of land covering the section around the Portage Falls on the Genesee River fifty miles south of Rochester are now known as Letchworth State Park. Here, due to the interest and foresight of the late William Pryor Letchworth, have been assembled an old Indian council house which formerly stood at Caneadea, the log cabin of one of Mary Jemison's daughters, and a bronze statue representing Mary as a young woman, over her burial place. It is easy to understand why Mary came to love this beautiful valley and why, to those who know her story and go on pilgrimage there, her spirit still lingers "by the Great Falling Waters."

For generous help in the preparation of this book I am deeply indebted to: Mr. Elrick B. Davis of the Cleveland

Press *for his initial suggestion; Mr. R. W. G. Vail, New York State Librarian, for first bringing the story of Mary Jemison to my attention, and for constant help and encouragement; to Dr. Arthur C. Parker, Director of the Rochester Museum of Arts and Sciences, and Dr. Clark Wissler, Curator of the American Museum of Natural History, for their helpful interest in reading the book in manuscript and checking it, as well as my illustrations, for accuracy; to Prof. Wm. P. Alexander, Buffalo Museum of Science, for checking portions of the manuscript dealing with wild animal life for accuracy; to Mr. Noah T. Clarke, New York State Archeologist, and Miss Bella Weitzner, Assistant Curator of Anthropology of the American Museum of Natural History for checking details; to Mr. Milton L. Bernstein for the loan of several early print views of the Portage Falls; to Maud Hart Lovelace, Beatrice de Lima Meyers, Miriam Elizabeth Bass, G. W. Walker and others for helpful suggestions.*

A careful study of Seneca Indian material was made at the American Museum of Natural History, the Rochester Museum of Arts and Sciences, the Museum of the American Indian at New York and the New York State Museum at Albany. I wish also to thank the Buffalo Museum of Arts and Sciences for its generous loan of pictorial material.

Lois Lenski

Greenacres
Harwinton, Connecticut
April 4, 1941

I *Come What May*

M
olly-child, now supper's done, go fetch Neighbor Dixon's horse."

Molly looked up at her father. At the far end of the long table he stood. He was lean, lanky and raw-boned. Great knotty fists hung at the ends of his long, thin arms. His eyes looked kind though his face was stern.

"All I need is another horse for a day or two," the man went on. "Neighbor Dixon said I could borrow his. I'll get that south field plowed tomorrow and seeded to corn."

"Yes, Pa!" answered Molly. She reached for a piece of corn-pone from the plate. She munched it contentedly. How good it tasted!

Corn! All their life was bound up with corn. Corn and work. Work to grow the corn, to protect it and care for it, to fight for it, to harvest it and stow it away at last for winter's food. So it was always, so it would be always to the end of time. How could they live without corn?

The Jemison family sat around the supper table. Its rough-hewn slabs, uncovered by cloth, shone soft-worn and shiny clean. A large earthen bowl, but a short time before filled with boiled and cut-up meat, sat empty in the center. Beside it, a plate with the leftover pieces of corn-pone.

"You hear me?" asked Thomas Jemison again. "You ain't dreamin'?"

The two older boys, John and Tom, threw meaningful looks at their sister, but said no word. Betsey, tall, slender fifteen-year-old, glanced sideways at their mother.

Molly colored slightly and came swiftly back from dreaming. "Yes, Pa!" she said, obediently. She reached for another piece of corn-pone.

Inside, she felt a deep content. Spring was here again. The sun-warmed, plowed earth would feel good to her bare feet. She saw round, pale yellow grains of seed-corn dropping from her hand into the furrow. She saw her long, thin arms waving to keep the crows and blackbirds off—the fight had begun. The wind blew her long loose hair about her face and the warm sun kissed her cheeks. Spring had come again.

"Can't one of the boys go?" asked Mrs. Jemison. "Dark's a-comin' on and the trail's through the woods . . ."

"Have ye forgot the chores?" Thomas Jemison turned to his wife and spoke fretfully. "There's the stock wants tendin'—they need fodder to chomp on through the night. And the milkin' not even started. Sun's got nigh two hours to go 'fore dark. Reckon that's time enough for a gal to go a mile and back."

"But it's the woods trail . . ." began Mrs. Jemison anxiously. "'Tain't safe at night-time . . ."

"Then she can sleep to Dixon's and be back by sun-up," said the girl's father, glancing sternly in Molly's direction. He sat down on a stool before the fireplace and began to shell corn into the wooden dye-tub.

"Mary Jemison, do you hear me?" he thundered.

"Yes, Pa!" said Molly again. But she did not move. She sat still, munching corn-pone.

Jane Jemison said no more. Instead, she looked down at her hands folded in her lap. Her hands so seldom at rest. She was a small, tired-looking woman, baffled by both work and worry. Eight years of life in a frontier settlement in eastern Pennsylvania had taken away her fresh youth and had aged her beyond her years.

Little Matthew, a boy of three, climbed into his mother's lap. She caught the brown head close to her breast for a moment, then put him hastily down as a wailing cry came to her ears. The baby in the homemade cradle beside her had wakened. The woman stopped wearily, picked him up, then sat down to nurse him.

"Ye'll have to wash up, Betsey," she said.

Molly's thought had traveled far, but she hadn't herself had time to move. She was still sitting bolt upright on the three-legged stool when her ears picked up the roll of a horse's hoofs.

Nor was she the only one. The others heard, too. As if in answer to an expected signal, the faces turned inquiring and all eyes found the door. All ears strained for a call of greeting, but none came. In less time than it takes for three words to be said, the door burst open and a man stumbled in.

It was Neighbor Wheelock. He was short and heavy. Like Thomas Jemison, he too had the knotty look of a hard worker, of a frontier fighter. It was only in his face that weakness showed.

Wheelock gave no glance at woman or children. He said in a low but distinct voice to Thomas: "You heard what's happened?"

The clatter of a falling stool shook the silence and a cry of fear escaped. Betsey, white-faced and thin, clapped her hands over her mouth. Mrs. Jemison, the nursing baby still at her breast, stood up. "Let's hear what 'tis," she said, calmly.

Chet Wheelock needed no invitation to speak. The words popped out of his mouth like bullets from a loaded gun.

"It's the Injuns again!" he cried, fiercely. "They've burnt Ned Haskins out and took his wife and children captive. They've murdered the whole Johnson family. They're a-headin' down Conewago Creek towards Sharp's Run, a-killin', a-butcherin' and a-plunderin' as they come. There ain't a safe spot this side of Philadelphy. I'm headin' back east and I'm takin' my brother Jonas's family with me."

4

Thomas Jemison looked up from his corn shelling, but his placid face gave no hint of troubled thoughts. A gust of wind nipped round the house and blew the thick plank door shut with a bang. The children stared, wide-eyed. Jane Jemison sat down on a stool, as if the load of her baby had grown too heavy and there was no more strength left in her arms.

"What are we a-goin' to do, Thomas?" she asked, weakly.

"Do?" cried Thomas. "Why, plant our corn, I reckon."

"You won't be needin' corn, neighbor." Chet Wheelock spoke slowly, then he added, his eyes full serious: "You ain't aimin' to come along with us then?"

Thomas Jemison rose to his feet. He thumped his big doubled-up fist on the table—his heavy fist that looked like a gnarled knot in an old oak tree. "We're stayin' right here!" he said.

"But, Thomas, if Chet says the Indians're headin' this way . . ." began Jane.

Thomas stood up, tall and gaunt. He laughed loudly.

"I ain't afeard of Injuns!" he cried. "I've lived here for eight years and I ain't been molested yet. There's been Injuns in these parts ever since we first set foot in this clearing. We've heard tell of so many raids, so much plunderin'—I don't put much stock in them tales. No . . . I don't give up easy, not me!"

John and Tom, the two boys, laughed too. "Who's

afeard of Injuns? Let 'em come!" they cried in boastful tones.

Jane put the baby down quickly in its cradle. She caught her husband desperately by the arm.

"Don't you hear, Thomas? Chet says they've murdered the whole Johnson family . . . We can't live here with Indians on all sides . . . devourin' the settlement. Forget the corn . . ."

"We're stayin' here, I said!" repeated Thomas. "Come what may, I'll plant my corn tomorrow!" His voice rang hard, like the blow of a blacksmith's hammer against the anvil.

In the silence that followed, Jane's hand fell from her husband's arm. Molly ran to her mother's side and put both arms about her waist.

Thomas's voice went on: "As soon as the troops start operations, the Injuns'll run fast enough. They'll agree to a treaty of peace mighty quick. Then our troubles will all be over. We've stuck it out this long, we may as well stay for another season. Leave a good farm like this? Not yet I won't! I'll plant my corn tomorrow!" His words were cocksure and defiant, but they brought no comfort to his listeners.

The baby began to cry and Neighbor Wheelock went out. In a moment he was back, addressing Mrs. Jemison.

"I brought my sister-in-law and her three children along with me, ma'am. Her husband, my brother Jonas, is with the troops and I'm takin' her back east. She won't stay in the settlement longer. Our horse was half-sick before we started and can't go no farther. Can ye give us lodgin', ma'am, for a day or two, to git rested up?"

None of the Jemison family had looked out or seen the woman. She stood by the horse, waiting patiently, with a boy of nine beside her and two small girls in her arms. Mrs. Jemison hurried out to bid her welcome, calling back to Betsey to put the pot on to boil.

"Boys, the chores!" called Thomas. Then he added, "Go fetch Neighbor Dixon's horse, Molly-child, like I told you."

Molly and her father walked out the door together. Despite his stern ways and blustering words, he had a great affection for his children and Molly was his favorite. He put his great, knotty hand on her head and rumpled her tousled yellow hair.

"Pa . . ." Molly hesitated, then went on: "Ain't you ever afeard like Ma?"

"Why should I be afeard?" laughed her father. "There's nothin' to be scared of. The Injuns'll never hurt *you*, Molly-child! Why, if they ever saw your pretty yaller hair, a-shinin' in the sun, they'd think 'twas only a corn-stalk in tassel and they'd pass you by for certain!"

Molly laughed. Then she turned her head and looked back—in through the open cabin door. She saw her mother and Betsey with Mrs. Wheelock and her little ones busying themselves in the big room. She saw the thick oak timber door, battened and sturdy. She knew it turned on stout, wooden hinges and was secured each night with heavy bars, braced with timbers from the floor. She wondered if, even then, it was strong enough to keep the Indians—the hated, wicked, dangerous Indians out.

Her blue jeans gown flew out behind her, as past the barnyard, on long, thin legs she ran. She passed Old Barney, her father's horse that had the devil in him and liked to kick, making a circle wide of his heels. She passed the grindstone and the well-sweep with the grape-vine rope. Then she ran the full length of the rail fence that bordered the field where the corn would soon be growing and rustling in the breeze. She flew past the bee-tree where, the autumn before, her brothers had caught the bear, his claws all sticky with honey.

Molly Jemison was small for her age. She looked more like a girl of ten than the twelve she really was. Her blue eyes shone bright from her sun-tanned skin and her hair was yellow—the pale, silvery yellow of ripened corn. She ran swiftly, her whole body swinging to the free and joyous motion.

Molly was glad to go to Neighbor Dixon's—anywhere, anywhere to get out of the house. There was always a load of anxiety there, reflected in her mother's face and her father's stern words. A load of worry which pressed down upon her naturally light spirits and brought sadness to her heart. This latest news of the Indians would only make things worse.

Then, too, there was always a fever of work in the house—so many things that had to be done. She wondered sometimes if her father and mother ever thought of anything else but work. It seemed to keep them busy from morn to night getting food and clothing for their large family. Had they no time for happiness?

Out-of-doors, Molly could get away from it all. She could forget there were such irksome duties as spinning and weaving, cooking and sewing; and worst of all doing sums and reading in books. Betsey could do these things. Betsey "took to them," as their mother said. She did not bungle as Molly did.

But out-of-doors Molly could watch the birds, the butterflies, and all the wild things. She could be one with them. She could pretend she was as wild, as free, as happy as they. When she had work to do out-of-doors she worked willingly enough. She thought now of the happy days to come—working in the corn, plowing, planting, weeding . . .

Molly ran on. Soon she was in the woods. She knew every inch of the trail, each stone, each stump, each tree. She ran fast and reached the Dixons' cabin before the slanting rays of the setting sun were blotted out by the trees.

* * * *

"'Tell her to make me a cambric shirt,
Without any seam or needlework.
Tell her to wash it in yonder well,
Where never spring-water nor rain ever fell.
Tell her to dry it on yonder thorn,
Which never bore blossom since Adam was born.'"

Molly's voice, thin and piping, broke through the quiet of the forest. Her heart sang, too, as her lips formed the words. The song was an old one of her mother's. Many songs her mother had used to sing. Why was it now she sang no more? Was it fear that had stopped her singing?

It was early the following morning and Molly was on

her way back from the Dixons'. The sun had not yet risen. In the woods, the light was dim and uncertain—the early light before dawn. The morning air smelled clean and freshly washed. The birds were awake, chirping and singing. A gentle breeze stirred, rustling the branches of tender green.

The trail wound in and out among rough, jagged tree stumps. The borrowed horse slowed down from a trot to a walk. His hoofs beat gently on the soft dirt trail. Molly bent her head, pressing her nose into the horse's mane, as an overhanging branch scraped her shoulders. She straightened her back again.

Then suddenly the horse stopped. He stood still, his whole body quivering. Molly's song died on her lips. Her face turned pale. She leaned forward and gave the horse a pat. The sharp, sweet tones of a bird song rang out through the quiet. A fallen branch crackled beneath the horse's feet, as he stirred nervously. Then all was still.

Underneath the oaks it was black and dark. Molly stared into the blackness. The trunks of many trees crowded close and seemed to press upon her. Was something moving there? Her breath came short, as her happiness faded away. The forest had changed from a world of beauty to a world of fear.

The girl glanced back quickly over her shoulder, as if a glimpse of the Dixon home, which she had so recently left, might give her comfort. Here, between the reality of the neighbor's log cabin and the unreality of the unknown

dark forest she paused, sensing danger. Here anything might happen. Here wild animals prowled, Indians hid, and evil lurked.

Molly went white about her lips. She turned her head and looked on all sides. She saw no movement, heard no sound. The sharp, strident bird song rang out again, piercing in its sweetness. Was it a note of warning or a word of comfort?

Then strangely, a vision of her home rose before the girl's eyes. She saw her tall, lanky father in the big kitchen with her mother—and her mother was scared as she had been last night, as she always was when there was talk of Indians. Molly pulled on the horse's bridle and urged him forward. Keeping her eyes on the trail ahead, she rode on, faster and faster, as fast as the trail would permit. She was fearful now—not for herself, but for her family. What if the Indians had come in her absence?

It was sun-up when she came out of the forest and entered the clearing. She circled the barnyard slowly, staring at the unchinked log out-buildings as if she had never seen them before. She saw her two older brothers grinding a knife at the grindstone; her father shaving an axe-helve at the side of the house. She rode up close to the cabin and bent her head to look in through the torn paper of the kitchen window. She let herself stiffly down on the door-log.

A scene of bright happiness confronted her. Everything was just as she had left it. Mrs. Wheelock was dressing her children in the corner. Her mother and Betsey were starting breakfast. Nothing had happened. The world was a beautiful place after all, and all her fears were groundless.

Neighbor Wheelock came out of the house, stamping on the door-log.

"There, gal! Let me have that horse!" he cried, taking the bridle from Molly's hand. "Mine's sick—no better this morning. Got to go back to my house to fetch a bag of grain I left there."

"Better wait till after breakfast, Chet!" called Molly's mother from within. Her voice sounded cheerful as if her fear were gone.

"I'll be back 'fore the corn-pone's browned on one side, Mis' Jemison," replied Wheelock, with a laugh.

"Take your gun along then," called Thomas from beside the cabin. "Might be you'd meet some of them Injuns you was a-tellin' us about. Might be they'd git a hankerin' for your scalp!"

"Don't know but I will . . ." Wheelock disappeared inside, then came out, gun in hand. "It's not the Injuns so much," he answered. "They ain't come this fur *yet*. But I might pick up a wild turkey for the women-folks to cook. With all this big family to feed, they'll need all the game they can get." He mounted the borrowed horse and rode away.

Molly entered the cabin and closed the door behind her.

The window paper, once slick with bear's grease, had split from drying. The morning sun came through the torn openings and brightened the dim interior. It rested on the tousled quilts on two large beds at the end of the room, on the great spinning-wheel and the small, on the home-made loom in the corner. It lingered on the somber homespun and soft deerskin clothing hung from wooden pegs in the wall. It made spotty patches on the uneven puncheon floor. It was traveling toward the fireplace where the corn-pone lay tilted up on a board. Soon the light of the sun would mingle with the shooting gleams of fire.

Molly stood motionless, watching. Then, out of the corner of her eye, she was suddenly conscious of her mother's actions. Time seemed to stand still as she waited. She saw her mother walk across the room, carrying a stack of wooden trenchers toward the slab table. She saw her mother open her lips, as if about to speak. She knew what she would say before the words came. She had heard them often enough before: "Stop your dreamin', Molly, and git to work!" But this time the words were never said.

The room was very quiet and the words were never said. For, through the stillness, a volley of shots rang out, and fear, turmoil and shock came that moment on all. Molly, still standing where she was, saw her mother drop the trenchers and snatch the baby from its cradle. She heard her mother's words: "God help us, they've come, just as Chet said!" She heard nine-year-old Davy Wheelock cry, "Indians! It's the Indians!" She saw Davy's mother sink limply in a chair, fainting, then rally and gather her children together and start a piteous wailing. She watched Betsey as the white-faced girl bent over the fire mechanically and turned the corn-pone, to keep it from burning. She watched it all, for her feet refused to move.

Then everything happened at once.

The door, the heavy battened oak door, built to keep the Indians out, opened to let them in. The morning sun shone on them, too, and made their skins shine like flashing copper. Above the noise and din which came with them, the baby's crying could be heard.

Out through the door, open now, Molly saw a scene she was never to forget. A man and horse lay dead beside the well-sweep. She wondered who it was. It couldn't be Neighbor Wheelock, who had gone laughing from the house so short a time ago. No, it couldn't be. He was safe, back at his house on Sharp's Run, fetching a bag of grain he'd left behind. He was far away, safe. There was not time

enough for him to go home and be back again so soon. But there, there on the ground, lay his coon-skin cap with the striped tail a-dangling. There at his side lay a horse—a horse of the same color as Neighbor Dixon's horse. Was it only this morning she rode him through the woods?

Molly covered her eyes so she should not see. But the sounds, these she could not shut out—the shouts and whoops of the Indians, the cries and moans of Mrs. Wheelock and her mother, of Betsey and the little ones. She wondered vaguely where her father was and where the boys had gone and why they did not come to help.

Then she saw her father's long rifle hanging on pegs above the fireplace. Had everybody forgotten it? She rushed over, climbed a stool and took it down. Some one must help. She would do it herself. Then, as quickly, a heavy hand was laid on her shoulder; the gun was jerked from her grasp and looking down, she saw that the corn-pone was burnt to a crisp.

The next moment she was in the bright sun, out in front of the cabin, weeping about the corn-pone which should have been their breakfast. They were all there with her, the two women and all the children. She turned away from the well-sweep and it was then that she saw her father. He was standing still, making not the slightest struggle, while two Indians bound him round with thongs. She wondered where the boys were. She looked toward the grindstone, but they were gone. Had they run away in time? She watched the Indians rush through the cabin, overturning chairs and tables, breaking and destroying; she saw them bring things out—bread, meal, and meat. Was this what was called plundering? Had the time, the dreaded time, of which she had heard so much, come at last?

They all stood together, huddled in a pack, waiting. Soon the Indians left the house and crowded round. The glaring, painted faces came up close and Molly's heart almost stopped beating. Though none but her father was bound, she realized now for the first time that they were prisoners. Then she saw that with the Indians there were white men, dressed in blue cloth with lace ruffles at their sleeves, speaking French in hurried tones. She counted. There were six Indians and four Frenchmen. Were the Frenchmen wicked, too, like the Indians?

What was going to happen next? What would their captors do with them all—this little band of women and children, and a man with arms tightly bound? Would they soon all be stretched out on the ground like Neighbor Wheelock? Or were the Indians making ready to be off with them?

Molly looked at her mother, but her face was so changed by grief and fear, she scarcely knew her. She looked at her father, who had so recently boasted there was nothing to be afraid of and she saw that he was afraid. With fear in her eyes and in her heart, she cried out weakly, "Ma . . . Pa . . ."

But they neither looked at her nor answered a word.

II   *The Long Journey*

"O h, where are they taking us?"

The words, an anxious cry, rose to Molly's lips, but no one there gave answer.

Words poured from the Frenchmen's lips in swift torrents, while they waved their hands and arms. The lace ruffles at their sleeves made changing patterns in the air, as they pointed up and down the valley. Indian voices now, deep-throated and guttural, were mixed with the Frenchmen's high-pitched, nasal tones. Over their shoulders, Frenchmen and Indians stared backward. Were they alarmed and anxious?

A decision arrived at, the command, *"Joggo!"*—"March on!" was given. The confusion of words faded away and heavy silence came down. Only the shuffle of moving feet—feet shod with hand-cobbled, cow-hide shoes, pressing the bare earth of the farmyard, and now and then the gulp of a stifled sob. Huddled together, tramping on each other's heels, like a flock of uncertain sheep, the frightened people walked.

Molly turned back her head and looked. For reasons known only to themselves, the Indians had not burned the house. There it stood just as always, homelike and inviting in the morning sun, with smoke still coming from the stick-and-mud chimney at one side. There stood the well-sweep, the grindstone, the corncrib. There stood the barn—behind those walls of log Old Barney, the cows and calves, the sheep—all left alive, alone, with none to feed or tend them.

Past the well-sweep the little crowd walked, past the log buildings, the bee-tree, the zigzag rail fence—the rail fence that bordered the corn field. Molly loved the corn best when the stalks were high above her head. She loved its gentle rustling, the soft words it spoke, as she walked between the rows, pulling the ears off one by one. She loved to feel the soft, warm earth ooze up between her naked toes. At the sharp memory of it all, she was seized with sudden pain.

"Oh, Pa!" she cried, but her mouth, so twisted and crooked now, was scarce able to form the words. "Oh, Pa! You said come what may, today you would plant your corn! The seed-corn was shelled and ready—the whole big dye-tub full. You said we'd stay and you'd plant your corn today. We must have corn to eat. We can't go away . . . like . . . this . . ."

But her father walked like a man in a dream and if he heard, he gave no sign. Outwardly he looked the same. He wore the same fringed deerskin hunting shirt and leggings, the same coon-skin cap upon his head. But his forceful, fiery, boastful spirit—that was gone.

"Hush, child!" said Mrs. Jemison. "'Tis best not to speak to your father now." She shifted the baby to the other arm and took Molly's hand in hers.

Molly stared over the rail fence and took one last look at the field that was not plowed, at the field that would not, despite a man's brave boasting, be planted to corn that day. Would it ever be plowed, she wondered? Would it ever be planted to corn? A grim foreboding seized her and she gripped her mother's hand the tighter.

No more words were said, for there was not time to speak. The Frenchmen and Indians divided themselves into two groups. One group went ahead of the prisoners, the other followed after. They seemed to have but one idea—speed. They went ahead and followed after, urging, pushing, rushing the little band forward, ever forward.

Perhaps they wanted to put many miles between themselves and Marsh Creek Hollow, where stood an empty cabin, with door a-gaping wide, with the smoke from a cooling chimney dying out to a lean, thin thread. Perhaps they feared that the restless horse in the barn or the helpless cows and sheep might cry out and tell the story of what had happened; might call to a handful of resolute neighbors to be up and follow after and avenge the wrong done there. Perhaps even, they had seen two boys drop a knife beside the grindstone, leap to their feet and run for help. Whatever the reason, on and on they pushed the little band.

A tall, gaunt Indian, straight as an arrow, led the way. Another, short and stocky, with bowed legs, walked behind, whip in hand. When the children lagged or stopped for a moment to draw breath, he lashed the whip around their legs. An old Indian followed still further in the rear. With a long staff he skillfully picked up all the grass and weeds broken down by the hurrying feet, to blot out all signs that along this way two families had so unwillingly passed. At first, Molly wondered where they were going. Not on any known trail, of that she was certain—not on the trail through the woods to Neighbor Dixon's, not on the Sharp's Run trail or any of the others. Below the clearing, they were herded along, wading through the waters of Conewago Creek, and down the bed of the stream for some distance. Then through a thicket and into an unknown meadow, heading west, with the morning sun full on their backs. Molly knew there were mountains to the westward and soon saw blue ranges ahead, looming high up on the sky-line.

After that, the girl neither knew nor cared where they went. All she knew was that they kept on moving, walking and running as fast as they could go, suffering sharp blows from the whip of Bow-Legs, with each attempt to snatch forbidden rest or ease the pain of too-quick breathing.

At first, hunger had pierced her and the thought of not having eaten since the night before seemed unbearable. Then hunger passed and with it all other sensations. There was only one thought now—to keep going, to keep going without pause or rest.

Betsey, who had been carrying three-year-old Matthew, suddenly dropped him. Heavier and heavier he had grown with each step until he fell from her tired arms. His short legs, sturdy enough at most times, were not equal to a flight like this. They wavered unsteadily, then the forward thrust of a Frenchman's leg threw the child headlong.

There was no one to catch him up but Molly—her mother already had one baby in her arms, her father's hands were bound and useless. Mrs. Wheelock and Davy had their two small girls to hustle along. There was no one to catch up little Matthew but Molly. She bent her back and with a wide curve of her arm, swooped him up. She pressed her chin into the warmth of his soft brown hair and held him close. By and by his sobs grew fainter and he slept on her heaving shoulder.

Long afterwards, there was one thing that Molly was to remember—the tender beauty of that fair spring morning on the Pennsylvania meadows—April 5, 1758. More than the terror of the Indians' war-whoop, more than the shock of sudden death and capture, the pain and suffering of rushing flight—or by very contrast with these horrors—the beauty of that April day stayed always with her. The beauty of that sweet April day, when all the buds were bursting, was shattered by what happened and cried out in protest against it.

All day long, the captives traveled without food or water, never stopping once to rest. Westward they moved, climbing up and down the hills, pushing their way through tangled brushwood and deep forest, splashing through brooks and streams. Night came at last when they could see and move no more.

In an open spot in the woods they fell down upon the ground, exhausted. Although the Indians carried food which they had taken from the Jemisons' own cabin, none was brought forth or offered. No fire was laid, no shelter built. There was only the ground, a hard and bitter resting-place, to give cold comfort. There they slept within a narrow circle surrounded by their ever-watchful captors.

Too soon, too soon did marching orders come again, before tired muscles had renewed themselves. Long before daylight the weary people were started on their way, hurrying as before. At sun-up a stop was made for breakfast. Packs were opened and bread and meat were passed around. Famished now, after a whole day's starving, the women and children ate.

Molly moved to a place beside her father's knee and held out a piece of bread. It was rye-and-injun bread, baked in the Dutch oven at home, bread that spoke, as she could not speak, of home. She held the bread to his lips— his bound hands could not hold it. But he turned his head away and would not eat. Silent despair engulfed him. He would not eat or speak. Did his boastful words of so short a time ago come back to taunt him now? Did he wish he had listened to Neighbor Wheelock's warning, to all the warnings that had come before?

So little time was taken for breakfast that by mid-morning Molly could scarce remember they had stopped at all. Hunger struck her with full force and she wondered if she had ever eaten and what their meal had been. Somehow the taste of food—her mother's wholesome, home-cooked food, was gone forever from her tongue. She took turns with Betsey, carrying little Matthew, until her arms, benumbed and aching, could carry him no more.

At noon, as the captives approached the nearest mountain, they saw a small fort nestling at its foot. But hopes of rescue died before they were born, when they saw the place deserted. The once-strong logs were sagging, the corner look-outs sunken and decayed. 'Twas then that Thomas Jemison spoke. "That might be Fort McCord," he said. "I heard tell the Indians took it a year or two ago." That was all. His lips were parched and dry. The sound of his voice was dull and lifeless and struck terror to Molly's heart.

Towards evening speed was slackened and again they came to a halt. Through thick overhanging branches, they followed their leaders into a cheerless swamp. Water oozed up as each foot pressed the grassy hummocks. Out from the moss-covered, black water, spikes of skunk cabbage poked their ghostly heads. It was not a place to camp, not a place to rest or sleep—oh, why should they stop here? But at the word of command, the tired people sat down.

Bread and meat were brought, but no woman or child reached out a hand. The food lay in a heap, untouched.

Suddenly Mrs. Jemison spoke and her voice had a spark of her old energy and spirit. "Children! We must eat the food that's set before us and thank God for the gift. There's no knowin' what we face tomorrow, but whatever 'tis, we need our strength. We mustn't lose heart—we must keep up courage. Now's the time to be brave. Give us bread, Molly, we will eat while we can."

The little ones stopped crying when bread was put into their mouths.

"Oh, Pa, won't you eat, too?" asked Molly.

She held bread, sweet, inviting bread up to his mouth, but again he would not eat or speak. He looked once at his daughter, but his eyes seemed not to see her.

When the food was gone, there was naught to do but keep on sitting there—sitting there in a little circle on the wet and soggy ground, leaning on each other for comfort and support.

They hadn't sat long when the old Indian shuffled up. He came to Molly, where she sat at her father's side. Bending over, he took off her shoes and stockings.

He handed her a pair of deerskin moccasins and pointed to her feet.

"Oh, Ma!" cried Molly, filled with fear and dismay. "Oh, Ma, what is he doing? *What are the moccasins for?*"

Then she saw little Davy Wheelock standing beside her—Davy Wheelock, wearing soft moccasins on his feet.

Silently Molly slipped one moccasin on, then the other.

"They're prettier than shoes," said Davy, shyly, almost proudly. "I like the pretty colors. And they feel soft. My feet was gittin' so tired, a-walkin' so far in my cow-hide boots. I like soft moccasins better, don't you, Molly?"

Before she had time to reply, Molly heard her mother speak. She heard her say the name *Mary*, which she used only on rare occasions.

"Mary, my child . . ." Her mother paused, as if to catch her breath. Molly turned to look at her. Above the full-gathered homespun gown, with snow-white kerchief and apron, she saw the deep blue of her eyes. She heard her mother speaking in hurried, breathless words, each word weighed down with pain. But under the pain was a kindness, a kindness so deep and

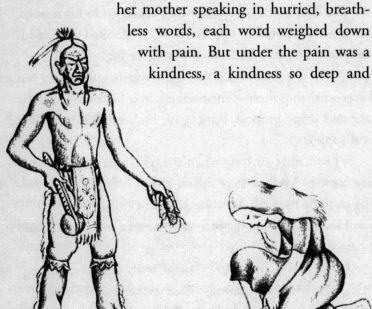

complete it pierced her heart. Molly was to remember those words of her mother's and how she looked when she said them, to the very end of her life.

"Mary, my child," her mother said, "the Indians are a-takin' you away from us . . . You and Davy . . . are a-goin' on with them . . . What's to become of the rest of us, only God knows—we are in His hand. It looks as if your life would be spared . . . but they're a-takin' you away from your family, from white people of your own kind, from everything you've ever known!

"I don't know where they'll take you, but no matter where it is, may God go with you! Make the best of things and be happy if you can. Don't try to run away from the Indians, Molly; don't try to git away and come back to us. They'd find you for certain and kill you . . . Oh, promise me you'll never try it . . .

"No matter where you are, Mary, my child, have courage, be brave! *It don't matter what happens, if you're only strong and have great courage.* Don't forget your own name or your father's and mother's. Don't forget to speak in English. Say your prayers and catechism to yourself each day the way I learned you—God will be listening. Say them again and again . . . don't forget, oh, don't forget! You're a-goin' now . . . God bless you, Mary, my child. God . . . go . . . with . . . you . . ."

The words fell like heavy blows on the girl's numb spirit. They fell so quickly, so unexpectedly, she could scarce comprehend their meaning. But her body, so straight and strong, went suddenly limp. Like a young tree bent well-nigh to breaking by the rush of a mighty storm, the girl trembled from head to foot, then recovered herself and stood up straight again.

She saw Davy standing in front of the old Indian and knew they were waiting for her to come. As she hurried to join them, the pain in her heart became so great she could not bear it and she burst into tears.

"Don't cry, Mary!" called her mother's voice behind her. "Be brave, my child, be brave! God bless you . . . farewell . . . farewell . . ."

Then Molly looked back at the little group through her tears. She had to look—how could she go off and leave them sitting there? She saw Mrs. Wheelock on her knees stretching straining arms to her boy Davy. She saw white-faced Betsey with the baby in her lap—and all the little ones. She saw her mother with a look of not fear or pain, but only kindness on her face; and she knew that her mother would save her from all she was to suffer if she could.

She saw her father—her father whom she loved so dearly. He seemed to come out of his stupor for a moment and to realize what was happening. He lifted his head and smiled at Molly, and words came again from his dry, parched lips: "The Injuns'll never hurt *you*, Molly-child! Why, when they see your pretty yaller hair a-shinin' in the sun, they'll think 'tis only a corn-stalk in tassel! They'll never hurt *you!* Remember that, Molly-child!"

Molly smiled back, thinking of the happy time when first he had said those words. Then, with her family's calls of sad farewell in her ears, she walked along with Davy and the old Indian and soon left them far behind.

It was a long time before the old Indian stopped. At last he found a comfortable camping-place and spread beds with soft hemlock boughs. Was he not cruel like the others? Was he trying to be kind? For the first time he spoke and his words were English. "Go sleep. No be scairt!" he said, pointing to the beds. Molly looked up into his eyes astonished.

All night long she kept her arm round little Davy's shoulder, while the Indian watched near by. The children said their prayers and cried together, then they talked awhile.

"Oh, Molly, he's fallen asleep now. Let's get up and run away. I want to go back to my mother," begged Davy.

"Ma said we'd only be killed if we tried it," answered Molly. "She said 'twas best to stay with the Indians."

"Let's go back to Marsh Creek Hollow then," said Davy. "My father will be there by now with the troops. He'll chase the Injuns away."

"Davy," Molly spoke slowly, "we could never travel in the wilderness without a path or guide. We'd die . . . we'd starve with no food to eat. If we stay, the Indians will feed us, I think . . ."

"But I can't walk on again tomorrow," protested Davy. "My feet are sore and bleeding."

"The nice soft moccasins will help," said Molly. "Yours are prettier than mine."

"Oh, won't I ever see my mother again?" cried Davy.

"The others may catch up with us in the morning," replied Molly, but she said it with a sinking heart, remembering her mother's farewell words.

"Molly, I don't want to go with the Indians, I'm afeard . . ." wailed Davy.

"Don't be afeard, Davy, don't be afeard!" said Molly.

She remembered how great was her mother's fear of the Indians before they came; and how, when they came, she met them with calm courage. Courage was better than fear, Molly said to herself. Courage helped not only yourself but others. She must have courage, not only for herself but for Davy. "Don't be afeard, Davy, I'm here with you." She urged him to lie still until morning and was relieved when at last the boy fell fast asleep.

The next morning there was no sun and fog patches were everywhere. The Frenchmen and Indians who had been left behind came up, and Molly and Davy saw that their families were no longer with them. What had become of them? They pressed questions on the pitiless Frenchmen, on the old Indian who had spoken the few words of English, but received no answer. After a breakfast of meat and bread, rain began to fall, but it did not stay their progress. The Indians led the two children on as fast as they could travel, still taking every precaution to conceal their trail.

At the end of the hard day's march through the pouring rain, night came and with night, rest. For the first
time, the Indians laid a good fire and built a shelter of
boughs. The children huddled close to warm their chilled,
shaking bodies and to dry out their dripping clothes.

The days passed one after the other until Molly Jemison lost count. Each was like the last in the haste, the in-
frequent stops, the hurried meals. With Straight Arrow
leading the way, the Frenchmen, the other Indians and the
children followed, walking single file in strictest silence,
moving fast but always with great caution. No hunting
was allowed, no gun was fired, no unnecessary noise was

made to betray their whereabouts. It was indeed a silent, ghostly passage. Behind the children Bow-Legs walked, whip in hand. His constant presence told Molly, as nothing else could, that the Indians were their masters and there was but one thing to do—obey.

The fog lifted, it grew colder and a light snow began to fall, but even that did not slow up their pace. Molly and Davy ran all the time to keep up. Davy seemed to grow stronger from the strenuous exertion, but it was not so easy for Molly.

Snow fell in earnest as they made their weary way over the mountains, climbing the steep heights and running down the abrupt slopes, wading rocky brooks and waist-deep streams. Nowhere was there any sign of a road. Molly wondered how the Indians found their way or whether they knew where they were going. She thought of tales she had heard of the dangers of crossing the great mountains to the westward and she knew she was crossing them herself on foot.

Her blue jeans gown caught on branches and brambles. Her bare legs were lashed and scratched by thorns. Her yellow hair hung tangled and uncombed. She remembered how long ago she had studied her reflection in the shining bottom of a tin pan at home. But now she gave no thought to her appearance. She forgot that people washed their faces and combed their hair. All she lived for was to push on, ever on—to sleep for a while and eat sometimes to gain strength to push on again.

Blinding snow drove in their eyes and the wind whipped their clothing tight about them. Molly knew they were in the heart of the mountains now—only at a great height could there be so much snow in April. Her strength fast failing, a vague hope upheld her—the hope of reaching the lower plains and somehow there to find warmth and rest.

At times she was conscious that someone was kind to her and it was always the old Indian. With their bare bodies and red-painted faces the others all looked alike, but the old one was different. Once when she fell, tripping on the string of her moccasin, he stopped, picked her up and tied the strings for her. Once when she could not rise from fatigue as the word to march was given, she saw the shadow of an arm uplifted, holding a tomahawk over her head.

At the moment she wished the blow would fall to end her misery. But when the old Indian quickly knocked the weapon from the hand and gave its owner a kick, she was strangely grateful. Although she did not realize it, his friendly smile was a constant encouragement and she thought of him as trusty and dependable, like a strong, straight tree—a shagbark hickory, the straightest in the forest—a tree to lean upon.

At last she could go no farther and it was the old Indian, Shagbark, who insisted upon rest. Though the others seemed unwilling, at his orders they stopped, and built a more permanent shelter. Shagbark wrapped the girl warmly in a blanket and while she slept, sat by and watched. There they stayed for three days and she rested and regained her strength. On the last day a deer was killed, dressed and roasted, and they all ate heartily.

Just as they left the shelter to resume their march, another party of Indians joined them—a raiding party like themselves, six Indians returning from the Pennsylvania frontier. They brought with them one white captive, a young man of twenty.

Molly stared at the newcomer and hope—the hope of escape returned. He was a full-grown man, he was strong, he could speak English, he would know how to help. Her

eager thoughts tumbled over themselves in anticipation. When they were left alone for a moment, she questioned him. But the young man sat dejected, and exhausted from the weight of the heavy burden on his back. He looked up at her with blank eyes and did not answer. And Molly knew that he was more in need of help than she; that only she could help him.

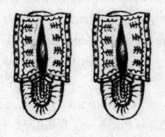

III   *Fort Duquesne*

"Oh, Molly, are we never going to stop walking?" asked Davy, looking down at his feet. The once bright-colored embroidery on his moccasins was faded now and covered with mud.

"I wish I knew," said Molly sadly. "I feel as if we've been walking all our lives . . . But see how tough our feet have grown!"

"Why did they make us run so fast?" asked Davy.

"They were afeard of being followed, I think," replied Molly. "Like as not they knew there were white men on our trail. Like as not John and Tom ran to Neighbor Dixon and he gathered the neighbors from Marsh Creek Hollow together . . ."

"Oh, why didn't they come to save us?" wailed Davy.

"They couldn't catch up," answered Molly slowly, "we . . . went . . . so fast . . ."

She stole a glance at the young man captive, whose coming had brought back her hope. If only she could rouse him . . . He talked a little now, as they walked down the mountain side. He said his name was Nicholas Porter and he came from Piney Mountain near Shippen's Town, only a few miles as the crow flies from Marsh Creek Hollow.

He told how one morning his mother wanted squirrel for pot-pie. He insisted that squirrel pot-pie, made by his mother, was the best dish in the land. He told how he went out hunting to take a few squirrels for pot-pie and how he'd been caught like a squirrel himself, by hunters stronger than he. He kept on talking about the squirrel pot-pie that his mother would never make again and he himself would never, never eat. He told the tale so often that Molly wearied of it. If only he could forget his suffering—there were more important things to think of. If only he could fasten his mind on the idea of escape . . .

All the time now the slopes went downward, as the highest mountains were left behind. Though the party moved at more moderate pace and no attempt was made to conceal the trail, they rarely paused or stopped. A day came when the hills behind were but a blue haze in the distance and they walked across a wooded plain.

At the brink of a steep hill they halted to gaze on a wandering stream below—but only for a moment. Down the rough, precipitous trail they plunged to the red clay shore of Turtle Creek. The current was strong and the waters were high from recent springtime freshets, but not even an angry stream could hold them back. The Indians brought out a bark canoe which they found concealed near the shore and the creek was crossed in safety. Another climb up the steep hill opposite, and the party came out on the plain again, following in single file the trail that skirted the shore of the Allegheny River.

One day in mid-afternoon they saw ahead across the flat river bottoms a large log stockade. To Molly the sight was welcome. She wondered what fort it was. Eagerly she watched the lips of Frenchmen and Indians, hoping to catch its name. Then she heard it—two words she had heard before on the lips of the white trader, Old Fallenash. There, before her, on the point of land between the arms of two great rivers, the Allegheny and the Monongahela, touched by the afternoon sun, lay Fort Duquesne. This, she knew, was the fort which the French had built only a few years before, when they claimed for their own the whole vast territory drained by the River Ohio.

Fort Duquesne! Fort Duquesne! What fate did it hold in store for Molly Jemison, the white girl captive brought over the mountains from Marsh Creek Hollow? She shaded her eyes with her hand to keep out the sun and stared at the uninviting, harsh, gray walls. At the corners, the garrison-houses loomed up, emblems of strength and terror, making bold, stark patterns against the blue April sky.

"It's Fort Duquesne we've come to," Molly whispered to Davy Wheelock. Davy stood beside her, wearing the same brown-checked home-spun garments, torn and shabby now, that he wore when snatched from his

mother's side. She gripped his hand tightly in her own. "If there's any help coming, we'll find it here," and she began to tremble at the prospect.

At the end of the village the Indians halted and Molly, too, was obliged to stop, restraining her impatience.

She stood there in the pathway, looking hard at the fort which she knew held for her either freedom or captivity. Dirty, disheveled, browned by exposure, with her clothing torn to shreds, she shifted from one tired foot to the other, as she stared at the fort. The setting sun picked up glints of light in her tousled yellow hair and shone into her eyes to blind them. She tried to read a message in the

41

cold, hard stockade walls, but they gave no hint of their secret.

Then she saw that the time to enter had not yet come and she must wait. Preparations of some kind were being made by the Indians, so she sat down, doubling her knees beneath her and watched.

The Indians laid a fire and gathered wood to pile upon it. A pole was raised near by, tomahawks were struck into it, and a string of wampum—a belt of beads with design of sacred meaning—was hung at the top. The twelve Indians stood about the fire, smoking peacefully, while the Frenchmen and the three captives waited. The smoke signal seen, an Indian messenger soon advanced from the village. Seeing the peaceful intent of the newcomers, he bade them welcome and the ceremony was concluded, but still the party was not ready to advance.

The old Indian, Shagbark, friendly as before, approached Davy and Nicholas and motioned them to sit down. He brought out a crude bone comb from his pack and painstakingly combed their blond hair. He combed out briars and tangles, then shaved their heads clean except for a strip from forehead to neck, which he dressed in Seneca fashion.

Molly's hair he left hanging loose and free about her shoulders, a shower of shining gold. Then he mixed paint in a shallow stone mortar and with the cloth-covered end of a stick dauber painted broad streaks of red across the captives' faces.

Molly put up her hands and hid her face in shame. Then she looked at Davy and Nicholas, scarce recognizing them. A strange picture the three captives made—a young man, a half-grown girl, a little boy—their white, white faces streaked with red. What did it mean? What was going to happen? Were they being prepared for something worse?

"All we need now is black hair!" said Davy, bitterly.

"And black hearts!" added Nicholas, with a flash of insight.

"They can change our faces," said Molly, "but our hearts they cannot change." She looked down at the red paint which had rubbed off on her hands, and the tears rose to her eyes.

They stopped for a moment upon

the banks opposite the stockade gate for further parley and the captives watched the two mighty rivers as they flowed into one. There it lay, the great divided river, shining bright and peaceful in the sun. On all the shores the hills were lined with forests—forest trees in the first full burst of tender green. At the river's edge, the trees grew downward, reflected in the mirror of the silent, peaceful waters.

"The French call it the River Beautiful," said Nicholas Porter. "O—hi—o! River Beautiful!"

"It *is* beautiful!" exclaimed Molly, watching it thoughtfully. "But how do you know?"

"'*La Belle Riviere,*'" Nicholas repeated to her surprise. "I heard them say it in French."

"Do you understand French?" asked Molly.

"A little," replied Nicholas, falling into silence again.

The Indians came to take them into the fort. The walls grew taller as Molly approached. They grew taller and more unfriendly, until she felt they would fall and crush her. For one wild moment she wanted to rush away—anywhere, back to the wilderness, anywhere to get away. She would live in the forest, eat of its roots and berries, be a friend to the wild beasts. Her thought that moment sprang to action and quickly her feet obeyed. Before her masters suspected her intention, away she rushed from their grasp. Round the corner like a whirlwind she dashed on flying feet that scarcely touched the ground.

But her escape was only a vain hope, for stronger pursuers followed close. She felt the jerk of a cruel hand that threw her prostrate and the lash of a stinging whip about her legs. With wild tears falling and body shaking, she was dragged back to the spot from which she had run. There, still standing motionless, Davy and Nicholas welcomed her back with eyes that spoke pity.

Then Molly found herself walking across the drawbridge. Inside the log stockade there was a deep ditch and on its banks thick walls of squared logs and earth rose up. Store-houses, dwellings and barracks built of logs lined the side walls between the tall garrison look-outs. A six-sided stone building stood in one corner. The buildings were bustling with people and a babble of men's voices, speaking in French, could be heard. All these things Molly scarcely noticed as she entered the fort enclosure, but other things she did.

Certain things, certain little things she saw and always remembered long afterward when Fort Duquesne had faded to a dim and uncertain memory. An outdoor bake-oven and several well-sweeps stood before the row of doorways. A boy carried a pailful of water across the yard. Near a corner, from a log building, two cows put out their heads, mooing contentedly. A Frenchman went whistling past the door, carrying hay on a wooden pitchfork. Beside the barn was a tiny garden where plants and fruit trees grew in rows. One of the trees was a peach tree and because it was April, the tree was in blossom.

Molly's homesick heart gave a leap as she saw it. Silhouetted against the deep blue of the sky, the beauty of the pink blossoms overwhelmed her. There had been a peach tree long ago beside the log cabin at home, a peach tree that stood so close you could touch the blossoms from the doorstep. She stared at the blossoming tree in the fort yard. She could only stare at it—stare at it so hard she would never forget it. She had no time to touch a pink blossom now, to smell its delicate fragrance. Impulsively she reached out her hand—and saw red paint upon it. She turned quickly, for the sight of it filled her with horror.

Important-looking French soldiers and Indian chiefs in full regalia bustled out of the largest cabin to meet the arriving band. Words passed and the three captives were hustled indoors without delay. They were taken down a damp hatchway into the cellar of one of the garrisons. Bread was brought, the door was closed and locked, and they were left alone.

All night long the captives sat on a hard wooden bench, staring into darkness. They dared not sleep for fear they might be wanted for some unknown purpose. They talked a little, to cheer each other with the comfort of human words. For a time they were hopeful and dreamed of freedom—the happy thought of walking out of the fort without their masters—the thought of home and family, food and comforts. Then they wondered what they could do with freedom if they had it—where could they go if they were free? To the westward and on all sides lay an unexplored wilderness. To the eastward, behind them, were the mountains which they had just crossed. They knew—

sane reason told them—they could not go back alone, defenseless, following unknown trails, surrounded by wild beasts. So hope died within them.

Back to their tired minds came thronging all the stories they had heard of Indian punishments and tortures, and they wondered if they'd been brought thus far to suffer such a fate. After a time, Davy began to cry for his mother and Nicholas to talk of his hunting trip. With a heavy heart, Molly took a hand of each in hers and cheered them as well as she could.

Morning came at last. The door opened and their Indian masters entered, beckoning Davy Wheelock and Nicholas Porter to come out with them. Obediently they rose and followed.

Molly walked behind them as far as the hatchway door and watched. She saw that the two boys were turned over to a group of strange blue-coated Frenchmen—Frenchmen like the others who wore lace ruffles on their sleeves. Little Davy looked up inquiring, but Nicholas walked as in a daze.

Their backs turned toward her, without a sign or gesture, Molly watched them go, never guessing it was for the last time she had looked upon their faces. Those dear friends who had suffered with her and looked to her for comfort—if she had known, could she have let them go? But they never knew it was a parting, nor did she, till they had passed without the gate. Then she ran back to the wooden bench, buried her face in her hands and fell sobbing to the ground.

Alone she lay there, but for how long she neither knew nor cared. The loss of her companions seemed unbearable and yet she knew that she must bear it.

She prayed to God for strength and guidance on the long, dark path that lay before her. She repeated to herself her mother's last words and admonitions and after a while she dropped asleep.

She wakened to hear the sound of whispered voices. Looking up, she saw two figures at the door—women's figures, bunched in clothing; the first women she had seen since she parted from her mother. The light behind them threw dark shadows on their faces and the words they spoke were strange. They stood a while, looking at her keenly, talking to themselves. Then they came closer and she saw that their faces were not white faces but Indian.

The women walked toed-in, bent forward, with shuffling gait. No white woman ever did that. They wore buckskin leggings like men and embroidered moccasins on their feet. No white woman, even in the wilderness, did that. O for the sight of a full-gathered homespun gown with snow-white kerchief and apron! O for the sight of blue eyes of a white woman, eyes of pity and love in a white woman's face. Would she never see that again?

The faces that came so close and peered so keenly were not white—they were Indian. The eyes that looked out were not blue but brown—dark brown, and they showed neither pity nor love, only cold appraisal. The two women lifted the girl from the ground, set her for a moment upon the bench, then bade her rise. She stood still and let them examine her. Why should she care what happened now? Like a frontier farmer looking over a horse or cow he meant to buy, so they looked her over. Were they about to buy her too? They noted her strength of limb and body, the toughness of her muscles, the firmness of her skin. They pinched her cheeks, they looked into her mouth and counted her even white teeth. They kept nodding their heads with approval, smiling shyly and making low soft sounds.

They seemed to be pleased. But the thing that pleased them most was Molly's hair—her pale yellow, shining hair, the color of ripened corn. They took it in their hands; they blew upon it and tried to braid it; they let it rest like corn-silk soft upon their palms. They looked at it as if they had never seen such hair before.

After a while they went out, returning again in a moment. This time Molly's Indian masters entered with them. The morning sun made a streak of light down through the hatchway door—a bright patch in the darkness. The air was filled with words, soft, deep-throated Indian words, spoken with care and deliberation. When the old Indian, Molly's friend on the journey, spoke, the others listened with respect. Were they making a bargain? What were they talking about?

Soon it was over. Then they all went up the steps and out once more to sunshine. They walked out from the fort enclosure. But before the great log gate swung to behind them, Molly caught one glimpse of the blossoming peach tree, the tree that had bloomed for her. She saw it standing not where it really was, but close beside the door at home.

Then she was out on the river banks and she saw two bark canoes drawn up close to shore. Her former masters, the old Indian with them, took their places in the larger canoe; the two women and Molly in the smaller. Not till then did the girl realize that she had changed masters. It had been a bargain. She belonged no more to the men who had brought her over the mountain, but to the women in whose canoe she rode.

The paddles made soft, gentle sounds as they were lifted up and down, the small canoe following in the wake of the larger. Behind, the gray, cold stockade walls of Fort Duquesne grew smaller and smaller, till the fort was only a dark spot in the distance and that, too, faded away. Ahead lay the wide expanse of shining water, the great River Ohio, the River Beautiful.

Where were they taking her?

Molly sat up straight and tense. She grasped the sides of the canoe with her hands. She lifted her chin and looked ahead. For, through her terror, she heard her mother's voice, saying: "Have courage, Molly, my child, be brave! It don't matter what happens if you're only strong and have great courage."

IV   *Seneca Town*

*T*he River Ohio was fair to look upon that day. So fine and broad it was, so quiet and peaceful, it gave no hint of storm or perilous wave. Molly's eyes saw it, but her mind took nothing of it in.

From the heavily wooded banks great sycamore trees, ghostly white, stretched giant arms across the water. Beneath, dimmed by flickering shadows, the tall, straight trunks of hickory, oak and walnut rose to touch the sky, topped by a canopy of twisting vine and pointed leaf—the wild fox grape. Long, thin branches of pale yellow willows drooped to the waters along the shore. Over all lay a heavy solitude, untouched by signs of human life.

Once at the mouth of a river branch, smoke from an Indian village a short distance inland could be seen; but nothing more, except now and then the cry or movement of creatures of the wild. Sometimes a slippery muskrat swam out of the hole in a floating log and sat up to look at the passers-by. Sometimes a green-frog croaked. Once a blue jay darted out from the leafy shore, a flying flash of sharpest blue, and passed so close that Molly might have touched it. But she did not see it for her pain.

The course was crooked and winding for the stream had many bends and at various points, tributaries poured in. Now and then a green island rose up in the middle to cut the broad river in two. The current was strong and a contrary wind blew up, but the Indians with careful paddling kept their canoes in the course.

After a time Molly raised her eyes and looked at the Indian women as their strong arms rose and fell. They were both young and sturdy, and were dressed in deerskin garments, richly embroidered. They looked enough alike to be sisters and yet there was a great difference between them. Molly sensed it at once. One was plain, the other beautiful to look upon. One was cross, the other kind.

They both wore strings of beads about their necks, silver ear-rings in their ears and silver bracelets on their arms. Their hair was dressed alike, parted in the middle with a streak of bright red painted on the part, and fastened behind in single braids, doubled back upon themselves and tied. The kind sister had a smooth, soft face. Her cheeks glowed like blushing apples, with a redness that obviously came from a smooth stain of red paint. The plain sister's face had more lines in it, lines either of age or ill nature.

At midday, the plain sister brought food from her pack.

"Oh! I'm so hungry!" cried Molly. Her tongue found words for the first time. Impulsively she put out her hand.

The plain sister frowned, divided the food with her sister, but offered none to Molly. The kind sister took pity and handed the girl a piece of meat, only to have the cross one strike out with her fist and knock it from Molly's hand. Over the side of the canoe it fell with a splash and went floating down the stream. With a burst of words the kind sister scolded, then gave Molly a better piece.

Soon after midday Molly curled up and dozed, soothed by the gentle motion and the grateful warmth of the afternoon sun. She was vaguely conscious that the cross sister was scowling and would have wakened her, had not the kind sister kept close watch. At last she fell asleep and forgot them both. She slept on undisturbed—the sleep of fatigue and exhaustion—and when she awoke, felt refreshed.

It was late afternoon when the Indians beached their canoes on the north shore at the mouth of a small creek. The hills, so close before, had now receded inland, and on either side of the creek's mouth the land lay low and un-wooded, river bottoms covered with rich, black soil. The Indians, the six men and two women, made fast their ca-noes at once. They tried to explain something by word and gesture, then quickly made their way inland.

Molly was left alone, still sitting on the floor of the ca-noe. The place was very quiet—only the gentle lapping of water over stones could be heard; in a tree close by, the twitter of birds and in the creek's shallow water, a chorus of noisy spring peepers. Molly saw smoke rising from beyond the low bushes and she wondered if they had come to an Indian village. An Indian village! A white girl captive in an Indian village! Would she have to live as the Indians lived?

The two women soon returned, chuckling under their breath, the kind one smiling broadly. Over her arm she carried a girl's suit of deerskin clothing, soft, clean and new. The skirt was made in an oblong piece, to be folded round the waist, lapped over and belted in. The tunic slipped over the head, had fringes down the sides and a pattern of porcupine quill embroidery round the neck. Ankle-length leggings and a pair of new moccasins completed the outfit.

Molly looked at the new clothes as the women held them out. Her blue jeans gown, whole and good when she had started on her long journey, was torn now to rags. There was scarcely enough of it left to cover her. She must have something to wear.

The women laid a fire and put water on to heat in an earthen pot which they had brought along. When the water was warm, they threw in a handful of herbs and stirred it well. Then they undressed Molly and gave her a good scrubbing. The touch of the warm water felt soothing and pleasant. It was good to be clean again.

First the leggings were pulled on over the poor

scratched legs. Then a twist of the deerskin about her waist and the skirt hung down over her knees. A thrust of her head through the slit in the tunic and the Indian clothes were on. They were on before she knew it—before she was ready to put them on. At her feet she saw the little pile of homespun clothing which she had worn on the journey, the clothes her mother had spun for her and woven and sewed. They were only a pile of rags now, but they were all that was left to her of home. As she looked, the cross Indian woman picked them up and trotted off, walking briskly toward the river's edge.

"Don't! Oh, don't!" cried Molly, dashing after her. "Oh, don't throw away my clothes!"

She knew now what they were doing. They were taking away her homespun clothing and putting deerskin upon her. They were making an Indian out of a white girl. She made up her mind she would never, never let them. Her feet ran fast, but not fast enough. For when they reached the shore, the little pile of ragged clothing was floating down the stream. The last thing, the only tie that bound her to her home, was gone. She had nothing now to wear but Indian clothing. She fell down upon the ground and sobbed as if her heart would break.

The cross Indian woman pulled a switch from a tree, but the kind sister snatched it from her and broke it to bits. The two women stood at a distance and watched, but did not try to stop the girl's wild crying. Waiting till the sobs came fainter, they picked her up and washed her face

again. They combed her yellow hair, braiding it in two long braids, then beckoned her to come.

The cross sister, clumsy and stout, walked first; the kind one, slender and graceful, next. They started off on a deep-worn trail through the thick, brambly bushes beside the creek. Molly saw that they meant for her to follow. She walked behind them, dressed in soft deerskin clothing like an Indian—she who was no Indian—down the deep-worn trail. What could she do but follow on with them?

They came to the Indian village, Seneca Town. A group of scattered lodges stood in an open meadow, but Molly took no notice of them. The women entered a long house and she followed close behind. They bade her be seated in the middle of the hard dirt floor, so down she sat. She hated the sight of the deerskin clothing. She closed her eyes so she would not have to see it.

Time passed. Then suddenly she was aware that the room was filled with women—Indian women, young and old, fat and thin, sour-looking and pleasant—and all were looking at her. They had come in so quietly, she had not heard them and it was a shock to find them there. They crowded close, pointing with their fingers, patting her on the back and making queer sounds in their teeth.

Then they turned away from her and began to wring their hands and weep. One woman, larger and more commanding than the others, recited chanting words at length, half-speaking, half-singing, while the rest gave strict attention. Whatever she was saying, her words brought forth tears of sadness and gestures of deepest grief.

Molly sat on the floor motionless. She could not move for terror, expecting at any moment that punishment would fall. She must be guilty of some wrong, but of what she knew not—only the wrong of being a white girl, white among the Indians. The women waved their arms more wildly, made stranger and more queer sounds. Molly sank down close to the floor, praying each moment for strength, awaiting the blows that never came.

Not till long after did she understand what they were doing, did she know that the occasion had been a ceremony. She learned that they were mourning the loss of a young Indian, their son and brother, who had been killed on the Pennsylvania frontier. It was because of his death which had occurred during the year previous, that the two women had gone up to Fort Duquesne to receive there either a live prisoner or an enemy's scalp. It was the ancient custom of the tribe, a religious duty to fill the place of the one who was lost, and it was Molly Jemison's lot to be brought back for this purpose.

After a time their grief subsided and they rejoiced to remember that their brother had gone to the Happy Hunting Grounds above the sky. And so they turned to Molly, to welcome her in his place. They gave every expression of joy as they adopted this new sister into the Seneca tribe of the Iroquois. In Indian words they chanted:

"Our sister has come—
Then let us receive her with joy!
She is handsome and pleasant—
Our sister—gladly we welcome her here.
In the place of our brother she stands in our tribe,
With care, we will guard her from trouble;
Oh, may she be happy
Till her spirit shall leave us!"

As they sang, all traces of sadness disappeared. Tears were dried and smiles bloomed on every face. The women crowded round the white girl, rejoicing over her as over a lost child found again. They touched her white skin, they stared into her blue eyes, they caressed her soft, silky hair. It was her hair that pleased them most. It made them think of blooming corn-stalks, of soft, fresh corn-silk, of pale yellow ripened corn—the dearest things in life. So when they gave her a name, there was only one that they could think of. They called her *Corn Tassel* that day and for many a long day thereafter.

But Molly did not know. She did not know the meaning of the ceremony, their kindness of intention or the name that they had given. All she knew was that the time of frightening terror had somehow passed and now for reasons that she did not understand, the women once more were friendly. Could their friendliness be trusted or should she be on guard? She thought again of all the things that white people said of the Indians—the hated,

wicked, dangerous Indians—she trembled to think she
was alone and helpless in their hands. She covered her eyes
and shivered. Their too-friendly smiles were like grimaces
and made her feel the more distrustful.

The crowd of women went away and Molly was left
alone with the two sisters who had brought her there. After a time they went out the door of the long house and
started across the meadow. Unbidden, she followed in
their tracks. She had learned that where they went she
must follow, for now she belonged to them. As she walked
across the meadow, her curiosity was stirred. She had

never been in an Indian village before, so she looked to see what it was like.

The village sat on the banks of the small creek, and bark canoes were lined up on the shore. It sprawled at the edge of the forest, for, like soldiers guarding, tall trees of maple, ash, poplar and beech loomed up behind. Between the village and the great river were fields of rich black earth, cleared of underbrush, all worked and ready for planting.

The Indian long houses were built on pole frameworks, with sides and roofs covered with great sheets of elm bark. Some were of great length, with rows of holes in the roof, from which streams of smoke poured forth. Here and there were smaller houses built of squared-up logs. All the buildings stood about haphazard around a central open space. Open platforms for storing hides and meat loomed up close by; and piles of firewood lay before the doorways. The whole scene had a bleak and cheerless aspect and Molly's heart grew faint.

The two women came to a lodge at the edge of the village. Over the door hung the carved head of a deer, to show that all within belonged to the Deer clan.

The women pushed aside the deerskin flap and went in. Close at their heels followed Molly and at once the flap fell down behind her.

It was dark inside and for a moment she could not see. The room was filled with smoke, for the wind was blowing it down through the hole in the roof. Molly coughed and rubbed her smarting eyes.

Then she looked up and saw a woman, an older woman, poking at the fire, stirring it up to give it a better draught and make it burn more brightly. She saw that the fire was built in the middle of the floor and not in a fireplace. It was built on the hard dirt floor and the hole in the roof overhead was the chimney. She had never seen such a funny way of building a fire before and it almost made her laugh. No wonder the room was full of smoke! Had the Indians never heard of a chimney made out of sticks and mud?

The woman took a great wooden spoon with a curved handle and dipped something from an earthen pot that sat by the fire. With a broad smile on her face, she dipped it out all steaming and piping hot and put it in a dish. Molly stared as she did it. No, it was not a pewter dish, not a wooden trencher—it was a round-bottomed wooden bowl.

The smell of the food that was cooking made Molly feel suddenly faint. She remembered the piece of meat on the river voyage, but that was long ago. She pressed her hand on her stomach, to ease the pain of her hunger. Then, somehow, she was sitting on the floor—there were no stools to sit on, no benches even, no crooked puncheon boards. There was no place to sit but on the hard dirt floor, on a piece of skin stretched out.

The woman placed the bowl of food in Molly's lap. Molly touched the side of it with her hand and comfort-

ingly warm it felt. She picked up the wooden spoon and dipped it. What was it, corn or meat, or both? Slowly she sipped and slowly began to taste. She held the spoon in the air for a minute while she swallowed. Then carefully back in the bowl she placed it and did not lift it again. The food, whatever it was, was queer and tasteless. Was it only because her mother had not cooked it? Would nothing ever taste good again?

She set the bowl down on the ground at her side, hoping no one would notice. She must not hurt the woman's feelings, the woman who had smiled so broadly while she filled up the bowl. Then Molly saw that the room was full of people and all were looking at her. But she could not eat. She covered her face with her hands.

The cross sister, whom she had not seen since they entered, snatched up the wooden bowl hastily, and as she did so, spilled its contents on the ground. Several dogs came running and quickly ate it up. Taking no notice, the older woman, who seemed to be the mother of the two sisters, went back to the pot and, smiling as before, filled another bowl to the brim. She handed it out to Molly, but Molly could only shake her head. She wasn't hungry any more.

She looked at the other Indians standing about the room. She saw the kind sister talking to a tall, older man, perhaps her father. She saw women, two or three with babies strapped to their backs, and children crowding round. A young boy pushed out from behind, an Indian boy of eight or nine, about the size of Davy Wheelock. They all stared at her and though there were smiles on their faces, her heart began to beat in fear.

They talked in noisy tones and while they talked, she looked at the curious room. It was a long, open hallway, with gabled roof above and a double row of bunks lining the sides. The hallway was divided into compartments and a fire was burning in the middle of the floor of each. Did all the crowding people live in the rooms beyond? Molly looked at the bunks on the sides—the lower but two feet off the floor, the upper high under the roof. Bark barrels stood on the upper platforms and hanging about were bundles of herbs, dried pumpkins and squashes and hanks of dried tobacco. But, most important of all, Molly saw endless rows of corn hung along the roof-poles above— long rows of pale yellow corn braided together and hung up to dry. Up there, under the darkened roof, the corn glowed like warm sunshine, and she could not help but re- member. Along the beams at home, above the fireplace, Pa hung his corn to dry. Oh, would she ever again help him to hang it there?

The crowding people talked in noisy tones. Molly wondered if the words could possibly have meaning or were only a mixed-up jumble of queer sounds. The people stared at her and kept on talking. They pointed to her hair and sometimes touched it with their hands. Then, after a while they seemed to forget she was there, but still they kept on talking. The noise grew fainter as if it came from far away. At last, Molly forgot where she was as, worn out with fatigue, she lost herself in sleep.

Sometime later, half-awake, she realized that she was being carried. For a moment, she felt her father's strong arms about her, lifting her up to his shoulder and carrying her into the house. Then she saw it was not her father. It was the old Indian, Shagbark, carrying her over the mountain on the journey that had no end. No—she rubbed her eyes again—it was neither. She was not at home, she was not on the mountain. She was in an Indian lodge for the first time in her life.

The Indian woman, the woman with the kind and beautiful face, had picked her up from the ground and was lifting her into a bunk. The brown eyes looked down at her tenderly as she smoothed the bed and covered her up. Tired, oh, so tired, Molly gave one grateful glance, then closed her eyes and under the soft, soft deerskins, fell fast asleep.

V   *Lost in Sorrow*

Molly was sitting beside her mother. They were spinning flax together and the whirring of their wheels made a gentle, pleasant hum. Molly was to have a new gown as soon as the cloth was woven, a new summer gown of soft, cool linen. Her mother had promised to color it yellow with the bark of sassafras.

Ka-doom! Ka-doom! Ka-doom! The sound of heavy blows repeated in quick succession came to Molly's ears. She rubbed her eyes and turned over. She drew the covers close under her chin and slept again. Pa said the new gown should match the color of her hair . . .

The booming sounds broke through her sleep. She lifted her head and listened. Then she remembered. It was only a dream. Molly would never sit at her mother's side and spin again. She would never wear a linen gown colored yellow with the bark of sassafras, colored yellow to match her hair. She was in an Indian bed; she had slept in an Indian lodge. She turned her face to the wall and cried.

Ka-doom! Ka-doom! What was the dreadful noise? Why did it never stop? What were the Indians going to do? She wondered if morning had come.

Molly looked about her. There was little light to see by, for the bed was closed in on all sides. At the edge hung long curtains of buffalo robe. At head and foot were slab bark walls. Overhead, she could touch the bottom of the upper platform which was made of slats laced together. Molly's eyes grew accustomed to the darkness. On shelves across the foot wall and hanging over her head she saw a curious lot of things—quilled bark boxes, piles and bundles of valuables and clothing. The bed had belonged to some Indian before her.

The booming noise went on and the girl became more and more frightened. Then she heard a sniffling sound and felt a movement at her side. The curtains stirred. Was some one coming to wake her up? Would a brown hand push in rudely and take her by the shoulder? She was ready to scream . . . No—it was only a small white dog. He poked a cold nose to her face. He jumped up and licked her cheek. Was he, too, hungry for affection? Molly put her arm about his neck, as he snuggled down beside her. He was one of the dogs who had eaten her supper last night. She was glad she gave it to him—he seemed to like it so much.

The booming noise went on, but nothing seemed to happen. What were the Indians doing? Molly pushed a corner of the curtain aside and peeped out. The bunks across the room seemed empty, but in one someone was still sleeping. Someone was sleeping under a heap of skins and blankets, with the deerskin curtain pushed back. On the wall above hung bows and arrows, tomahawks, war clubs, pipes for tobacco, belts and pouches. It must be the woman's husband. Was that where he kept his things?

Molly looked up through the hole in the roof and saw a patch of blue sky that told her it was morning. Her eyes followed the light as it streaked down through the dim interior. It fell on the bent figure of an Indian man. He was on his knees, brushing away the ashes, preparing to lay a fire. Carefully with his hands he scooped out a pile of earth, making a hole in the middle of the circle of stones. Over the hole he laid thin, dry twigs, arranging them in neat order.

Then he picked up a fire-drill and rested the lower point of the shaft upon a block of dry wood. He pulled the bow against the drill several times and got a spark started. He blew it to a flame and fed it with thin strips of bark. In a moment the fire was ablaze and, after adding some larger sticks, the man went into the adjoining room.

Molly saw the Indian woman come in—the older woman of the night before—with a load of wood upon her back. She put the wood on the ground and fed the fire as it burned more brightly. She brought water and poured it into the large earthen pot which sat on the stones at one side.

Molly looked down along the length of the bark house. The other families were stirring, too. Other fires were being made and children and grown-ups were tumbling out of their bunks. Molly shrank back into her corner, not daring to move or speak, not knowing what to do. How could she get up and be one with this Indian family? How could she eat their uninviting food? How could she talk when she knew not a word of their language? How could she bear the rude stares of all the people? How could she live in a place where everything was strange?

Suddenly the Indian woman gave a call and threw a handful of bones to the ground. The dog that was so friendly leaped from Molly's arms and jumped down. He ran to the woman and eagerly snapped at the bones.

The woman turned to the bunk. Her sharp eyes had seen the dog jump out. She saw Molly's scared face peeping, so she came over and pushed the curtain back. Without a smile or a word she beckoned the girl to get up.

Slowly Molly obeyed. She put her feet to the ground and drew on her moccasins. She stepped out from behind the curtains ready-dressed, wearing the Indian clothing they had put on her the day before. The woman threw the curtain onto the upper platform and spread the deerskin coverings out to air. With scared eyes Molly watched her, not knowing what to do. Uncertainly she stood, shifting from one foot to the other.

She heard the man's loud snoring from the bunk against the wall. She heard the booming sounds that never, never stopped. She heard the sounds of voices coming from the adjoining rooms. She thought of early morning at home and she wondered if the Indians had a wash basin. Did they never wash their faces? Never comb their hair and put on fresh, clean clothing? Did they always sleep in their clothes at night?

A wailing cry from somewhere behind gave her a start. Swiftly she turned to look. A flat board was hanging by a strap to the bunk pole. On the board a brown Indian baby was fastened with wide bands of embroidered cloth. Its hands were covered up and only its head could be seen. The sharp memory of her baby brother came to Molly and quickly she turned away.

The woman threw a log on the fire. She pointed out the door and said a few low words. The deerskin flap was fastened back. Molly stepped out into the sun. The air felt clean and cool after the smell of smoke within. *Ka-doom! Ka-doom!* The booming noise was near at hand. Molly looked to see what it was.

Beside the lodge door the two sisters were pounding corn. In front of all the lodges roundabout, Indian women were pounding corn and the booming sounds made a low, deep chorus. In oaken logs hollowed out to form deep holes or mortars, they pounded corn with heavy wooden pounders. The grains of corn had been boiled in lye water to loosen the hulls, then sifted and dried. Now they lay on the round bottoms of the mortars and were pounded until they were ground into meal.

It made Molly think of the corn at home. Long ago her father had rigged up a mortar, with a pestle attached to the end of a bent-over sapling. The swinging branch

73

helped to lift the heavy pestle up and down. But they had not used it for long. After Ned Haskins started his mill on Conewago Creek, it was easier to pile the bags of corn on Old Barney's back and ride thirty miles to mill to have it ground. Yes, it had been a long time since Molly had seen corn ground to meal in a mortar.

Up and down, swirling round, up and down the pounders went. Molly watched in fascination. The booming sound was a pleasant tune now in her ears, as she watched the meal being ground finer and finer. The plain sister was the first to lay down her pounder. She brought out a long, wooden mixing-trough and a sieve basket. She set them down on the ground beside her mortar. Then she brought water in a bark water vessel.

"Oh, corn-pone!" exclaimed Molly, clapping her hands. "You're going to make corn-pone—the way Ma makes it at home!"

The cross sister frowned at the girl as she heard her speak. Leaving her work, she took up a piece of fire wood and gesticulated. She pointed to the wood-pile which was getting low. She waved her arm toward a grove of trees behind the lodge. With a volley of scolding words she made Molly understand she wanted her to go to the grove and pick up wood.

Molly wanted to see the corn-meal mixed and made into cakes. She wanted, more than anything else in the world, to see cakes of yellow corn-pone lying tilted on a board in front of a fire, burning hot. The kind sister was still busily pounding. She did not once look up. Molly stood, uncertain, for a moment . . .

But a kick, a sturdy kick on the shins from the cross Indian woman, sent her flying off on the path to the woods. She held her hand down to the bruise to ease its pain. She must get wood and bring it back. Somehow she must find wood to burn, wood, wood, she must find wood. Unconsciously she repeated to herself the word in Indian. The woman had said it over so often, she could not forget its sound or meaning. The word for "wood" was the first Indian word that she learned and she learned it because of a kick.

In the thicket at the edge of the deep woods she looked about on all sides. She stumbled over dead branches lying on the ground, but never thought to pick them up. She had a vague idea that somewhere she would come on a neat pile of cord-wood, piled up the way Pa piled it at home. But what could she do if she found it? Four-foot logs would be too heavy to carry and she could not split or chop them shorter, without a hatchet or an ax.

Then she saw a patch of white on the ground in the distance. Eagerly she ran ahead, to find blood-root in full bloom! A patch of white blood-root blooming in the woods, as pretty a patch of blood-root as any in the woods at home. She fell on her knees before it, touched the white glowing petals with her hands, then buried her face in them.

It was there the kind sister found her and beckoned her to return.

"But I can't find wood! There is no wood!" cried Molly in distress.

The Indian woman shook her head and repeated the word in Indian. Then she stopped where the dead branches were lying and broke them up into short lengths. She worked fast and soon had a great pile ready. She passed a long strap of bark around a bundle of wood and laid it across Molly's back. She talked quietly in Indian words and somehow made Molly understand that when there was work to do, she must help. On her own back she bundled the rest of the wood and together they walked back to the lodge. The cross Indian woman was there waiting. Silently she looked on. When they put the wood down on the ground and pulled out the straps, it made a great pile.

"Here's your wood!" cried Molly, proudly. Surely now, no matter how cross she was, the woman would be pleased.

But she scolded again. The sound of the English word in Molly's mouth made her angry. Repeating the word in Indian, she cuffed Molly and gave her another kick.

Molly scarcely felt the blows. She was thinking of the corn-pone. Was she too late? Had she stayed too long in the woods, looking at the blood-root? Eagerly she ran into the lodge to the fireside, expecting to see the corn-pone lying tip-tilted on a board. Eagerly she sniffed to smell its rich crust browning. Then she started back in dismay, for there was nothing by the fireside, no board, no corn-pone, nothing.

Oh, what had they done with the meal, the soft,

crumbly meal? It wasn't long until she learned the answer to her question. With a round, flat, longhandled paddle the woman dipped into the pot that was boiling on the fire, as she had done the night before. She brought out several wet, dripping corn-cakes and placed them on a bark platter. She handed it out toward Molly.

Molly looked at the Indian women and children standing about and wished they would go away. Some held bowls in their hands and supped soup noisily. Others stood and stared at her. Did they eat whenever they pleased? Did they have no regular meals?

Molly took a cake and held it in her hand. It was an inch thick and about six inches across. But the cake had been boiled in water—it wasn't corn-pone at all! Dry, crisp, crunchy corn-pone, with a sweet brown crust that was good to bite upon. Would she never taste that again? Molly looked at the wet cake in her hand. She lifted it to her lips, she sniffed it with her nose, but again, she could not eat. Down she threw it into the fire and, sullen and defiant, watched it burn.

A look of horror went round the circle. The Indian women stared at each other and spoke in shocked voices. Although Molly did not know it, she had violated an old tradition. Corn must be treated with respect. Corn must never be burned. It must be eaten, not wasted. No person may abuse a gift of the Three Sisters. Molly saw the women's angry looks and trembled. She knew she had done a dreadful thing.

79

The little white dog came near and wagged his tail. Molly took him into her lap. She put her arms about him and buried her face in his shaggy fur.

The older woman's anger passed. With her large ladle, she dipped into the steaming pot and filled a small bowl with the soup, the liquor in which the cakes had been boiled. She handed the bowl to Molly. But the girl shook her head in angry refusal. How could she eat their terrible food?

Raising her eyes, Molly noticed that the man who had been sleeping in the bunk against the wall, was up. Very straight and tall he stood on the other side of the fire. She wondered if he had come for food or whether he had had his breakfast. His nose was long, his forehead high, his mouth wide. His eyes were bright and piercing. As she studied him Molly was struck with his noble appearance. She had not known before an Indian could look so fine, so wise, so good. As he walked across the room his gaze met Molly's and somehow she felt ashamed. He said no word but his clear eyes told her he disapproved of her bad behavior and expected better things. Then he went out the door.

The moment he was gone, Molly pushed the dog off her lap. She stumbled to her feet and picked up a wooden bowl. She held it out to the woman, who filled it up with soup. The soup had no taste, but Molly ate it to the last drop.

She took a corn-cake from the platter. The corn-cake, like the soup, was made without salt and had no taste. The corn-cake was wet and soggy, but Molly knew now that she was hungry and greedily she ate. Smiling, the Indian woman watched her.

But the morning had only begun. As soon as Molly's meal was over, the cross Indian sister came up. She handed Molly a bark water vessel and pointed to a spring at the edge of the woods. Water had to be carried each day for cooking, washing and drinking. A white girl captive was useful for chores such as these.

"Water! Water!" said the woman, in Indian. "Go fill the vessel with water and bring it back!"

Molly hurried off toward the spring. She found the water bubbling out from under a pile of rocks at the base of a low hill. Stooping down she filled the vessel, then set it on the ground.

Suddenly she was tired, too tired to carry the water back to the lodge. She walked a little way into the woods, found a fallen log and sat down. She knew she mustn't stay. The cross sister would come and find her, kick her and take her back. Off she started into the woods, where the trees grew larger and the shade was deeper. She would go away where the woman could not find her. She could never live with the Indians. Everything there was hateful. She would never go back to the lodge again.

Aimlessly she pushed through the rough undergrowth, not knowing or caring which way she went. It made her think of the mountain journey. Trees, bushes and branches barred her path on all sides. The bushes were full of thorns. Their rough branches tore at her hands and arms. They were trying to hold her back. It was no use—no use to try. She was tired, too tired to push through any further. She had never been or felt really rested after the long mountain journey. She dropped to the ground dejected.

Now she knew. She knew why her mother had begged her not to try to come back. She knew why Indian captives, especially women and children, stayed and lived with the Indians, why they never went back to their homes again. The forest was a cruel enemy. The forest was no place for traveling. The forest kept her from going home. She leaned against a tree and cried.

It was very quiet except for the movement and chirping of birds, but Molly did not hear. She sat there for a long time, lost in sorrow. The memories of her parents, her brothers and sisters and the log cabin home pressed down in pain upon her. The tears came and sobs shook her forlorn little figure.

Through the stillness, a strange noise came singing like a flash. A sharp whizzing sound of swift movement passed over. Molly glanced up to see a bush stir beyond her, then hid her face again. Moments passed, then came the regular beat of quiet footsteps. Nearer they came and nearer. When they stopped, Molly knew that some one was watching and a queer feeling went through her. Would it be the kind sister come to help? Or the cross one to punish and take her back again? She trembled from head to foot, not daring to look up. She listened. Whoever it was, they seemed to be only standing and looking. Whoever it was, they came no nearer.

Slowly Molly raised her swollen, tear-stained face. No, it was neither of the two Indian sisters—it was only an Indian boy. It was the same boy she had seen in the crowd about the fire when she arrived the night before. He had soft brown eyes and they made her think of Davy Wheelock.

She stared at him from head to foot. He wore deerskin leggings and waist-cloth, but his broad, brown shoulders were bare. His black hair hung loose to his shoulders. His forehead was low and his eyes were narrow. He had a quiver of arrows strapped on his back and he held a bow in his hand. He looked at Molly sympathetically. Then he pointed to his bow, making motions as if to ask where his arrow went.

Molly rose from her seat and looked beyond the tree where she was sitting. In a moment she had found the arrow beside the bush and brought it back. She held it in her hand and looked at it. A shaft of red willow it was, with a sharp bone point and red feathers fastened on at the end. She handed it back to the Indian boy and saw a broad smile spread over his face.

She sat down again disconsolately. She leaned against the tree and the tears began to come. He was only an Indian boy. He was the same size as Davy Wheelock, but his skin was red and his words were Indian. She listened as he spoke. He pointed to his bow and arrow and seemed to be

talking about them, but the words, to Molly, sounded harsh, strange and meaningless.

Then a sturdy red hand found her own and gave it a tug. The Indian boy, with swift determination, pulled the girl to her feet. He pointed out the direction and started off. Slowly Molly lifted her feet to follow. He was taking her back to the Indian village and she didn't want to go. He kept just a step ahead, turning now and again to make sure that she was coming. Each time he turned, he smiled a smile of encouragement.

She hadn't gone far at all. By the path that the Indian boy took, it was only a short way back to the village. The deep forest was left behind and the two came into the thicket. There at the edge was the spring and the water vessel where Molly had left it.

The boy flung himself down on the ground, made a

cup of his hands under the dripping water and drank. Then he motioned to Molly and she did the same. How good the spring water tasted! She was thirsty and had not known it. She washed her face in the water and it felt fresh and cooling.

The boy pointed to the filled water vessel and, obediently, Molly took it up. The water was heavy, but he did not offer to help. He walked on ahead and once more she followed at his heels. Soon they were back at the lodge. Molly set the vessel down and watched the boy, as he ran off toward his home. She watched to see which lodge he entered. She saw him stop beside the door, turn and smile, then disappear from sight.

With a deep sigh, Molly picked up the vessel of water and walked slowly into the lodge.

VI   *A Singing Bird*

"Tell her . . . to make me . . . a cambric shirt,
Without any seams . . . or needlework . . .
Tell her . . . to wash it . . . in yonder well . . .
Where never spring water . . . nor rain ever fell . . ."

Little Turtle, the Indian boy, heard the faltering words and hurried faster. The new captive girl was singing. She was singing a strange song of the white people. She must be happy today. She had put her sorrow aside at last.

It had not taken Little Turtle long to find out that when the white girl was sent to bring water from the spring daily she ran off to the forest, sat under the walnut tree and cried for hours. He wondered that Squirrel Woman and Shining Star allowed it. Every day he expected to see Squirrel Woman, cross and ugly, march out and with kicks and blows fetch the girl home. But she did not come. Perhaps she knew as he did that the white girl's sorrow must wear itself out. There was no hurry. As each moon passed, her unhappiness would fade. There were many moons to come. But in the meantime he did what he could.

Day by day he followed Corn Tassel to the woods, and when she had dried her tears, took her by the hand and coaxed her home. Day by day he talked to her patiently in the Seneca language, pointing out objects and repeating their Indian names over and over, in the hope that some day she could speak to him in reply. Surely if she could speak his language she would feel happier in her new home.

Today she was singing. But the sadness, as he came nearer, wrung his heart. The words were happy words—he could tell that by the sound—but the voice that sang was still filled with pain. Corn Tassel! Her name was as beautiful as her hair! If only she could be happy!

Suddenly the song broke off in the middle. Molly looked up. Little Turtle held out a silver brooch. He smiled expectantly. Surely a piece of shining silver cut in delicate design would please any woman or girl-child. "Here! This is for you!" he said.

But Molly did not so much as look at it. She rose to her feet and instead of waiting as usual for him to go first, she ran back to the village as fast as she could go.

With the silver brooch still in his hand, Little Turtle stared after her, shaking his head. He wished he understood her better. If only she could speak in Indian . . . Deep in thought, he watched her as she ran, then started swiftly in pursuit.

As he approached the lodges, he heard a buzz of excitement. A hunting party which had been out for a short trip was returning along the trail by the creek. Some of the women and children who had gone out to meet the hunters followed behind, laden down with game and dried meat.

But Little Turtle gave no heed. Running swiftly, he caught up with Corn Tassel as she was about to enter Squirrel Woman's lodge, and took her by the hand. He pulled her along behind him with desperate determination.

Little Turtle approached the largest lodge in the village. He gave a call as he stood before the door. When the answer, *"Dajoh,* enter!" came, he lifted the flap and went in, pulling Molly along behind him. The boy and girl found themselves in the presence of a group of men who were sitting about a fire. All eyes were fixed on one man, the Chief.

Chief Standing Pine was the most important man in the village. He was strong and handsome, wise and thoughtful. No one entered his presence lightly. He had no time for trivial things. He sat on the ground, with his feet crossed under him. His face was turned toward the fire in quiet meditation. Attentively a woman handed him his pipe and a martenskin pouch. Then she stood behind him, ready always to anticipate his needs and serve him.

The Chief nodded his head and the men left the room. Slowly he took tobacco mixed with savory red willow bark and carefully filled the pipe. Little Turtle now ran forward, took it to the fire and laid a hot coal on top of the bowl. Then he handed the pipe back to the Chief.

Molly waited in the corner, staring. She wondered why Little Turtle had brought her there. The room was quiet and nothing was said. She wished she had not come. After a long period of waiting, the great Chief turned to the little Indian boy and the two began to talk. Molly listened, for she knew they were speaking of her.

"What is it, my son?" asked Chief Standing Pine.

Little Turtle, young as he was, knew it was not wise to approach the subject dear to his heart too directly. He would lead up to it by slow, careful steps.

"When a hunter traps a raccoon or a fox, O Chief," said Little Turtle quietly, "he uses the dead-fall. As soon as the animal eats the bait, the small log falls and kills him at once. Is it not so, O Chief?"

"Yes, my son," answered the Chief.

"The dead-fall is better," went on Little Turtle, "than a trap or contrivance which allows the animal to suffer great pain. A hunter should not be wantonly cruel. That is true. Is it not, O Chief?"

"Yes, my son. You are indeed wise for a hunter so young," replied the Chief.

"A hurt animal in a trap cannot go free," said Little Turtle. "That is true, is it not, O Chief?"

"Yes, my son. You have observed well."

"A white girl captive is like an animal in a trap, suffering great pain. Is it not so, O Chief?"

Chief Standing Pine made no answer. Then Little Turtle was bold. To the great Chief, so wise and thoughtful, he made a suggestion. Not many dared be so bold, but he did it for Corn Tassel's sake.

"Can we not help a poor captive go free, go home to her people?" The anxiety he felt never once broke through the boy's voice. "If she drowns herself in her tears, is it well to keep her here, O Chief?"

Little Turtle trembled, not knowing what he must suffer for saying such words. The old Chief looked hard at him, then at the white girl who cowered against the wall.

"My son," he spoke with great patience, "you are too young to understand. You do not know the ways of war. War is a cruel master. War is never kind to the enemy. We take the life of a man only when his tribe is at war with us.

"The pale-faced people come in mighty streams from over the great waters. They come to our forests, our streams, our meadows. They kill our men, they kill the animals the Great Spirit has given us for food and clothing. They spoil our hunting. Their horses and cows eat the grass our deer used to feed on. They have no respect for the forest. They chop down trees, not for use, but merely to destroy them. They build houses where our lodges once stood. They are pushing us out of the lands of our fathers. They come, not as friends, but as enemies, taking from us things that are rightly ours.

"We raid, sack and burn their settlements as they do our villages. It is kill or be killed. We fight for our very life. We take scalp for scalp, captive for captive—no more. Our religion tells us that for every scalp or captive taken by the pale-face, we must take a scalp or captive in return. That is justice. It is the ancient law come down from our fathers, by which we live. These things you will understand and accept as you grow older. You are young, my son.

"It is hard to see the grief of the pale-faced captive. Yours is a noble impulse and I forgive you. But there is nothing you can do. Time alone can help. Time, the destroyer of every affection, will dry the tears in the white captive's eyes. Before many more moons have passed, the little one with hair like waving tassels of golden corn will be happy. Before many moons, she will forget her sorrows, forget the pale-faced people and be happy with the Indians. I have spoken. Go, my son!"

Little Turtle's face was as sad as Corn Tassel's when they came out of the lodge together. He knew the Chief was wiser than all men and he knew his words must be true. Only one thing he did not accept—the thought that there was nothing he could do. He was determined to help Corn Tassel more than ever before.

Although she could only guess what he had said, Molly knew that the Indian boy had been interceding for her with the Chief. She knew that he was sorry for her and she felt between him and herself a bond of understanding. She was filled with a new kind of content when the boy was with her, a content she felt with no one else.

They walked along slowly together. Just when they reached the lodge, Squirrel Woman rushed out in haste, as if she were looking for Molly. She sent Little Turtle away abruptly. Then she brought out Shining Star's baby strapped to his baby frame. Seizing Molly by the arm, the woman quickly placed the baby on the girl's back and laid the burden-strap across her forehead. She lifted up to her own back a heavy basket of seed corn. Then she started off to the field, calling to Molly to follow.

It was planting-time, Molly knew. She had seen Red Bird, the older woman, and Shining Star, the kind sister, go off earlier with baskets of corn on their backs. She knew they were making ready to plant corn.

Molly had never carried a baby on her back before. The baby was about six months old, she guessed, much larger and heavier than her tiny baby brother at home. But she had never dared look at him or touch him. She stayed as far away as possible.

The load of the baby was heavy and the burden-strap cut cruelly against her forehead. Molly poked her head forward, stooping to lessen the weight. Then she knew she

was walking like an Indian woman. Was she turning her toes in, too?

Suddenly she hated the Indian women and the way they walked. She hated the Indian baby tied fast to a hard, flat board. She moved the burden-strap a trifle with her fingers as the tears filled her eyes. Then she saw Squirrel Woman stopping in the path ahead, waiting for her to come up. She bent her head forward and, stooping, hurried on.

In one of the fields corn was already up. The fresh green blades like slender grasses made a dotted pattern over the hummocks. A second field was ready for a later planting. The women were working busily, Red Bird, Shining Star and others, under the direction of Bear Woman, the matron and overseer.

Squirrel Woman took the baby off Molly's back and hung the baby frame up on a limb of the nearest tree. There she left the Indian baby swinging in the breeze. Molly glanced up in astonishment, then turned quickly away. Why should she care what they did with their baby?

Squirrel Woman brought Molly over to the field which had not been plowed at all. Rich black earth was piled up in hills about two feet high, placed a "long step" apart. The hills were in rows and the women walked, each in a row, planting corn in the tops of the hills. They worked rapidly, making holes in the earth, dropping in grains of corn and closing the holes again.

Squirrel Woman handed Molly a short stick, to the

end of which a piece of elk bone had been tied. She pointed to the row of corn hills and walked off.

How different it was from planting corn at home. Molly held her stick in her hand, not knowing what to do with it. Did the Indians know nothing of plows? Was her stick supposed to be a hoe? How could anybody plant corn with a stick? A vision of her father's field, behind the zigzag rail fence, and the wooden plow lifting the soil in clean, even rows, came back to her. A vision of the field he had not plowed or planted to corn . . . because of the Indians.

Molly looked about and she saw Bear Woman, the overseer, standing at a distance, looking at her. She saw Squirrel Woman advancing rapidly in her direction. Molly's eyes were dry now and her lips set in a tight line. She was afraid of neither of the women. Did they think they could make her plant corn—plant corn for Indians to eat? If they did, then they were sadly mistaken.

Down she threw her hoe that was only a stick of wood. Out of the field she ran. She stumbled over the loose earth hummocks, scattering the dirt with her feet. She kicked over a basket, spilling seed-corn in all directions. Past the tree where the Indian baby hung swinging, she ran as fleet as the wind. The baby was crying now but she did not care. She would never look at an Indian baby, never touch him, never carry him again on her back.

She ran into the woods. She had only the woods to run to—there was no other place to go. When she heard

someone coming swiftly behind her, she knew before she looked who it was. She had only one good friend, only one friend who cared what she did—Little Turtle.

The boy asked no explanation. Sensing that something had gone wrong, he tried to make her forget it. He led Molly down by the creek. They followed it upstream and into a shallow brook, where on sunwarmed rocks mud turtles lay basking. Little Turtle lifted his bow and aimed under them. Each time the arrow hit the rock, the turtle flew several feet up in the air. Up they flew and down they fell. Before she knew it, Molly was laughing.

"Is that why—*you*—'Little Turtle'?" she asked, venturing a few halting words in the Seneca language.

Little Turtle beamed. She had spoken at last. "Yes, Little Turtle, me! I shoot little turtles!" he answered, happily. "When I grow up I shall earn a new name for myself. I shall be a great hunter and a great warrior!" He puffed out his chest with pride.

Molly's laugh pleased the Indian boy greatly. Her face shone like the sparkling sun when she was happy. Never must she be sad again. Close by in the woods the boy pulled a long strong grape-vine, climbed up a tree and tied it fast for a swing. Molly sat on it and soon she was swinging happily back and forth. Like the happy sound of falling waters, her rippling laughter rang through the forest and fell pleasantly on the boy's ears.

When they came out of the woods Little Turtle led the way to a small lodge of logs that Molly had not noticed before. An old man was sitting inside the door carving a ladle of wood.

"This is Grandfather Shagbark!" said Little Turtle.

Then he stepped back in surprise, for the old man and the captive girl seemed to be already acquainted.

They looked at each other and smiled. Molly could scarce believe her eyes, for before her she saw the old Indian who had befriended her on the mountain journey. She had not seen him once since she came to the Indian village. The other Indians in the large canoe had sailed on down the River Ohio and she had supposed he had gone with them. Now she was glad he had stayed behind.

Shagbark began to talk about his work. He pointed out many things which he had made during the winter, before he left on the expedition to the Pennsylvania settlements—wooden bowls, ladles, dishes, spoons, snow-shoes, as well as stone and pottery pipes.

Little Turtle held out his bow proudly. "Shagbark made it for me," he cried eagerly. "He is teaching me to be a great hunter. Soon he will make me a real man's bow and

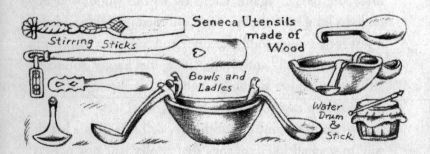

arrows; won't you, Grandfather?"

"Slowly, slowly," said Shagbark, his placid face smiling. "First we must learn how to shoot. How does one learn?"

"I will tell you how he teaches me," Little Turtle replied, turning to Molly.

Then, just as if Molly understood every word, he explained how Shagbark first hung a coon's foot high at the smoke-hole for him to aim at. Then the coon's foot was thrown to the top of a high tree and Little Turtle learned to hit it there. Down to the creek to practice on mud-turtles came next, and there the boy had earned his name. After that, in the woods he had taken his first squirrel.

Molly followed his words closely. The boy spoke slowly and made meaningful gestures. Suddenly, to her great surprise, she realized that she *understood every word that he was saying!* She smiled to herself. As Little Turtle's and Shagbark's words flowed back and forth, she listened quietly.

"So now, Grandfather," asked Little Turtle, "may I have a man's bow, and arrows with flintheads?"

"Slowly, slowly, my son!" replied Shagbark. He paused and looked critically at the wooden ladle in his hand. He held up the unfinished handle for the children to see. "What will it be?" he asked.

"A bear!" cried Little Turtle.

"A turtle!" suggested Molly, at which they all laughed.

The old man kept on shaving off tiny chips of wood,

shaping the handle carefully, without speaking.

"When may I have my new bow and arrows, Grandfather?" asked Little Turtle again.

"Oh ho!" answered Shagbark, laughing. "This boy never forgets. Well, my son, a real hunter's bow and arrows are not easily made. First, the flint must be quarried and carefully selected for the arrow-heads. Then the blanks must be made and the finished points chipped. But that is not all, oh no. The arrow-shafts must be cut from red willow withes and dried under weight to prevent warping. And still that is not all, oh no. A bow should be split from tough hickory saplings or red cedar. The wood must be buried for so many moons to season it. Then it must be given the right shape . . . Oh, the making of a bow is no easy task.

"But most important of all, an Indian boy must learn to shoot, so he can bring home game to help his mother. At first wooden arrow-heads are best because he loses so many. Then bone or antler when he is sure he can find each one . . ."

"I found one for Little Turtle," cried Molly.

"Yes, Grandfather, Corn Tassel found one for me . . ."

"You did not see where it went yourself?" asked Shagbark, his face grown suddenly sober.

"No, Grandfather. I did not see where it went." Little Turtle hung down his head.

"Then you are not ready for arrow-heads of flint!" said Shagbark, with a note of sadness in his voice.

"You are right, Grandfather," said the boy. "I will be patient."

The old man held up the ladle he had been working on. The carved ornament on the handle was complete. "What is it now?" he asked.

"A bird!" cried Molly, clapping her hands.

"A singing bird," added Little Turtle shyly, "to keep Corn Tassel always happy!"

For the boy already knew that Shagbark had made the ladle for the white girl captive. He knew that his grandfather wanted her to be happy as he did himself. So he was

not surprised when he saw Corn Tassel holding the pretty ladle with the bird on the handle between her two white hands. She had a ladle of her own now to keep. The bird on the handle was the sign for all to see and know that the ladle belonged to Corn Tassel.

"A singing bird—to keep Corn Tassel—always—happy!" Softly, haltingly, Molly repeated the words in the Seneca language.

"She speaks! She understands!" cried Little Turtle, in great excitement.

It was true. All the time they had been talking, Molly had understood what they were saying. Due to Little Turtle's helpful teaching, she had gradually learned some of the important words and phrases of the Seneca language. All through the long journey and all through the long weeks of her stay in the village, her ears had been growing accustomed to the strange sounds and now, suddenly, she could understand. How strange it was—a new world opening.

Molly looked at Little Turtle and Shagbark and smiled. They understood. What good friends they were!

The time had passed so happily that she had forgotten to be sad. It had passed so happily that she had forgotten the unpleasantness of the morning. It was when she was on her way back to the lodge of the Indian women that she remembered. Her unwillingness, her disobedience, her running off to the woods—all these came back to her. What would they do to her now that she had been away all day? She looked down at the ladle in her hand and the feel of the soft wood gave her courage, as she thought of the old Indian who had made it.

She hurried into the lodge, suddenly hungry. She had not eaten since morning. They were all gathered about the fire. The baby hung from the bunk pole as usual. The family was larger tonight. The husbands of the two sisters, now returned from the hunting trip, were there. Red Bird, the mother, and Swift Water, the father—they were all there.

Molly stood in the doorway and watched. She saw Red Bird dip the ladle into the big clay pot, fill a bowl and hand it to one of the men.

"The succotash is good tonight," the woman said. "When one has worked hard and is hungry, the succotash lies well on the tongue."

The words fell on Molly's ear as clearly as if they had been spoken in English. Words that had before been only a jumble of queer sounds suddenly took on meaning: "The succotash is good tonight . . . when one has worked hard and is hungry . . ."

Molly stepped forward, picked up a wooden bowl and walked over to Red Bird. She reached out her hand, displaying the new ladle proudly. All eyes round the circle turned to look, not at the ladle but at Molly.

"Grandfather Shagbark made it for me," she said in the Seneca language. "A singing bird to keep Corn Tassel happy."

It was the first time she had spoken to them in Seneca. But no one appeared to notice. In silence, Molly handed out her bowl to be filled with succotash—hot, steaming succotash, made of corn and beans cooked together.

But Red Bird did not lift her hand. She did not look at the bird on the handle of the new-carved ladle. She pointed to the door where stood the baskets that in the morning had held seed-corn. She pointed to Corn Tassel's bed, then she looked at the girl.

"When one has worked hard and is hungry," she repeated in a quiet voice, "the succotash lies well on the tongue."

Molly climbed into her bed, tearless. Well had she learned her lesson, a lesson she would not forget. She climbed into her bed without her supper. She had learned that from now on she must work if she would eat.

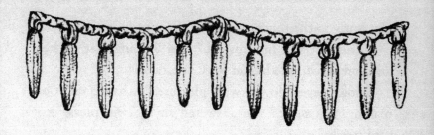

VII   *Slow Weaving*

A basket for me?" asked Molly in surprise.
"When the corn is ripened for picking," said Shining Star quietly, "you will
see there are not baskets enough. It is always good to have
one more. A basket is useful for many things—for gather-
ing the fruits of the earth, for carrying loads, for storing
supplies."

Shining Star looked very beautiful this morning. Her
blue skirt and bright red leggings were made of broadcloth
and were richly embroidered with bead designs. Her figured calico over-dress was fastened down the front with a
row of shining silver brooches. Above the colorful cos-
tume, silver earrings dangled from her ears and her face
beamed with honest kindliness.

Putting her baby in Molly's arms, she sat down under
a shady tree beside the lodge. From the top of a pile of
splints cut from the black ash tree, she picked up an unfinished basket and began to weave. The dry splints rattled

pleasantly to the touch of her deft fingers.

"Today it will be finished," said Shining Star, in her low, soft voice, "the basket for Corn Tassel."

Molly's eyes glowed with pleasure. "A basket of your making, my sister," she answered shyly, "will please me very much."

Molly made a new nest of fresh, dried moss in the baby frame. Then she wrapped the strong, kicking baby in a blanket and lashed him fast with two broad beaded belts, one red, the other blue. The baby-frame was the finest in the village. Its foot-board was carved as well as the hoop or bow which was placed arching over the child's head to protect it in case of a fall. Molly folded and placed at one side the cloth which was sometimes drawn over the bow for shade.

Then she, too, sat down upon the ground. As the wind began to blow, the play trinkets hanging from the arched hoop set up a merry tinkle. The pretty shells knocked gently against the tiny wooden hoops filled with knitted webs of nettle-stalk twine.

"What are the spider webs for?" asked Molly, pointing with her finger.

"To keep away evil," answered Shining Star. "As a spider web catches each thing that touches it, so the knitted webs will catch flying evil before it can harm little Blue Jay. Grandmother Red Bird made them. She is well versed in wisdom."

"But how can he play," asked Molly, "with his hands

tied tight? How can he learn to use his hands if they are always tied tight in blankets?"

Shining Star raised her head and smiled. "It is the Indian way," she said simply. "The Senecas have always done so."

Molly was fast learning how different Indian ways were from white people's. It seemed strange there could be such different ways to do the same things. At home her baby brother was left free to wave his arms, crawl or kick at will.

"The Indian child grows strong and straight," Shining

Star went on, "with his back to the hickory board. The Indian child, with his hands tied close, learns patience. Before he can walk alone he has learned a hard lesson."

"All he can do is open his mouth and cry," said Molly, looking down at him thoughtfully, "but he doesn't do that very often. Tied up in a tree and left swinging, no wonder he imitates the call of the blue jay! "

"His first words were spoken to the birds in the tree," said Shining Star softly. "That is good. His life will be spent in the forest. The birds and the beasts will be his friends. He will learn many lessons from his brothers of the forest. He will follow the trail with the scent of the bear or the wolf. He will build more wisely than the beaver, climb with more daring than the raccoon. He will work more faithfully than the dog; crouch more closely and spring more surely than the panther. He will learn cunning from the fox, the power of swift feet from the deer.

"He will learn to be as brave, as uncomplaining as his brothers of the forest. The hurt dog, the wounded wolf or bear, the dying deer never cries out in pain. The beasts bear their pain in silence, giving no outward sign. They go forward bravely to meet danger. They shrink not from pain or suffering, sickness or death. When little Blue Jay learns to be as brave and uncomplaining as his brothers, he will be a brave man indeed."

Shining Star looked at Corn Tassel thoughtfully. Was she thinking, not of a wounded animal, not of Blue Jay, but of a white girl captive who was in need of courage?

Shining Star had chosen her words with care. She seemed to know that a conflict was going on in the white captive's mind.

As Molly listened, she looked away from the Indian woman. She wanted to close her ears to the words and yet she wanted to hear them. They gave her a sense of peace she had not felt before and at the same time she feared them. One part of her mind wanted to listen. The other part steeled itself hard against the woman and all that she stood for.

A voice in Molly's heart kept crying out to make her hear: "You must not love Shining Star. There is a purpose behind her kindness. If you listen to her words and love her, she will turn you into an Indian." An answering voice cried out: "How can a girl torn away from her people live without affection? How can I live without someone to love?"

"But I don't *want* to turn into an Indian!" The words leaped out of her mouth before she knew it, tell-tale words that gave Shining Star a glimpse deep down into her aching heart. The tears came and Molly could not hold them back.

"An Indian child never cries," said Shining Star, calmly. "Loud sounds of grief might attract a wolf or panther or some enemy of the Senecas. Like his brother in the forest, the child must learn to bear his pain and give no sign. He must have courage to suffer bravely. Can you be as brave as a wounded deer?"

Shining Star knew the white captive carried sadness in her heart. Shining Star was trying to help her. Molly dried her tears quickly. Surely a white girl could show courage like an Indian . . .

"Come, we must go to the corn-field," said Shining Star, laying aside her work. She always knew when they had talked enough.

"After all—I shall not finish the basket today. Better to weave more slowly . . . but more surely . . . Then there will be no need to unravel what has been woven before."

Molly looked into her face, surprised. Was there some hidden meaning behind the words?

She picked up the heavy baby frame and with the woman's help, loaded it onto her back. She was accustomed to the burden now and took it up without thinking. As day by day it grew heavier, she knew she was growing stronger, too, to bear it. As she was used to the burden, so was she growing used to all the Indian ways.

Already in four moons she had learned so much. She had learned that by prompt obedience she avoided punishments, even Squirrel Woman's ever-ready kicks. She had learned that Indian words spoken instead of English brought forth pleased smiles. She had learned that when she worked hard, she was given good food to eat. She had learned that an Indian baby can be as lovable as a white one. Now she had learned one thing more—that the cold look on the face of an Indian was not indifference. She knew now that he suffered as much as others, but he bore his pain without a sign, because he had great courage.

When they reached the corn-field, they met a group of women and children carrying water vessels, hurrying toward the creek. Behind them walked Bear Woman, slow and majestic. Her face was wrinkled and stern. With many winters upon her head, her back was bent with age.

"The corn stands still," she said with sorrow in her voice. "It does not grow for want of water. We must quench its thirst." After a moment she added, "There has been no rain for twenty suns."

"This field was planted later than the others," said Shining Star, "after my sister and I returned from Fort Duquesne. The right time to plant corn is when the first oak leaves are as big as a red squirrel's foot. Well do I remember, the oak-leaves were half-grown when these seeds were sown. Grandfather Hé-no is not pleased to have us plant corn so late."

"Grandfather Hé-no has forgotten us," said Bear Woman, sadly. "Now we must suffer his punishment." She walked away, following after the women and children.

"Grandfather Hé-no?" asked Molly. "Is he a Chief whose name I have not heard?"

"Grandfather Hé-no is the Thunder God," explained Shining Star. "He brings rain to make the corn, beans and squashes grow. Today Shining Star will make a song, asking Hé-no for rain."

Shining Star took Blue Jay from Molly's back and hung him up on a limb. Then she and Molly joined the water-carriers. They brought many vessels of water which they poured at the feet of the corn-stalks, soaking the ground thoroughly.

Then the women and children stood by and listened while Shining Star talked to the Thunder God:

"Oh Hé-no, our Grandfather,
Come to us and speak kindly,
Come to us and wash the earth again.
When the soil is too dry
The corn cannot grow.
The beans and the squashes are dry and withered
Because they are thirsty.

Hé-no, our Grandfather
Does harm to no man;
He protects his grandchildren
From witches and reptiles;
He washes the earth,
Gives new life to the growing corn.

For all thy gifts
We thank thee, oh Hé-no!
Come to thy grandchildren—
Bring rain! Bring rain!"

That evening, after Shining Star and Molly had eaten, they heard the noise of a soft rumble, like thunder far away. They hurried out to look, followed by the rest of the family. The sky that had all day been cloudless, began to darken.

"Hé-no has heard us," said Shining Star, with a happy smile. "He is coming to visit us."

With amazing swiftness the storm rolled up, a dense black cloud sweeping furiously eastward. Over the Indian village, thunder soon broke with deafening peals and lightning flashed in sheets of flame.

Molly ran back to the lodge door, frightened. The sky made her think of a hymn the white people had sung in Marsh Creek Hollow:

"Day of wrath! O day of mourning!
See fulfilled the prophets' warning,
Heaven and earth in ashes burning!"

She ran to get away from the fury of the storm, from the anger of this unknown god of the Indian people. But Shining Star came after her, took her firmly by the hand and led her forth again.

Looking about she saw the Indians, men, women and children, standing in front of their lodges in perfect calm. They had no thought of danger. They gazed at the changing sky in delighted wonder, as the crashes of thunder shook the air and flashes of lightning broke across. When the rain began to pour down in heavy torrents, they held out their hands to welcome it. "It is good! It is good!" they cried. "The corn that was dying of thirst drinks again!"

"Hé-no has come!" said Shining Star softly, and something of her calm and wonder passed into the white girl who met her gaze and held tightly to her hand.

"We thank thee, oh Hé-no!
Thou hast come and spoken!
Thou hast washed the earth again,
And brought water
to the thirsty corn
to the beans and the squashes.
We thank thee, oh Hé-no!"

* * * *

The thunder-storm ended the drought and from that time on, the corn grew apace. Each day, as Molly walked between the rows, she could almost see the corn-stalks grow. First, they were knee high, then up to her waist, then abreast of her shoulder, so she could barely look over the top of the waving sea of green. Then came a day when the corn-stalks blossomed in tassel. The field of corn, with green tassels nodding, was a pleasant sight to the Indians, but to no one more than to Molly.

"Oh, how beautiful is the corn in tassel!" cried Shining Star, as they walked between the rows together.

Molly looked up with a puzzled expression. She had

long ago noticed that the Indians called her by an Indian name. She had grown used to the sound, but she had not questioned its meaning. Now she heard Shining Star use it when speaking of the tassels on the corn.

"Corn Tassel?" she asked, using the Indian word.

"Yes," replied Shining Star. "When first we saw your pale yellow hair, there was only one thing we could think of—a stalk of corn in tassel. So we gave you its name—Corn Tassel!"

"Oh, thank you, Shining Star!" cried Molly. "Thank you for the beautiful name."

Through her mind came singing sweet words she had heard on her father's lips: "The Injuns'll never hurt *you*, Molly-child. Why, when they see your yaller hair a-shinin' in the sun, they'll think 'tis only a corn-stalk in tassel!"

A corn-stalk in tassel! He must have known the Indians would treat her kindly. Corn Tassel—they had named her Corn Tassel because they loved the corn so much. How pleased her father would be if he knew! Where was he now? She had not thought of him for days. Molly's eyes filled with sudden tears; then with the back of her hand, she brushed them away.

"I like to work in the corn," she said. "I always worked in the corn at home."

"It is time now you worked for Bear Woman," replied Shining Star. They walked through the rows till they came to the overseer.

"Is she ready to work?" Bear Woman glared at the

white captive and her voice was gruff like a bear's. "She ran away before."

"She works well now," answered Shining Star. "She works like an Indian woman. She wants work to do in the corn-field."

The old woman's face and figure bristled with fierceness and Molly trembled to see Shining Star go off and leave her. But Bear Woman's voice, gruff though it was, held kindness as she talked to Molly about the corn.

"The corn, the beans and the squashes are Three Sisters," Bear Woman explained. "We call them Our Life, because it is they who sustain us."

She pointed to the south side of the corn-hills where the women had planted beans and squash seeds. The vines grew thick around the hills, the beans curling their tendrils about the corn-stalks, the squash plants a mass of broad green leaves spread out on the ground.

"In the same hill the Three Sisters grow," Bear Woman went on. "They take the same food from the earth; they drink the same moisture. They love each other so dearly that they grow better when planted together. They can never be separated without pain."

"Three Sisters!" cried Molly, her eyes shining. "Three Sisters always happy together!" She had never heard anything like this from the white people.

"The corn has enemies, too," continued Bear Woman. "First there are the weeds, rank and tall, who try to choke its roots. They must be pulled out and destroyed. After

three weedings the corn is safe. Now that the ears are beginning to form, there are thieves who come to steal—
birds, squirrels, field mice, crows, deer."

"Do the Indians have to fight to save their corn as the
white people do?" asked Molly.

"Yes," said Bear Woman. "Long and hard they must
fight for the precious corn."

She led Corn Tassel to a tall covered platform built of
poles. When the girl climbed up the ladder and looked,
she could see far out across the waving tassels. It was like
looking over an ocean that ebbed and flowed with soft,
gentle movements.

"You will come here for part of each day," said Bear
Woman, "taking turns with the other children. The worst
offender is Kah-Kah, the crow. Wave the blanket and
shout, but throw no stones, lest you kill him. He is our
friend, however mischievous. To frighten him off is
enough. Long ago, Kah-Kah lived far away to the south-
west. One day he took a grain of corn in his beak and
brought it here to us. He brought us our first grain of corn
for a gift. So to Kah-Kah we must ever be grateful."

Days passed, hot summer days, in which Molly pulled
weeds with the Indian women and took turns with the
children on the platforms, guarding the grain and frightening marauders away. In the corn-field she was happy
and for her work won frequent praise from stern-faced
Bear Woman.

As the days came and went, bringing hot summer sunshine and cooling rains, Molly watched the beans bloom and the pods begin to form. She saw the squash plants open their great yellow blossoms, then drop their petals to grow their fruit. She saw the ears on the corn-stalks grow fuller day by day, watched over with constant care by sharp-eyed Bear Woman. Each day without fail, with Corn Tassel by her side, the woman looked to see how big the grains had grown. Each day she shook her head and said to the questioning Indians, "It is not ready." The whole village waited, as eagerly as Molly, for the ripening of the corn.

On a pleasant morning in mid-August, Bear Woman announced that the corn was ready. The ears, now grown to full size, were in the soft, milky state best for roasting. She called the Indians together to celebrate the Feast of the Green Corn. Always, she explained to Corn Tassel, the first fruit of the corn that was fit to use was made a feast offering by the Senecas.

Molly went into the corn-fields with the women. The new splint basket, which she carried strapped upon her back, she filled with ears of corn for roasting. She took them to the fires where the Indians danced and sang in honor of the ripening harvest.

The festival lasted four days—a season of general thanksgiving to the Great Spirit, of feasting and rejoicing among the Indians themselves. Important men of the tribe made speeches and burned ceremonial tobacco. There were games and dances for men, women, and children in the great open space in front of the lodges and each day at twilight, a feast.

Huge kettles were hung over great smoking fires and everyone ate his fill of the bounteous, delicious food. In addition to boiled beans and squash, green corn was cooked in a variety of ways. It was both boiled and roasted in the ear; some was cut from the cob and cooked with beans to make succotash; some was made into a special kind of green corn bread, used only on this occasion.

At first, Molly watched the strange proceedings, wide-eyed and curious. The muffled beat of the drums, the shaking of the rattles and the shuffling movement of the dances filled her with a strange excitement. Then, suddenly, she felt out of place. The music beat on her ear with an alien note. She was not an Indian like the others—she was still a white girl. She was the only white person in the whole village.

She hurried away to the corn-field. There she worked diligently, pulling off ears of corn as fast as she could until her splint basket was full to the brim. Then she carried it back to the fires. Always more corn was needed. The amount that the Indians were able to eat was astonishing. Back and forth she hurried, emptying the corn from her basket onto the ground beside the boiling kettles.

Up and down the corn-rows she walked, pulling ears off one by one. Her arms grew tired, her back began to ache, but still she worked. Work—that was what she needed. Work, to fill her mind and heart. Work, to make

her forget the sorrow that lay only covered—not dead. Work, to make her forget . . .

But, oh, she must not forget! How near she had come to forgetting! For the first time in days, her mother's voice came back to her, saying: "Don't forget your own name or your father's and mother's. Don't forget to speak in English. Say your prayers and catechism to yourself each day. . . Say them again and again. . . don't forget, oh, don't forget. . .

She must not forget. She would never let herself forget. She dared not speak English in the presence of the Indians. She must contrive to be alone more often. She must not forget the English words she knew. *What if one day a white person should come to the Indian village to take her home again?*

Slowly she walked down through the corn-rows, where all was silent, and slowly she said the names over: "Thomas

Jemison, Jane Jemison, John, Thomas, Betsey, Mary, Matthew and baby Robert." Her prayers and her catechism came next, then the names again: "Thomas Jemison, my father; Jane Jemison, my mother; John and Thomas, Betsey and Mary, little Matthew and baby Robert, of Marsh Creek Hollow in Penn . . . syl . . . van . . . ia . . ."

The rustling leaves whispered familiar memories in her ears and took her back in spirit to Marsh Creek Hollow. Sheltered by the huge green stalks of corn, she could almost believe she was there. Perhaps at the edge of the field when she came out, she would find a zigzag rail fence to climb over . . .

Slowly she walked along as darkness fell. "Thomas Jemison, my father; Jane Jemison, my mother . . ." The names made a sing-song rhythm on her tongue.

She had not guessed that anyone was near, so absorbed had she become in the sound of the English words and the pleasing picture of a loved one called up by each. Unconsciously she paused. Then, like a thunder-storm breaking the still beauty of a summer day, disaster fell. Squirrel Woman, running softly and swiftly up behind, heard sounds that were not Seneca words, sounds of English that enraged her.

"So you come alone to the corn-field," she cried, hot with anger, "to say aloud to yourself words of the pale-face!"

She took the girl by the arm and began to shake her. She shook her till her teeth chattered in her head. She shook her till, limp and exhausted, she fell upon the ground. Only then did she let go her hold.

After a moment Molly staggered to her feet and looked up at the Indian woman, but there were no tears in her eyes. Like an Indian, she was learning to bear her pain. She looked at Squirrel Woman, but she saw in her place a neighbor from Marsh Creek Hollow—a woman whom everyone knew as a scold. She had seen her shake her children in just the same way.

She turned to Squirrel Woman and spoke calmly: "Like a rushing tornado, like the wind through the trees in winter, you come running up behind me. Like a white woman, you shake a defenseless child. Till her teeth rattle and fall out, you keep on shaking!" She paused to draw breath, then went on: "Squirrel Woman acts like a white woman, an angry white woman, a torment, a scold. Squirrel Woman is the only Indian in the village who, like a pale-face, gives loud expression to hot anger!"

The Indian woman stirred uneasily, staring. But Molly had more words to say: "If you speak to me in reason, I will listen to your words. Shining Star speaks words of wisdom, Red Bird does the same, and so do all the others. I listen when they speak. I try to heed their words."

Squirrel Woman's arms dropped, with a sudden movement, to her sides. At Corn Tassel, this new Corn Tassel, she stared in open-mouthed surprise. Perhaps the truth of the accusation reached and hurt her. Perhaps it would help her to mend her ways.

Then suddenly Molly saw Red Bird there, standing beside her daughter. Had she seen and heard all?

"As it is wrong to punish a child with a rod or a whip," said Red Bird to her daughter, "so it is wrong to use any sort of violence. Water only is necessary and it is sufficient. If Corn Tassel has disobeyed, plunge her under. Whenever she promises to do better, the punishment must cease at once."

The quiet words were unexpected. Molly turned, still expecting a shower of blows to rain down upon her head. She stood still a moment, waiting. But none came. She waited a moment longer, then ran fast, out of the cornfield, back to the lodge.

A dreadful thing had happened, a thing that overwhelmed her. Her rudeness to Squirrel Woman was wrong, she knew, but that was not the thing that gave her pain. A more dreadful thing than that had taken place. She ran to her bed and, filled with shame, hid her face in the blankets.

A dreadful truth like a burning fire consumed her. Molly Jemison had begun to think like an Indian, to see white people from the Indian point of view. Molly Jemison was turning into an Indian. What could she do—oh, what could she do!

VIII   *A Second Captivity*

*A*s Molly stood in the doorway, she knew they were talking about her. She had heard the sound of her name. She had heard the word *journey*. She looked at them in confusion as their voices died away. Two strange men stood by the fire with the others; one of them looked at her and frowned. Where were they planning to take her?

Nothing more was said. For days, she lived in the shadow of a dark secret; then Shagbark called her to his lodge and had a long talk with her.

"The real home of the Senecas," the old Indian explained, "is not here, but far away to the northeast, in Genishau or Genesee Town, by the Great Falling Waters. The Senecas are of the *Ho-dé-no-sau-nee,* the People of the Long House. The Five Nations are the Senecas, the Cayugas, the Onondagas, the Oneidas and the Mohawks. These tribes look upon each other as brothers and in time of war fight side by side.

"They are like families living together in one great Long House, with a door at each end. The Mohawks are the Keepers of the Eastern Door and the Senecas are the Keepers of the Western Door. The Oneidas and the Cayugas are our younger brothers; while in the center, the Onondagas keep the council fire always burning.

"The Senecas have the power of swift feet. They can outrun any animal in the forest. And so, beside their camp-fires they are never content to remain. Far and wide over the face of the earth they roam, protecting their people, putting down their enemies, and searching always for good hunting-grounds.

"The Senecas have built villages by the River Ohio because here the soil is black and rich. In the winter they sometimes go as far south as the mouth of the River Scioto to hunt, because there the hunting is good. Always there are Senecas making the long journey from Genesee Town to the River Ohio and back again."

"Is it a long journey over the mountains?" asked Molly, remembering.

"It is long and hard," answered Shagbark kindly, reading the girl's thoughts, "but not over the mountains to the eastward. It is in a northeasterly direction. Part is taken by canoe and part on foot. All is through the trackless wilderness, so it is well that the men know the way. They have traveled it many times going to and returning from the Cherokee wars.

"The two strange men who have come to your lodge

are Red Bird's sons, Shining Star's brothers. Good Hunter and Gray Wolf go and return every season. They have wives and children at Genesee Town. The Senecas who live on the Ohio are often urged by those at Genesee to come and live with them. It is this way—Genesee Town is *home* to all the Senecas. Good Hunter has come again to ask his mother and her family to go home with him. But Red Bird and her daughters have once more refused. They do not wish to go. They are contented here. The corn grows tall in Seneca Town by the River Ohio."

"But why, then, do they make preparations for a journey?" asked Molly. "They have pounded parched corn and mixed it with maple sugar. They have put meal into a bag . . ."

"Shining Star's two brothers are soon to make the return journey to the village by the Falling Waters," replied Shagbark. "Others in Seneca Town are going home as soon as the corn is harvested. Shining Star and Squirrel Woman will accompany their brothers as far as Fort Duquesne, there to buy needed supplies and return. If Shining Star wished to take her pale-faced sister along, would you care to go?"

"To Fort Duquesne?" asked Molly, in amazement. "To be given away to a Frenchman?"

"*Ohè!*" cried Shagbark, laughing. "What gave the child such a notion? Do you not know that you have been adopted into a powerful tribe of the Senecas? Do you not realize that no pale-face, not even a Frenchman, can take you away from the stronghearted Senecas? No—you go to Fort Duquesne and after two suns, you come back again to Seneca Town with the women."

Fort Duquesne! Davy Wheelock and Nicholas Porter! If only they would be there, if only she could talk to them again! Molly's face saddened. There would be no one she knew at Fort Duquesne, only Indians and blue-coated Frenchmen.

"If it is the will of Shining Star to take me," she said, dropping her eyes, "I am ready to go."

"You have spoken well, my daughter," said Old Shagbark. "Your Indian sister will be pleased when she hears."

The voyage was taken as before; the men in the large canoe leading the way, the two women in a smaller one following with Molly. Only one thing was different. Blue Jay went along, strapped to his baby frame, lying safely on the bottom of the canoe. There, with his eyes shaded by the covered hoop, he talked to himself or slept peacefully.

The forests on the hillsides were touched with patches of gay autumn color. Already the brilliant green of summer had begun to fade. Molly rested contentedly. The women did not ask her help with the paddling. For the first time in many long weeks she sat with her hands folded in her lap, idle. The sun beat down upon her golden head with pleasant warmth. After a time, she curled up on the floor of the canoe and like Blue Jay fell fast asleep.

The Indians beached their canoes on the shore opposite the fort and camped there for the night. Early the next morning they paddled across the river.

Fort Duquesne looked just the same. It had not changed at all. It looked just as it had looked five long months before in April. Molly's heart began to pound as she stared at the hard, gray stockade walls. Then she thought of all that had happened to herself. She who had said she would never be an Indian, had been living the life of an Indian girl. The fort was just the same—it was she who had changed.

The Indian men walked first, then the women with heavy packs of furs upon their backs. Molly followed at their heels carrying Blue Jay. Behind her head she could hear him chattering contentedly.

Soon they came to the Indian trading-house. It was built of hewn logs of great size, with heavy puncheons for the roof. It was a store and fort combined for the safety of the trader and the protection of his furs and goods.

Molly walked into the cabin at the end of the little procession. She saw the Indians pick out places on the plank floor and sit down. A Frenchman appeared who spoke some words in Indian. He presented each of the Indian men with tobacco. Pipes were lighted and the bits of tobacco left over were stowed safely away inside the men's tobacco pouches. The Indian men smoked and talked a great while among themselves. The women who had dropped their packs stood behind waiting patiently.

Arranged on shelves against the wall Molly saw a fine array of merchandise—blankets, store cloth, guns, tomahawks, and knives. Before her on the counter a pile of trinkets was displayed—balls, rings, bells of brass, brooches of silver, and piles of small glass beads in brilliant colors. She walked up closer, staring. She had never seen such things before.

"Go outside!" snapped Squirrel Woman, stepping up behind her. These goods and baubles were made by white men. To look upon them might be harmful to a white girl captive. "Go outside!" the woman cried. "A trading-house is no place for such as you."

Blue Jay began to cry. The men looked up in surprise to see a crying baby there.

"Go outside!" Shining Star joined words with Squirrel Woman. "Let Blue Jay watch the birds. Then will he be content. Keep watch near by, within sight of the door. When the trading is over, we will come to you."

Obediently Molly went out the door. She walked along the path, jogging Blue Jay up and down to quiet him. There were no trees at hand, no flying birds to show him. Molly walked along the path, passing by the few scattered bark houses for Indians and soldiers which made up the village.

She stared at the great fort whose walls loomed high above her. Once they had held out hope—a false hope which brought no freedom. Here she walked, a white girl, carrying an Indian baby for a burden. She looked down at her hands and arms. They were as brown as Little Turtle's. She knew her face must be the same.

Closer and closer she came to the fort entrance. Blue Jay's cries had died away. He was sleeping now upon her shoulder. She would go up to the entrance—the gate stood open wide—the gate through which Davy Wheelock and Nicholas Porter had walked, never to return. She would take one look inside. No one need know. Sleeping Blue Jay would not betray her. In a moment she would return before the Indians had finished their trading, before they had a chance to miss her.

Yes, it looked just the same within the fort enclosure. There stood the bake-oven, the well-sweeps, the log houses with their doors open wide. There stood the barn in the corner, but no cows were looking out. There was the garden—a few cabbages had not been pulled—and there the peach tree. Long ago its blossoms had wilted, covering the ground with petals of pink. Long ago, tiny pale green tips had turned into long green peach leaves, curling and browning now in the late summer sun.

Had the pink blossoms borne fruit? Had there been time for the hard green ball of a peach to turn into red-cheeked softness? Time enough for a white girl to turn into a brown one. Time enough for a girl to forget the family she loved. Was it time enough to grow a peach?

Before she knew it, Molly had crossed the drawbridge and entered the fort yard. The tree, like a magnet, drew her on. She could not go away till she knew. With her head pressing forward to ease the burden-strap, taking short quick steps, she ran. The leaves hung thick and heavy, curling and burning in the midday sun. She pushed them aside with trembling hands to look. The sight of a ripe, red peach against the blue sky—only that could bring her comfort . . .

She was all alone in the fort yard. Even if anyone should see her, they would think it was only an Indian girl with a baby. They would turn and pass her by. But a voice broke through the stillness. As the first sound struck her ear, she crept under the shadowy branches.

"Why, hello!" the voice said. "What are you doing here, little girl?"

The words echoed through Molly's excited mind and it took a moment or two before she realized they were English—before she sensed their meaning and the friendly tone. Still she cowered beneath the branches.

Then she remembered Blue Jay. They must not see him—they must not see an Indian baby on a white girl's back. She wheeled about quickly, to give Blue Jay a covering of green branches.

Then she looked up.

She saw a white man, dressed in blue, with lace ruffles at his sleeves. His coat was a bright, deep blue like the blue of the sky in summer. It was edged with rich gold lace and had a row of shining buttons down one side. Four Frenchmen in blue—four Frenchmen with hard, cold faces had made Molly a captive. Was this one of them? She looked up into his face to see. No, he was a stranger. His face was not hard and cold. It was kind.

"Who are you, child?" the man asked, smiling. "Why don't you speak?"

He was not French at all. He was English. In spite of the blue Frenchman's clothes, he could speak in English.

Molly tried to swallow the lump in her throat, but she couldn't. She tried to find English words to say, but they refused to come. The man took her out from under the peach tree and, holding her by the hand, walked across the yard. The next thing she knew, she was in a room in one of the houses and a group of white women, dressed in gowns that sparkled in many colors, smooth like shining silver, were crowding round and looking.

"What lovely hair!" the women cried.

They touched her yellow braids—her pale yellow hair that had grown still paler, bleached by so many days spent in the burning summer sun. Molly had forgotten that her hair would tell the truth about her. The women did not think her an Indian at all.

Excited words fell thick and fast, some in French and some in English, and the English words struck deep into the confusion of Molly's mind:

"How can she live with the Indians? How can she endure the hardships of a savage life?"

"She's only a child! She can't be more than eleven, if that!"

"She's of delicate build—her hands and feet are small.

She comes of good parentage."

"How can she carry that heavy Indian baby?"

"How did she happen to be taken by the Indians? Won't she talk at all?"

The sound of the English words fell like sweet music on Molly's ear. The sounds were lighter, gayer, happier somehow than solemn Indian speech. As she listened, her heart leaped up in happiness. There was only one thing she wanted. She knew it now, without the shadow of a doubt. Her whole heart knew it—to be free of the Indians, to be a captive no longer, to go back to the white people, to her own dear family.

One of the women brought her a cup of milk to drink. Her trembling hand reached out to take it. It was the first cup of milk she had had to drink since she left Marsh Creek Hollow. She wondered if her hand could hold it, if her dry throat could swallow once again. She thought of the red cow in the barn that had given the milk—she wondered who had milked the cow that morning. The milk tasted sweet like honey upon her tongue. Perhaps it was the milk that helped the English words to come.

The man and the women who spoke in English took her away from the others. They took her out on the doorstep, into the sun. They put the questions slowly and at last she was able to answer.

"Tell us your name, child."

"Mary Jemison, sir. They always called me Molly.

Thomas Jemison is my father, Jane Jemison is my mother."

"When and where were you taken, child?"

"At corn-planting time . . . in Marsh Creek Hollow . . . in Pennsylvania." Then the whole story came out, bit by bit.

"Where are you living now?"

"In an Indian village called Seneca Town, a day's journey from here down the River Ohio."

As she said the words, Molly saw a black shadow fall. It fell upon the happy, shining day as well as upon her heart. Like animals bent upon seizing helpless prey, two Indian women had rushed through the entrance gate. With heads bent forward, stooping under heavy loads, with short, quick steps they came. Within earshot, they stopped.

"Oh, I must go!" cried Molly, as she saw them. "I stayed too long. They told me to wait by the trading-house door."

"Just a minute!" The man in the gold-laced coat glanced darkly at the women. "Are they looking for you to hurt you? To punish you?"

"Oh, can't we *do* something?" cried one of the ladies, in a voice of anguish. "Such a lovely child . . . Why do we just go on standing here?"

"They are looking for me, I must go," said Molly.

She broke away from the white people to go across the yard. With her moccasined foot still touching the door-log

she paused. She looked into the woman's lovely face. She did not want to go. She did not want to go back to the Indians. She wanted to stay with the white people and be a white girl for the rest of her life.

As in a dream, she heard the woman say, *"Why can't we keep her with us?* What would the Indians do if we did?"

Molly could not move. She did not want to go. At that moment her whole life hung in balance. Was she to be an Indian or a white girl?

Blue Jay began to cry. The next moment Squirrel Woman had Molly's arm in a tight grip and she was obliged to follow. She looked back only once. She saw the white people standing there, crowded about the doorway—doing nothing. They just stood there and watched her go.

"Pale-faces!" cried Squirrel Woman, hot with anger. "So you run off alone to talk to the pale-faces!"

Shining Star, greatly alarmed, looked down at Corn Tassel and there in her eyes, she saw that a seed of new hope had been planted. She turned to her sister. "There is a time to speak," she said, sternly, "and a time to be silent."

Squirrel Woman, angry as she was, held her tongue. Laden down with the stock of blankets, clothes and trinkets which they had received for their furs at the trading-house, the women took Molly between them and hastened to their canoe.

Swiftly they paddled across the river and came to the

place where they had camped the night before. The banked camp-fire was smoldering. In its still-hot embers, corn-cakes lay slowly baking. The women went on shore, leaving Molly and Blue Jay in the canoe. Far enough away to be out of the girl's hearing, they talked in low tones. Sick at heart, Molly watched them. She had never seen them so upset before. With motions of great alarm, they kept looking at her while they talked. Then they came to a quick decision. From out the embers they snatched their bread, climbed back into the canoe and paddled off.

The sun had begun to sink behind the wooded hills before Molly looked up. Then she gave a wild start of alarm, for she saw that the canoe was going not west, but east. It was going away from the setting sun, not toward it. Seneca Town lay down the river, to the westward—of that she was certain.

"Oh, where are you taking me?" she cried aloud, in great distress. "Where are you taking me?"

But the women would not answer. Squirrel Woman muttered under her breath and Shining Star turned away. Then Molly knew that something serious had happened to make the women change their course, to make them go away from their home, not toward it.

Although the women paddled with swift desperation, they were not able to put much distance between themselves and Fort Duquesne that night. They kept on the course until long after dark and stopped to camp on the

Allegheny River banks only when they could see no longer. There they made no fire but, wrapped in blankets, slept upon the ground.

The next morning they rose early, but did not start at once. They watched and waited, looking down the stream. At last they saw what they were expecting—the large canoe with their brothers and the men from Seneca Town. Molly stared as she saw them coming. What did it mean? Were the women going along, too, to the village beside the Falling Waters?

The men stepped ashore, as if expecting to find the women there. They stopped to eat bread and to have private consultation with their sisters. Then they came nearer and no longer guarded their words.

"You went away none too soon," said Gray Wolf, loudly. "The pale-faces came before you were out of sight, asking for the white girl captive. They searched along the shore to find where she was hid. They went back to the fort with tears streaming down their faces. You are fortunate that you still have your captive."

He turned directly to Molly. "Oh ho, little Pale-Face!" he cried. "You didn't get away that time, did you?"

"It is the will of the Great Spirit that Corn Tassel should be our sister," said Squirrel Woman, crossly. "The pale-faces cannot take her away from us."

"All that we have we will give to Corn Tassel," said Shining Star, her eyes lighting up with happiness. "I will love her as her own sister would."

Molly knew now why the women had paddled so fast. They had been afraid of losing her to the white people at the fort. The man in the gold-laced coat and the woman in the sparkling gown of silk had wanted to keep her, after all—to keep her for their child. They had followed the Indians to the opposite shore and tried to bring back the white captive girl. They had returned to the fort with heavy hearts, with tears in their eyes. They had seen Molly Jemison only once, but they had loved her enough to want her for their child.

Molly knew now why she was not returning to Seneca Town. The women had heard her tell the white people where she lived. They were afraid the white people would search out the Indian village and find her. They were going along with the men, taking her on the long journey to Genesee Town, where they had not wanted to go. They had changed their plans because of her. She herself was going on the long, hard journey of which Shagbark had told her—the long journey through the pathless wilderness. She was going to a place where the white people could never, never find her.

On a second journey, like that first one over the mountains, they were taking her—a journey of hardship, hunger, pain and distress. Through pathless woods, through flooding streams, through drenching rains she must go. At night no place to sleep but on the ground; by day, a heavy burden on her back, the Indian baby growing ever heavier as her own strength grew weaker.

And all for what? All for what? Molly could not lift her sorrowful head. For a second captivity, harder than the first. A second captivity more painful than the first, because her hope was gone.

IX   *By The Falling Waters*

*I*t was a lovely, mild day in late fall—the moon of falling leaves—when Molly came to the end of the long journey from Fort Duquesne.

The Indians followed the general course of the Genesee River northward, skirting the western shore until they came to the river gorge. Near the top of the cliff they stopped at an Indian camp site to rest. Molly took Blue Jay in his baby frame off her back and leaned the board against a tree. Then, with faltering steps, she walked to the edge of the cliff and looked down into the gorge for the first time.

Her tired eyes filled with wonder as she gazed at the great Falling Waters. She had often heard the Indians speak of the place, but nothing they had said had prepared her for its great beauty. So tired she could scarcely keep from falling, she stood there and drank it in.

The air was soft and warm, and a gentle breeze was blowing. With the deafening roar in her ears, Molly put her hands into the damp spray and forgot her fatigue. The noon-day sun struck down at just the right angle to make a rainbow spring, upward and outward, from the base of the falls. Breathless, Molly walked closer, stumbling through the wet, brown, fallen leaves.

It was then she saw the second rainbow, arching proudly, following the same curve as the first, both ringed in the most brilliant colors she had ever seen. Was it an omen? Were the rainbows meant for her? Was she here, in this beautiful spot, to find solace for her pain, peace to uplift her spirit?

Greatly comforted, she slept that night with the roaring of the waters in her ears. The next day she followed the

Portage Falls - from an old Print

women over rough and rugged hills to the Indian village, a half-day's journey farther north. Molly was sorry to leave the gorge behind, but the low rolling hills of the Genesee Valley were beautiful too. Composed of bark long houses and log cabins, the village was much like Seneca Town, though larger. It lay near the mouth of Little Beard's Creek, and it was called Genesee Town—Gen-ish-a-u, which in the Indian language signified a *Shining-Clear-or-Open-Place.*

Upon arrival, Squirrel Woman and Shining Star turned Molly over at once to Earth Woman, famous among the Senecas for her skills in dealing with all forms of sickness. Silently, Earth Woman looked at the girl's thin legs and arms, examined her scratched limbs and swollen feet. She saw that her toes were worn almost to the bone from the rubbing of sand which had collected in her moccasins while fording so many creeks. Slowly she shook her head. Then she scolded.

"Why did you not kill her and be done with it?" she cried. "It would have been more merciful. A wounded animal should be put out of its misery. Such a journey is only for a strong man to take—not a child and a pale-face at that! The daughters of Red Bird have shown little wisdom." She paused, then added, "But I will do what I can."

Rebuked by a woman older and wiser than they, the two sisters hung their heads and without reply, returned to their mother's lodge.

Earth Woman took the girl to the river bank and there

in a shallow place, gave her a thorough washing. Then back to her lodge she brought her and placed her in a bed. There, tired and ill, Molly was to lie for many days.

Earth Woman prided herself on being able to cure all manner of fevers, plagues and diseases. She knew the exact medicinal root or herb to perform the cure for each. She set to work at once. She steeped red oak and wild cherry bark and mixed it with dewberry root. This she gave to Molly to drink frequently and in it she had her soak her feet, at intervals, for days. When the girl did not improve, she tried various other decoctions, but nothing seemed to help. A troubled frown settled on the Indian woman's placid face.

Days passed one after the other, but Molly took no notice. Sometimes she heard Earth Woman start out the door on her daily trip to the woods or saw her come back again, her arms filled with roots she had dug or leaves and herbs she had gathered. Listlessly she watched as the woman mixed her medicines, setting them to steep or boiling them over the fire. Listlessly she watched, but her mind took in little or nothing of what she saw. She never spoke or asked a question.

The lodge seemed always quiet as if the other families had no children full of life and action. Or, perhaps all the other families had moved away. Perhaps they had all gone on the long journey, too. Sometimes a little white dog, like the one in Seneca Town, came whining to Molly's bedside. Sometimes Earth Woman was not herself at all. One moment she was Bear Woman, pointing out weeds on a corn hill. At another, she was Squirrel Woman, scolding and angry. Then she turned into a white woman, with full-gathered skirts of homespun and friendly eyes of blue. The white woman was always in a hurry, going away somewhere. And when she went, Earth Woman came back again.

Long hours passed when no one was there. The fire was out, the ashes were cold. Had they all gone away and left her? Had they set the broom against the door, a signal of their absence? Slowly Molly crawled out of her bed. Over the dirt floor she crept as far as the door. Then she forgot about the broom. She made up her mind she would go away from the Indians. She would find her way home again. But Earth Woman came, picked her up and carried her back to her bed.

One day Molly was surprised to find Little Turtle looking down at her. But it couldn't be Little Turtle—he was far, far away in Seneca Town on the River Ohio. She brushed her eyes to make sure she was not dreaming. The dream grew more real when Shagbark appeared. Then she knew she was back in Seneca Town. The long journey was the dream. She had never taken it. It was only a dream about Fort Duquesne and the white people there. They had not wanted her at all. There was no place now to go but home.

It grew more and more difficult to tell what was real and what was a dream. Molly could not think things out, her head was so hot; and Earth Woman's medicines were sharp on her tongue.

One day the air was suddenly filled with shouting, the beating of drums and the shaking of rattles. In through the lodge door rushed a number of queer-looking figures, their faces covered with grotesque masks, to represent woodland goblins or sprites. They plunged their bare hands into the fire, scattered the white ashes of the hearth and kindled a new fire.

It was like a queer nightmare to Molly. With a curious dream-like detachment, unmixed with fear, she saw one of the figures take ashes in his hands and sprinkle them on hers and Earth Woman's heads. Filled with wonder she watched the figures prancing and dancing in the firelight and listened to the strange noises they made. When they left the lodge and all was quiet again, Earth Woman explained that the ceremony was a purification rite; that the False Face Company had put on masks to drive evil spirits from all the lodges in the village.

"The demons responsible for your sickness have been

Seneca   False-Face
                          Society
                          Masks

driven off," said Earth Woman, confidently. "Soon now, your strength will return."

Even Earth Woman's words seemed part of the dream. Molly looked at her with glassy, feverish eyes and wondered what they meant. If only she would speak in English—then she might hope to understand.

Through everything, inside her mind only one thought remained clear—she must get away from the Indians. She must find her way home again. Only at home could she be happy. But each time she asked Earth Woman if she could go, she was told she was not strong enough; and so she waited.

Shining Star came sometimes and talked. Shining Star spoke of Red Bird and said she lived in Red Bird's lodge. Was it true that Red Bird and Swift Water had made the long journey? Yes, Shining Star explained. It was true. And so had Little Turtle and the members of his mother's family, as well as Shagbark. They had all come to the great Falling Waters and never meant to go back to Seneca Town again.

Then Molly understood why they had followed her to Genesee Town. They meant to keep her from going home. They were not her friends at all. They were Indians and meant to make her an Indian, too. But she would get away just the same.

One day Earth Woman sat by her bed, surrounded by dried corn-husks. The little white dog made a nest in them and slept. Earth Woman said that corn harvest on the Genesee was long over. All the ears in the great piles had been stripped down, the husks braided in bunches, about twenty ears in each. Now the fresh harvested corn hung high in the roofs of all the lodges, ready for winter use. From the scattering, loose husks left over, Earth Woman said that many useful things could be fashioned—moccasins, mats, masks, bowls and bottles. None of the husks would be wasted.

Earth Woman's fingers flew fast and beneath them the dry husks made a gentle rustling. Molly watched to see what would emerge. A few moments later, the woman handed her a corn-husk doll.

Molly stared at it dully. "A corn-husk baby," she said, slowly. "A baby made of corn-husks. But why has it no face?"

"If it had a face," explained Earth Woman, "that would complete the effigy and invite a spirit to come and inhabit it. You could not tell the spirit was hiding inside, because the corn-husk is so unlike flesh. If you dropped the doll or hurt it in any way, you would be hurting the spirit. That we must never do—so we put no faces on our dolls.

"Besides," Earth Woman went on, after a pause, "if it had a face with a set expression, the face would never change. With no face at all, the corn-husk baby can laugh, cry or sleep at will. Corn Tassel can see in its face whatever she wishes it to feel." Under the woman's strong fingers, the corn-husks began to rattle again.

Molly looked at the doll as it lay in the palm of her hand. It was not like a real baby at all, not like Blue Jay or baby Robert at home. It was like a miniature grown-up—a tiny, small-boned woman. Its arms were braided corn-husks, its clothes were strips of dried corn leaves. A handful of dried-up corn-silk was fastened to the corn-husk head.

She pressed it suddenly to her lips, then looked at it again. She was glad now it had no face—no dark brown eyes, no brown Indian skin, no shining black hair. She saw instead a fair white face with eyes of blue beneath the yellow corn-silk hair. A spirit *had* come to inhabit it. Her corn-husk baby was a white woman.

Then she thought of the white woman in shining silk at Fort Duquesne and her eyes filled with tears. "I see only sadness in its face," she said.

"By and by the corn-husk baby will smile for you," said the Indian woman. "She will smile to make you strong and well again."

"Will I ever be well again?" asked Molly. She knew in that moment that there are two kinds of sickness—sickness of the heart as well as the body.

A day came when Earth Woman lifted Molly from her bed and led her out in the sun in front of the lodge. The little white dog came, too. Molly took a few uncertain steps and stared at what she saw.

An Indian girl sat on the ground beside a pile of wet, smooth clay. She was the same size as Molly, but very brown. She wore garments of bright-colored broadcloth, embroidered with beads. Two long black braids hung down beside her cheeks. She did not raise her eyes. She took wet clay between her palms and rolled it into a long, slender rope.

"What is she doing?" asked Molly, sitting down beside her.

"She is making a cooking-pot," replied Earth Woman.

"What is her name?"

"Beaver Girl," answered Earth Woman. "Well has she earned it. She is industrious like the beaver. She is always busy."

Earth Woman sat down on the ground and began to pound a pile of rougher clay with sticks and after a time, knead it with her hands. Molly kept her eyes on Beaver Girl. Round and round she twisted the slender rope of clay in even coils upon a flat stone. Gradually each coil overlapped itself and the clay began to form the crude shape of a pot.

"Why does she not speak?" asked Molly.

"She is shy before the new white girl captive," said Earth Woman, "but she is anxious to be your friend."

"I saw no one make pots in Seneca Town by the River Ohio," said Molly. "Do all the Indian girls here make cooking-pots?"

"Alas, no!" replied Earth Woman sadly. "Only Beaver

Girl because I have taught her. Most of the women, even, have forgotten how. It is an old, old art, rapidly becoming lost. It is so easy now to buy brass kettles from the white traders. When I was young, we knew nothing of brass kettles. All the women made pots—beautiful pots to be proud of. As my grandmother taught me, so have I taught Beaver Girl."

Earth Woman paused in her work to watch the coils build up under the Indian girl's fingers. "So coils the forked-tongue," she said softly, "whose bite is like the sting of bad arrows. So coils the rattle-snake, ready to spring; but if a man be wise, he will heed the snake's loud warning. The sting of the forked-tongue is deep and the eyes of the heedless man will close in sleep, unless quickly he obtains help of our brother, the ash tree. A brew from the ash tree's bark will check the poison; a poultice from its bruised leaves will heal the wound."

Although Molly scarcely seemed to hear then, long afterwards the woman's soft words were to come back to her, plainly, yet unmistakably.

Silently she watched Beaver Girl's dark fingers work the clay coils together and smooth unevenness away. She saw her scrape the sides smooth with a piece of broken gourd. The shape of the pot grew more beautiful as she watched.

"Please, Earth Woman," she asked, suddenly, "could I not make a cooking-pot?"

"*Ohè!* You!" cried Earth Woman, astonished. "An ear

of corn not half filled out?" She frowned, then with all the appearance of anger, broke out: "Do you not know then that it is hard work to make a cooking-pot? That the fingers which shape it must be trained to skill? That only Earth Woman, of all the women in the village, has the skill to make a perfect cooking-pot? No! A fledgling that lingers in the warmth of the nest has not yet the strength to fly. By and by, perhaps . . ."

"But if Beaver Girl can make one . . . She's no bigger than I!" cried Molly.

"Ah, but Beaver Girl has dipped her hands in clay ever since she stepped out of her baby frame!" laughed Earth Woman. "And Beaver Girl is as strong as a beaver."

"But I grow stronger day by day," protested Molly. "See!" She held out her arm and doubled her elbow.

"*Ohè!*" Earth Woman laughed again. "Corn Tassel is as strong as a little humming-bird. Only a strong woman can do a strong woman's work. The making of a pot is not easy. The clay must be gathered from the banks by the river bed. First Earth Woman prays to Mother Earth for permission to remove it. Then she digs it carefully and brings it home. She spreads it on the stone slab, she beats it with her hands and with stones; she treads it with her feet. When the clay is soft and smooth, it must be mixed with ground clam shells or mica and be beaten smooth again. All this before the coils are rolled."

"When I am strong like Beaver Girl, then may I make one?" asked Molly.

"Yes, little humming-bird, then you may try," said Earth Woman, with a smile. "Meanwhile it is well to watch how a cooking-pot grows under hands of long experience. That is the best way to learn."

Beaver Girl carefully turned and shaped the collar of her pot, and made a scalloped design on the edge. Then she set the pot aside, with others, to dry.

"When the water has been drawn out of the clay by the sun," said Earth Woman, "the pots will be ready for firing. We will set them over a slow-burning fire and keep them there. The fire must not be too hot, because that would crack the pots. If it is too cool, it will smoke them. Oh, no—like all good things, a cooking-pot is not easy to make."

When Molly went back to bed, Earth Woman's sharp eyes noticed that she did not pick up her cornhusk baby, her little white woman, and look at it with tears in her eyes. Earth Woman's kind face beamed with satisfaction, for she knew that the white girl captive had forgotten, at least for the moment, her sorrow. She was thinking of the cooking-pot which one day she would make.

Ah, a cooking-pot was good in more ways than one. A cooking-pot could make a white girl forget to be home-sick. A cooking-pot could make a girl want to be well and strong again. Earth Woman was wise enough to know that a cooking-pot could do what all the herbs and medicines in the world could not. But there was no hurry—there were many moons to come. In time, in the fulness of time, the white girl would forget altogether.

Molly's body grew gradually stronger. Each day she lay on a blanket in the sun for hours. Then she began to walk about, taking longer and longer walks. A happy day came when she went as far as the banks of the Falling Waters, carrying her corn-husk baby with her and talking to it in English. There she rested on the leaf-covered bank and, as she watched the flying birds and the water's swift movement, the beauty of the place gave her peace and eased the sharpness of her sorrow.

* * * *

Restored again to health and strength, Molly returned to Red Bird's lodge, but still spent most of her days with Earth Woman. One day the Indian woman suggested a trip to the forest.

"Now that the frost has loosened the nuts of the shag-bark hickory," she said, "we must go out with the children and gather them before the squirrels carry them off. Some of the nuts we will store in pits for winter use; from some we will press out an oil to eat with bread or meat; some we will trade when the white trader comes. And before Hó-tho seals the ground up fast and hard, I must dig more roots for food and medicine. Beaver Girl will help me."

"Who is Hó-tho?" asked Molly.

"Hó-tho is Cold Weather," explained Earth Woman. "Every winter he takes his hatchet from his hip, waves it in the air and strikes the trees with it. That's what makes them crack with such a loud noise. But man has learned to outwit Hó-tho. Man builds fires, drinks hot drinks and keeps warm under blankets and fur coverings."

Earth Woman called the children together and they all started off with baskets on their arms. It was the first time Molly had seen the children and she was sorry Little Turtle was not among them. As Earth Woman told her their names—Chipmunk, Star Flower, Woodchuck, Lazy Duck, Storm Cloud, and others—they stared at the white newcomer with frank curiosity. Then they ran on and forgot her.

Most of the leaves had fallen and the trees were almost bare. The ground lay white beneath the straight shaggy hickory trunks, covered with nuts all free from their shells, nuts which had been showered down by the wind. The children ran off in all directions, but Molly stayed near Earth Woman and set to work to fill her basket. As they worked busily, Earth Woman talked and eagerly Molly drank in her words.

Earth Woman was wiser than any Indian woman Molly had known before. She had all the wisdom of Red Bird, Bear Woman, Shining Star and far, far more. Her wisdom reached out through the endless forest, up to the changing skies and deep, deep down into the earth. She knew everything about the earth, its plants and its creatures. She knew about the unknown world as well—the world of dreams and spirits. Molly saved up her words and grew stronger in more ways than she knew.

"I will tell you," said Earth Woman, "why there are so many trees in the forest. The squirrels plant them. Each time a squirrel buries a nut in the earth, he puts but one in a hole. If he should fail to return for his nut, it grows into a tree and then the forest has one tree more."

Then Earth Woman told how the chipmunk got its stripes and why the rabbit runs in circles. She had a story for everything.

One of the Indian girls, small and chubby, came running up with a frown on her face.

"What is the matter, Storm Cloud?" asked Earth Woman. "Why is it that you always pout?"

"A big dog chased me," replied the girl. "Or else it was a deer."

"Why, Storm Cloud!" cried Chipmunk, a boy somewhat older. "You are as stupid as a pale-face! The patter of a dog's feet sounds nothing like the tread of a running deer."

"But I saw it!" insisted Storm Cloud. "Maybe it was a wolf, then."

"A wolf!" laughed Chipmunk. "Wolves always howl—you can hear them a long way off."

Molly turned to Earth Woman. "Can an Indian tell what animal it is from listening to its hoofbeats? How does he know?"

"The Indian child goes to the forest to learn," replied Earth Woman, "to learn to see with his eyes and hear with his ears. He watches the young of the bear at play. The fawns come to eat from his hand. He coaxes the squirrels and rabbits from their holes. He is their brother, their play-fellow. The forest is the Indian child's home. He is more at home in the forest than in his own lodge."

Earth Woman paused, then she continued: "Every plant that grows in the forest was put there by the Great Spirit for some purpose. A girl who is soon to be a woman must learn their names and uses. Whenever you see a new plant whose name you do not know, bring it in to me and I will tell you about it."

"But I should have to bring my hands full every day!" laughed Molly. "I know so few. I know blood-root, trillium and jack-in-the-pulpit when they are in bloom. The pale-faces have no time to study all the plants in the forest."

"If you will bring in one plant each day during the summer, you will soon know a great deal," said Earth Woman. "The Indians find time for everything useful. The Great Spirit placed his children in the forest so that they might learn to understand and love it."

With their digging sticks in hand, Earth Woman and Beaver Girl walked away to a boggy place beside a small creek, to dig lily roots and green arum. For a while after she was left alone, Molly worked busily. Not a breath of air was stirring in the quiet woods. Now and then bright-colored leaves dropped gently to the earth. The hickory nuts made a soft clatter as they fell into her basket. Then suddenly she felt tired. Her strength was not so great as she had supposed. She picked up a nut from the ground and its slight weight felt heavy in her hand.

She sat down at the base of a large maple tree and leaned against the trunk to rest. Idly she watched a gray squirrel. It ran down the trunk of a tree, chattering noisily, picked up a nut and scampered back again. "Are you planting a tree, little squirrel?" asked Molly. Then she saw that he was burying his nuts, not in the ground, but in a hollow of the tree. He worked fast, putting aside his winter's food supply. "Take them, little squirrel," said Molly, softly. "I give them to you, so you will not be hungry when winter comes."

Molly thought of Earth Woman's story. It was pleasant to know that the squirrels had planted the beautiful forest. The Indians lived closer to growing things and to the animals than the white people did. They knew and understood them better. They accepted them as friends to be cherished, not enemies to be destroyed or conquered.

As she sat there, Molly could almost imagine she was back at Marsh Creek Hollow again. On the trail that led to Neighbor Dixon's there was just such a huge maple tree as the one under which she was sitting. Earth Woman's stories faded away. Molly liked them but they never quite filled up her mind. Always behind them and behind everything she did, lay her longing for home, unchanged—the homesickness that would not be blotted out. Sometimes she did not hear Earth Woman's words at all. She was living in two places at once, her body with the Indians, but her spirit where she wanted to be—at home with the white people. Once she and Betsey had sat down to rest under the maple tree on the trail to the Dixons' and had seen a deer run by so close they could have touched it . . .

Molly caught her breath. Was she dreaming? There before her, as if in answer to her thought, stood a deer—a tall and stately buck, with antlers like a growing tree upon its head. Molly's hand flew to her mouth, to smother her cry of surprise. The deer paused a moment, as if listening, looking past her into the depth of the forest. Then, with a bound, away into the forest it leaped. Molly held its picture in her mind long after it was gone.

Some moments later, she heard a movement inside the trunk of the tree behind her. She rose hastily, walked round the tree and soon found a long, narrow opening, wider at the bottom. The trunk was rotten inside and had been hollowed out. Along one side the bark was scratched and she could see the marks of claws.

"If I were an Indian," thought Molly, "I would know at once what animal it is. But I'm as stupid as four-year-old Storm Cloud."

She peeped into the hole. It was dark inside and she could see nothing. The movement continued. Seeing the Indian children not far away, she called and they came running.

"Bear cubs!" announced Woodchuck, wisely.

"Let's take one home!" begged Star Flower. "I want a cub for a pet."

"What?" asked Molly. "What do you want him for?"

"We will put a rope round his neck," answered Star Flower, jumping up and down. "We will teach the bear cub to do tricks. Once when the trader came, he brought a bear cub that could dance and do tricks."

"You would take the bear cub away from its mother," asked Molly slowly, "and make it a captive?"

"Yes," answered Woodchuck, coldly. "Why not?" This white girl who spoke in Indian was a queer person, indeed. Woodchuck scowled at her with disgust.

"Oh, you have to take him very young," cried Chipmunk, "if you want to tame him. If he's too old, he will stay savage and manage to get away somehow. Or else, the men will kill him before he does, for bear meat."

"Let us first ask Earth Woman," suggested Molly. "Earth Woman will not let you make a bear a captive. She will say it is better for the baby bear to run free in the forest . . ."

"How do you know what she will say?" demanded Lazy Duck.

"We will ask no one," said Woodchuck, firmly. "I am the eldest boy and I shall decide. We shall take the mother bear, too. Bear meat is good to eat."

"Bears have lots of fat," chimed in Storm Cloud. "My grandmother fries it out and makes a deerskin bag to hold it."

"Bear oil is good to spread on chapped faces in winter," added Star Flower. "Bear oil makes my hair lie smooth and black and shiny. Is bear oil good for yellow hair, too?"

Molly turned away from her and faced the two boys boldly. "How will you take the mother bear?" she asked with quiet patience.

"Kill her, of course!" answered Woodchuck, promptly. "My mother is always pleased to have bear meat brought to her lodge. What does a pale-face know about bears, anyhow?"

"I know this much," retorted Molly, hotly. "I know that to kill a bear you must at least have a bow and arrow!"

"Ho ho! A bow and arrow!" laughed Woodchuck.

"We might chase her home . . ." began Chipmunk.

"Here comes Earth Woman," said Molly quickly, as she heard footsteps rustling in the leaves behind her. "Let us ask her and do what she says."

"Oh, may we take the bear cub?" cried the Indian girls, together.

"Don't let them!" begged Molly. "Oh, please don't let them put a rope round its neck."

No answer came. Why did Earth Woman not speak? Molly turned and looked behind her. To her surprise she saw a huge black animal coming directly toward her.

"There's that big black dog again!" said Storm Cloud, pointing.

Molly gasped. It was not Earth Woman at all. It was not a dog, deer or wolf. Anyone should know that such awkward, clumsy motions could only be made by a heavy animal like the bear.

The children fell into sudden silence. "The mother bear!" said Woodchuck, in a low voice. "The mother bear is angry!"

Like falling leaves blown by a gust of wind, the children slipped noiselessly into the underbrush and disappeared. All but Chipmunk. Chipmunk and Molly stayed where they were.

Chipmunk was young and slim, younger even than Little Turtle. Bravely Chipmunk picked up a dead branch and shook it. He jumped toward the bear, to frighten it

away. Then gradually he backed up, as the mother bear approached the hollow maple tree where her cubs were. Molly ran to the other side and so did Chipmunk. The tree was wide enough to hide them from sight.

Chipmunk thought fast. He remembered Woodchuck's boasting that they would take the bear and the cub. But Woodchuck had run away. How could Chipmunk do it? Still waving the stick, he peered round the tree again. Molly looked, too. To their surprise they saw that the mother bear was running off, her cubs following. There were two of them, big, fat and roly-poly. Chipmunk

and Molly stared after them in silence. Soon they were lost to sight in the dense woods.

The children came back at Chipmunk's call. They looked in at the bed of dry grass in the empty hole in the tree where the cubs had been. Then Earth Woman and Beaver Girl came up. The children all talked at once, telling the exciting story.

"The mother bear was more scared than we were," cried Chipmunk. "Why didn't you kill her, Woodchuck?"

Woodchuck did not answer. He was still scowling.

"She had two fine cubs!" cried Star Flower. "And we didn't get one of them."

Earth Woman shook her head. "A mother bear is a dangerous animal," she said. "If you had tried to take one of her cubs, she would have started fighting. You had no weapons with you. It is best she ran away with her cubs."

"We have lost our pets!" cried the children, sadly.

"The cubs have no ropes about their necks," said Molly to herself. "They are still free. I'm glad they are not captives."

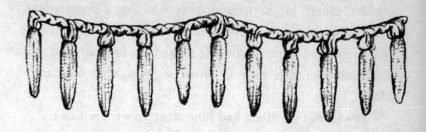

X   *Old Fallenash*

*H*ere, keep these for me!" Little Turtle dropped a few arrows on the ground beside Molly, who sat hidden under a clump of bushes in the forest. "I think the turkeys will soon be coming down to the river to drink."

Little Turtle walked cautiously into the woods again. He sat down upon a log and remained as motionless as possible. Then he began to sound his call on a turkeybone, imitating the get-together notes of the wild turkey, the way Shagbark had taught him: *"Keow-keow-kee-kee-keow! Keow-keow-kee-kee-keow!"*

Molly felt sure that no turkey would recognize it as a human cry. She did not have long to wait. A flock of wild turkeys came hopping and running through the woods, gobbling noisily.

Little Turtle held his breath as he picked out a bird and took aim. Putting his arrow to the bow string, he drew it and sent it flying. *Whizz!* The arrow hit the biggest gobbler square in the breast. After running a few yards with drooping wings, the bird tumbled over. Out from the bushes jumped Little Turtle. He picked the bird up by the neck and swung it round. Then he brought it over to Molly.

The rest of the flock had long since flown up into the trees and disappeared.

"I got him!" said Little Turtle, proudly. "I won't need the other arrows. You can carry them."

Molly clutched them tightly in her hand. Slowly the boy and girl walked back to the village.

"I expect Shagbark will have my new bow and arrows ready for me today," said Little Turtle. "He will be pleased to learn that I brought down a turkey with my first shot." The boy looked up at Molly and smiled happily. "I shall throw this bow and those blunt arrows away," he went on. "I shall never use them again."

All at once he noticed that Corn Tassel had not spoken. He looked into her face and saw how sober it was.

"What have I done to make you feel sad, Corn Tassel?" he asked. "Shagbark says that we should do no harm and bring no sadness to anyone. He says if we can make a person happy, we should do so. If we pass a stranger in the road, we should cheer him with a word of greeting before we pass on."

Molly looked down at the ground and said nothing.

"You need not speak," said Little Turtle. "I know what troubles you. You remember your loved ones always and you cannot forget them. In Seneca Town, I asked Chief Standing Pine to send you home to the pale-faces, but he said it was not possible. If I thought it would help any, I would speak to Chief Burning Sky."

"No—don't!" begged Molly. "I knew from the first you understood my trouble. It never leaves me, no matter where I go or what I do—but just now, it is the turkey that makes me sad."

"What!" cried Little Turtle, holding up his prize. "You are not happy then that I have killed this fine fat gobbler? The whole village will rejoice and tell me what a fine hunter I am. You are not happy that all the people in my mother's lodge will dip their bread in turkey gravy tomorrow?"

"It made me feel sick to see it die!" confessed Molly, in a whisper. "Oh, why did you ask me to come with you to the woods?"

"*Hoh!*" cried Little Turtle, puzzled. "That I do not understand. The spirits of the animals go up to the sky. 'Tis only their bodies we kill. Indian girls—Beaver Girl, Star Flower and the others—none of them weep. Do the pale-faces, then, never kill animals for food? Is a pale-faced girl different from Indian girls that it makes her feel sick?"

"*This* pale-face is different," said Molly. "Corn Tassel can only weep to see a bird suffer pain."

"Weeping is weakness," replied Little Turtle, sternly. "To be sick is weakness. To refrain from weeping is to gain in strength. Indian girls must be strong and well-hardened."

"But I am not an Indian girl!" Molly broke out, indignant. "I shall never be an Indian girl as long as I live!"

Old Shagbark was working busily, as usual, surrounded by his finished handiwork—bark barrels, wooden bowls, carved pipes and ladles. In his hand he held an arrow-point of flint. With a piece of deer antler he flaked it on the palm of his hand. The two children watched him in silence.

Soon he laid down the piece of deer antler and picked up a red willow shaft which had been smoothed with sandstone. With deer sinew he bound the arrow head fast to the shaft. Then he held it up.

"My son," he announced solemnly, "you may have your arrows feathered with the best eagle or hawk feathers, whichever you prefer, and dyed whatever color you choose."

"Feathers are useful," said Little Turtle, thoughtfully, "to make the arrow fly straight to the mark. But eagle feathers I do not care for, and hawk feathers are not to my liking. Could I not have turkey feathers, Grandfather?"

"Turkey feathers?" asked Shagbark, with all the appearance of surprise and a touch of anger. "Where, then, would we get turkey feathers, may I ask?"

"Here!" cried Little Turtle. With a proud, bold gesture, he lifted up the bird which he had killed and held it in the air.

"Oh ho!" laughed Shagbark. "So now I see! Where did the big, fat turkey come from, may I ask?"

With pride and delight, Little Turtle told his story and

to please him, Shagbark fastened turkey feathers in their natural color to the end of first one arrow shaft, then another.

"When your arrows fly through the air," said Shagbark, smiling, "they will sing always the song of the wild turkey. Through the air your arrows will go singing *gobble-gobble-gobble-gobble-gup!*"

Little Turtle pulled two long tail feathers from his turkey. Then he brought out his cap. "Please, Grandfather, could you not fix them in a socket on top of my cap, so that they will turn in the wind?"

"What splendid ideas fly through this young hunter's mind!" cried Shagbark, attaching the feathers as requested. When it was done, the boy put the cap on his head. "At night I will hang my feathered cap on the wall over my couch," he exclaimed, happily, "but as soon as morning comes, I will put it on my head."

"Your name is no longer Little Turtle!" announced Shagbark, picking up the turkey and weighing it in his hands. "From now on, your name shall be Turkey Feather for the turkey feathers from your first turkey which you wear in your cap."

"My happiness would be great, Grandfather" said the boy, "except for one thing. Corn Tassel weeps because the turkey is dead."

Shagbark turned to Molly, who had said no word since she came in. He drew her to one side and asked, "What lies heavy on your heart, little one?"

Molly gulped, then spoke haltingly: "It is good for Little Turtle . . . to have turkey feathers on his arrows . . . to make them go faster. It is good for him to have turkey feathers . . . to wear in his cap. But . . . oh, why did he have to kill the turkey? Its feathers were shining so brightly even in the dark forest and it was so happy, running fast to the river to get a drink of water. It only wanted to go on living and to have a drink of water. But after the arrow hit it, its wings began flopping and it fell over and died."

"I see what troubles you," said Old Shagbark, full of sympathy, "and I believe I can help you. An Indian never kills for the sake of seeing an animal die. Hunting is not a game—it is a necessity. A hunter kills only when meat is needed. Before killing, he asks permission of the animal's spirit, telling it that its body is needed for the good of the people. To the moose or bear, the hunter says in a low voice, 'Brother Moose. Brother Bear, I am sorry to take your life, but I need your flesh for food and your hide for clothing. It is your turn to die; some day it will be mine.' Afterwards, when he ties the tail or a tuft of hair to the twig of a tree, he offers the spirit his thanks.

"The wild creatures are our brothers and even the dangerous ones are not molested unless they make an attack. Little Turtle or Turkey Feather, as we shall now call him, will take the turkey to his mother. It will make a fine meal for all the members of his mother's family."

Shagbark looked at Molly and still saw sadness on her face.

"The Great Spirit has told the Senecas they may kill only enough animals for their food and clothing and no more," said the old man. "If the children of the forest had no meat, they would die. He placed his children in the forest and he gave them the animals for their food."

"Yes, I understand," said Molly, unhappily, "but . . . but it still makes me feel sick inside." Then she lifted her chin and cried out boldly: "It is not weakness to hate to see a cruel deed, as Little Turtle says. It is not bravery to make oneself hard and unfeeling and to close one's eyes to suffering. It is braver far to hate the sight of another's pain.

You call the animals your brothers . . . and yet you deny them the right to live . . . The animal's life is as dear to him as ours to us. It makes me weep to see an animal die. I will not be strong and hard like an Indian girl. I am not ashamed of my tears—I would save the animal's life if I could . . ."

Sobbing, she turned away, but Shagbark drew her back again.

"The Senecas are the richer for having a daughter like you, Corn Tassel," said the old man. "They have much to learn from the pale-face. Sympathy, love for our brother, is what we all most need. That you can teach us as no one else can, little one. Perhaps that is why the Great Spirit led you to come to us. Perhaps only you, in all the world, could do this for us and that is the reason that you became a captive!"

He paused, then continued: "Hunting is a man's work. It is not meant for women. Their tender hearts are better suited for the care of little children and for tending growing things—the corn, beans and squashes. It is man's duty to bring in meat for food and woman's to prepare it for eating. And now, let us see. This young hunter, who has brought a fine, fat turkey to his mother's lodge, has earned a reward. He shall have not only a quiver full of new flint-headed arrows, but a new bow as well. From now on, he shall hunt with bow and arrows fit for the best hunter in the tribe."

Shagbark brought out a strong, beautifully shaped, carved bow made of a hickory sapling and strung with sinew cord.

"See if you are able to draw this bow, Turkey Feather," he said to the boy.

Turkey Feather drew the bow easily. Shagbark handed him an arrow and bade him come outdoors. Pointing to a great hickory tree, he said, "Take aim at the topmost branch of that tree, but do not shoot."

Turkey Feather took his position and pulled the arrow back.

"Shoot that duck as it flies across!" said Shagbark, quietly.

Whizz! The flint-headed arrow went singing through the air and in a moment the bird dropped to the ground.

"One of these days," said Shagbark, solemnly, "Turkey Feather will be a great hunter."

"Please accept this duck for your supper, Grandfather," said Turkey Feather, running back with the bird in his hand. "May I always be worthy of the man's bow and arrows which you have seen fit to give me."

"We will go now to Chief Burning Sky's lodge," said Shagbark. "We will present the new hunter, Turkey Feather, to the Chief."

Dusk fell and evening came. The night air was cold with the fresh briskness of late autumn. Inside Chief Burning Sky's lodge, a crowd had gathered. A bright fire burned on the hard clay ground and threw flickering lights on the upturned faces. Several women moved silently about in the shadows, bringing in loads of hemlock and pine wood which crackled and sputtered as the fire consumed it.

Inside the door, Molly hesitated. She had not yet mixed with the people of Genesee Town. Except for the children, they were strangers to her. Perhaps they did not know that a white girl captive had been brought to the village. Then she wondered why they were so quiet. Something unusual must be about to happen. She looked over their heads. She saw Old Shagbark and Turkey Feather go into the adjoining room and speak to the Chief and his men. Then, in a moment, she forgot them entirely, for she saw something which took her completely by surprise.

She saw a man standing by the fire in the first room, leaning upon a long, thin rifle. He was a backwoodsman. He wore fringed deerskin hunting-shirt and leggings. On his head at a rakish angle, sat a raccoon skin cap, with its striped tail caressing his broad shoulder. A pouch for bullets hung from the man's belt, a hunting-knife was stuck in a sheath and a carved powderhorn was slung over his chest by a strap.

All these things Molly saw in a flash and in that flash, her Indian life faded completely away. The man was the same height and build as her father. The side of his cheek was stubbly with rough whiskers. His clothes were her father's clothes. Or, was she dreaming?

Molly took hold of a bunk-pole and gripped it tight. She stared at the rifle, at its shining metal, glittering in the firelight. Had she seen it before? Had she taken it once in her hands to point it at an Indian? But the man did not speak. He did not turn and look at her.

Then she could wait no longer. Past the waiting, astonished Indians, past the crackling fire, into his arms she rushed.

The man's face looked down at her and from his thin lips, a word of astonishment broke out. "Hello!" he said, weakly. "Who's this?"

Then she knew it was not her father. The voice was the voice of another man, who was not her father at all. But it had a familiar ring to it. Had she heard the voice before?

Molly's arms dropped weakly down and she almost fell to the ground, so limp had she become. She stepped back a little and looked at him keenly. Then she smiled, for the face took her back, back again swiftly to Marsh Creek Hollow. No, it was not her father. It was Old Fallenash, the white trader; and his words drawled soft and sweet, spoken as only backwoodsmen spoke them.

"Why, look-a-here!" cried the man, staring hard. "Seems like I've seen you before somewhere, but not in them clothes—not all decked out in Indian togs! Have they been tryin' to make an Indian out of a white gal with yaller hair? Seems like I can see you back down there somewhere, a-sittin' in a log cabin on a three-legged stool, dressed up in purty blue homespun. Now, ain't it a fact?"

"Oh, Fallenash!" Molly was in his arms again, unashamed. "Oh, Fallenash, have I changed, then, so much? Don't say that you don't remember. Tell me you know who I am!" The girl was sobbing now. The pain of

not being recognized stabbed her through and through.

The assembled Indians began to exclaim. Their cries of astonishment made a murmuring chorus behind the words of man and girl.

"If only you'd take off them Indian togs and put on blue homespun again," said Fallenash, lamely, "I'd know ye in a minute, gal. Sure as I'm a white man, sure as my name's Fallenash, I've seen them blue eyes somewhere. But your skin's gone brown now, too, just like an Indian's and my eyesight's gittin' dimmer each day."

"Oh, Fallenash, Fallenash! Don't say you have forgot!" cried Molly, unhappily. "Don't tell me you don't remember. I'm Molly Jemison from Marsh Creek Hollow! You used to come time and again! Each year you came . . ."

"To be sure! To be sure!" Old Fallenash settled his coonskin cap more firmly. "Now I know. You're Tom Jemison's darter, from Marsh Creek Holler in Pennsylvania. Many's the time I've sat on Tom's big hearthstone and talked far into the night. Remember? I'll say I remember. There's no other hair as yaller as Molly Jemison's along the hull frontier, and I'd orter know, I've traveled everywhere."

"Oh, Fallenash!" Molly hung to his arms and would not let him go. Like water from a fresh mountain spring, the words came pouring: "How long since you've been there? When did you see them last? Did they send a message along for me, in case you would find me? Did they send you to search me out? Oh, tell me they're well and hearty . . . Oh, tell me they think of me still . . ."

"Slowly, now slowly!" answered Fallenash. "This ain't no time to be talkin'. The Indians are anxious to trade and I must give them attention. There's Chief Burning Sky and there's Panther Woman a-comin'. She scares the gizzard out of me. I can't talk to ye now, but I will later, before I go."

Then, seeing the look of disappointment on the girl's face, he decided he might as well get the worst over.

"I ain't been to Marsh Creek Holler," he said, quickly, "not for a long, long time I ain't. I didn't know ye was took by the Injuns. Honest, I never dreamed of such a thing. The Chief's comin' now with his woman . . . don't forgit, I'll see ye by and by."

Just then Squirrel Woman darted out from behind the others and pulled Molly back into the crowd.

"Once more you rush forth to talk to a pale-face!" she scolded. "With shame I behold you, rushing out before the eyes of all the village. Only the Chief and men of importance may speak to the trader—children never. How oft must I tell you—you are an Indian, your lips are to form words only of Indian."

Squirrel Woman's words passed over Molly's head. Fallenash had not been to Marsh Creek Hollow for a long, long time. Fallenash did not even know, after all the long months, that she had been taken by the Indians. He had not seen her family. The news was crushing, but still there was hope. Perhaps then, he would be going there soon. Perhaps he would take her along. She watched the trading with impatience.

The Indians had brought packs of furs and hides, and baskets of nuts to trade. Fallenash passed tobacco around and the smoking and talking began. The trader brought from his pack several small shiny brass kettles and set them in a row on his blanket. He spread out rolls of bright-colored cloth and blankets, strings of gay, brilliant beads and a fine array of silver jewelry, tools and weapons.

The Indians stared at the objects, fascinated. After a long delay, the Chief gave the signal for the trading to begin and, one by one, the buyers approached.

"Beads are better'n porcupine quills," said Fallenash, lifting a handful and letting them fall in a shower. "You don't have to go to the trouble of dyein' 'em; they don't get sticky and crack like quills. Quills are all right for embroidering deerskin, but for this handsome cloth, you want handsome beads."

He unrolled a bolt of bright red broadcloth and held it up in the fire-light, while his coaxing, wheedling voice went on: "Good quality cloth in the brightest colors—every bit as durable as deerskin. Soon you'll forget how to tan your hides—you'll all be wearing cloth! As for earthen pots that break so easy, you've most forgot them already. See these brass kettles—you can kick 'em around! They'll bend, but they won't break! They'll last forever. Cheap, too—considerin' what you're gettin'. How 'bout some handsome silver bracelets for your women?"

Molly saw the greedy looks on the faces of the Indian women. She saw the frown on Chief Burning Sky's face grow heavier. Was he displeased with the trader and his wares? Did he dislike seeing the Indians buy white men's goods? How eager and greedy she herself would have been—at any other time! But now, all she could think of was Fallenash's news.

Log-in-the-Water, the laziest Indian in the village, seized a pair of silver ear-rings and held them up. After careful examination and long pondering, he offered a beaver skin to pay. Fallenash nodded and the exchange was made.

Big Kettle, known for his greediness, came next. For a fine steel tomahawk he reluctantly piled his skins higher and higher and grudgingly handed them over.

Gray Wolf, sullen and leering, demanded fire-water to quench his thirst. Fallenash shook his head and said quietly, "Soberness makes more money for a trader than drunkenness." Gray Wolf left the room, swearing.

Molly stood at the edge of the crowd and looked over the Indians' heads. Some of the women bargained endlessly for pieces of cloth, for beads and jewelry. Others walked away with shining brass kettles on their arms. Would the trading never be over? Gradually the trader's wares found their way into the Indians' hands, and the furs and nuts for payment were placed on the ground by his side.

Still the Indians lingered by the fire. They waited for Fallenash, who traveled over both frontier and wilderness, who had free entry to white and Indian camp-fires alike, to speak, for he was always the bearer of news. Molly hid behind a bark barrel to keep out of sight of the Indian women.

"Blood has indeed flowed red," Fallenash began in Indian, approaching the subject with grave caution, "to color the falling leaves with rich autumn brilliance."

Chief Burning Sky's face changed not at all. As if he were already acquainted with the news, or suspected in advance its import, he gazed quietly into the fire.

"Fort Duquesne has fallen!" announced Fallenash. "The French have lost it to the English."

He looked around the circle. The news was greeted with silence. Not a head was turned, not a word was said.

"Them English were too strong for them, even with the Indians' help," the trader went on. "The French, I am sorry to say, had to run, some down the River Ohio, others overland to Presque Isle and others up the Allegheny River to Venango. A friend of mine who was there told me about it. Fort Duquesne's only a mass of black and burning ruins. It's been completely destroyed."

"The fort?" cried Molly. Forgetting her caution, she ran to the man's side. "The fort with the peach tree in the yard?"

But Fallenash paid no attention to her.

"When them English under Forbes came rushing in, in three columns, they had nothing to do," he continued, his eyes upon the Chief's face. "They found the fortifications blown up and the barracks and storehouses burned to the ground. Only thirty chimney stacks were left standing. The French had to do it themselves—to keep it from falling into the hands of them English. Looks like they got good and scared and ran for their lives when they saw them English coming. The Indians ran, too, I suppose."

He paused, then went on: "Them English will have to build it up again, if they want a fort of their own there—at the forks of the River Ohio, and I reckon they do. Sir William Johnson, I hear, is no friend of the Frenchmen. He'll be takin' Fort Niagara next, if we don't watch out, and Quebec too, they say. Then a Frenchman's hide won't be worth a pinch of tobacco. Trouble is, the French need more help from the Indians than they've been gettin'."

As the trader spoke, he did not look once at the white girl there before him. Leaning on his knee, she drank in all his words and tried to comprehend their meaning. Fort Duquesne, with the cold, gray stockade walls, burned to the ground! Only the chimney stacks of the log houses left standing. The barn, the well-sweeps, the garden, the peach tree—all were gone. The Frenchmen were gone as well as the Indians. Now the English, the red-coated English were there. She could never go back again to Fort Duquesne— to the man and woman who had wanted to keep her.

"Which side will the Iroquois take, English or French?" asked Fallenash, bluntly, looking toward the Chief. "You Senecas will have to make up your minds. You want to hold them English back on the Atlantic seaboard, don't you? So far, you've been good friends of the French and they need you now worse than ever. You won't let them English talk you over to their side, will you?"

"That is a question I cannot answer," said the Chief. "The League of the Iroquois must decide. The People of the Long House must speak for themselves."

"Well, if you desert the French," said Fallenash, with a smile, "it means goodbye to all French agents and traders. Me—I ain't on one side nor t'other. I like the Indians better. But when this fightin' begins, I'll have to run fast to save my hide. Maybe I'll have to give up this wandering life and settle down somewhere—where there ain't no tomahawks flyin'!"

"Will you be going back to Marsh Creek Hollow then?" asked Molly, quickly.

But the question was not answered, for Squirrel Woman's hand grasped the girl's shoulder and away she was hustled to Red Bird's lodge.

Molly was determined to speak to Fallenash before he left the village. All night she thought over what she would say. All night she tossed and turned, trying to keep awake. At dawn, unheard and unseen, she crept from her bed and ran out the door. As she expected, the trader was already there. He was loading his pack-train as she came up.

"Take me with you, Fallenash!" she cried. "Oh, please take me away with you!"

"Why, gal, I can't do that," answered the trader seriously. "I feel mighty sorry for any white gal who's been took by the Injuns and can't git back to her folks again. But I can't do nothin' about it."

Molly watched as the man adjusted the ropes of bark that bound the burdens to the horses' backs.

"I could walk, if there's no room to ride on the

horses," she said, hopefully. "Ever since the white people at Fort Duquesne wanted to keep me, I can't seem to think of anything else. Somehow, I must get away from the Indians . . . I could stay with you till you go back to Marsh Creek Hollow again. I would help all I could and I can travel anywhere—I'm strong again, now."

Old Fallenash glanced at the girl's thin face and frame. Then he sat down on a stump and drew her down beside him. His weatherbeaten face folded into lines of anxiety and strain.

"I wish to God I could help you, Molly," he said, in a solemn voice, "but I can't. You see, I've got a trading-post on Buffalo Creek and that's no place for a nice white gal. Sometimes the Indians get drunk and angry and they cut up purty lively."

"I could hide till they went away," suggested Molly.

"Then, there's another reason," Fallenash went on. "I have . . . well, you see . . . I have an Indian woman living with me and she's not a very good housekeeper. It would be just another Indian home and not half as good as you have here. I know these Senecas well. They'll be good to you. Besides, if I took you, it would make the Senecas angry. I want to go on livin' a while yet. I don't want to lose my scalp. I'm not ready to feel a tomahawk stickin' in my back, either!"

"They would kill you?" asked Molly.

"They would kill me sure, if I took you away," said Fallenash. "No, gal, you stay right here and try to be contented. If you just make up your mind to it, you'll be happy enough. Say your catechism like your mother taught you, pray to God every day and try not to forget to speak in English."

"I do! Oh, I do!" cried Molly. "Ma said I must never forget and I don't mean to."

"Don't take it too hard," Fallenash went on, with real sorrow in his voice. "It's a fine, free, open life and you can be happy if you'll just make up your mind to like it. The Indians don't work half so hard as the whites and they get lots more joy out of life. In fact, I think Indian life is not half bad myself. I like it."

"You do?" asked Molly, her face brightening. "Do you mean what you say?"

"I do," said Fallenash. "That's why I got me an Indian woman and live as much like an Indian as I can." He paused, then continued: "Have you ever happened to think? The Indians don't make you read books or do sums. They don't make you knit and sew seams every minute. They don't sit in church all day long. They don't scold and think about their sins all the time."

Molly's thoughts flew back to home. Once there had been a time when knitting and sewing were irksome; when she had hated reading and doing sums. Betsey "took to" those things, but Molly bungled. If only now she could have a seam to sew or a stocking to knit—how well she would do it!

A shadow fell on her face as she spoke. "Oh, Fallenash, tell me. Do you think there's any way I can ever get home again?"

"Well, of course, there's always a chance somebody

might come . . . but I doubt it. No, there ain't no way," replied Fallenash, firmly. "You'd best try to be contented here. Once these Senecas have adopted you, they'll fight tooth and nail 'fore they'll give ye up. No, you'd better just forget about goin' home and be happy here."

The girl's thin white face fell again into despair. The trader with a conscience-stricken look of half-guilt, dug into his pack and brought out a shining string of glass beads. He leaned over and tied them about the girl's neck.

"There!" he cried. "When you see them purty beads, just remember Old Fallenash would help ye if he could."

Slowly he walked over to his waiting pack-train. At the signal of his shout, the horses started. The trader looked back at the white girl sitting on the stump, but she did not raise her head.

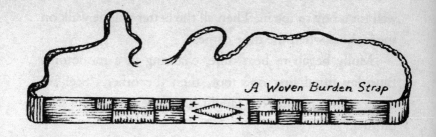

A Woven Burden Strap

XI   *Running Deer*

A burden-strap with moose-hair embroidery Corn Tassel shall have," said Earth Woman, softly, as if talking to herself.

Molly had just come in. She lifted Blue Jay off her back. Her cheeks, touched by the chill of late autumn winds, glowed faintly pink. She smiled, but did not speak. She stretched her hands out to the welcome warmth of the fire. Then she unbound the Indian baby and set him on his feet.

"See! Blue Jay walks!" she cried in excitement. "His back has grown straight from the hickory board. His legs have grown strong and sturdy. Now he walks alone."

The Indian woman chuckled. "He is not the first Indian baby who has learned to walk alone. My son was just so fine and strong when he was young."

"But see!" cried Molly, laughing. "He turns his toes in, just like a woman. A man should not walk so.

"*Ohè!*" cried Earth Woman. "Let him walk so. It is

well for a boy to toe in. Then all the better will he walk on snow-shoes when the time comes."

Molly began to beat time, chanting in a monotone. Blue Jay lifted first one foot, then the other. "See! He dances! Shining Star has taught him. She is indeed a wise mother."

"After dancing," said Earth Woman, smiling, "he will learn to swim. When the moon of flowers comes again, Blue Jay will swim in the river."

"His name will have to be changed to Blue Trout then!" said Molly.

While Blue Jay, chattering happily, explored the lodge, Molly sat down by the fire and began braiding three strands of coarse bark fiber together, twisting it hard, to make a strong rope. A kettle, filled with narrow strips from the inner bark of slippery-elm, covered with ashes and water, boiled on the fire. Skeins made up of small fibers of bark which had been boiled, dried and twisted, were piled up near by. Balls of finely twisted basswood cord lay on the floor.

"Yes, a burden-strap decorated with moose-hair embroidery is none too good for Corn Tassel," said Earth Woman again.

"But Blue Jay grows fast!" protested Molly. "I won't need a burden-strap much longer. Soon he will be too large for the baby frame. When he goes all day long on his own two feet, I will have no burden to carry."

"Your two sisters will soon see to that," replied Earth Woman. "They will give you a *burden* frame instead of a *baby* frame. They will see that you carry game or cooking-utensils or bark or skins. They will never let you run idle. But a beautiful burden-strap can lighten a burden, no matter how heavy."

A shadow crossed Molly's face. "Why do Indian men make their women carry heavy loads?" she asked. "A white man never does so. The white man takes the burden away from the woman. He tries to spare her."

"It is the Indian man's duty to provide meat," explained Earth Woman, "and to protect his family from the enemy. It is the Indian woman's duty to make the home and keep it. When they go together on a journey the men and boys must have their hands free, to be ready to kill game and to meet any lurking enemy. The women walk behind. They carry the young children and the burdens. It is the Indian way. The Indians have always done so."

Earth Woman worked rapidly as she talked. She picked up loose bark fibers from the pile, two at a time, and twisted them together, by rolling them back and forth under the palm of her hand on the calf of her leg. A thin but strong cord was produced which she rolled into balls and put away for future use.

"A fine burden-strap is made by finger weaving," Earth Woman went on, "with a needle of hickory. Only the finest strands of twine from slippery-elm bark are used. The belt in the center is the length of an arm and the width of three fingers. The ropes at each end are long and thin. Fine, delicate, but strong it shall be, with designs in bright colors for Corn Tassel's forehead."

A call came from outside.

"Enter!" cried Earth Woman, smiling happily. "More bark has come!" she added.

Shagbark and Turkey Feather entered the room, carrying loads of elm and basswood bark, which they had stripped from trees in the forest. They dropped the bark in heaps on the floor.

"More strings and ropes for Earth Woman to make" announced Shagbark. "A woman should never be idle.

Now that the corn is harvested, it is well to provide work for her fingers."

"Thank you for your kindness to one who has no man in her lodge," said Earth Woman.

"I am to have a new burden-strap," announced Molly, "with moose-hair embroidery. Earth Woman will make it for me."

"Put many bright colors on it!" cried Turkey Feather. "Put blue for the sky, red for the falling leaves and yellow for ripe corn, the color of Corn Tassel's hair."

"Weave them together with kindness!" added Shagbark, quietly. "Then the burden on her back will never cut her forehead or give Corn Tassel pain!"

It seemed very quiet in the lodge when the man and boy went out. Earth Woman's lodge was always quiet, for it was different from the others. She had no families living with her. In a room behind she kept her herbs, roots and supplies. No one but herself was allowed to enter. Molly knew now why it had always seemed so quiet during her long illness.

"Why have you no man in your lodge?" she asked,

Seneca Utensils made of Bark

suddenly. "If you had a man, you would not have to fell a tree for firewood. You would never have to strip bark and carry it in. You would always have plenty of deer meat to eat; you would never need know hunger."

The shadow of great grief fell across Earth Woman's face.

"Once I had many brothers and relatives, but they have all gone to the happy hunting-grounds beyond the sky, where fighting has ceased and hunting is easy; where the summers are not too hot and the winters never too cold." Earth Woman pointed to the wall. "There hang their bows and arrows and other weapons. My son went away with the warriors last year and never returned. Perhaps in good time the Great Spirit will give me another son to take his place."

"Who is the Great Spirit?" asked Molly.

"The Great Spirit is Hä-wen-ne-yu," replied Earth Woman. "He made the world and all that is good. He made the corn and the plants of the earth to grow, to blossom and bear fruit, so we may be happy. His brother is the Evil Spirit, Hä-ne-go-ate-geh. He made the snakes, the mosquitoes, the flies and all poisonous plants. He brings sickness into the world."

"Oh, yes! I remember now!" cried Molly. "Ma used to tell me something like that at home—only the names of the spirits were different. If you ask the Great Spirit for things, will he give them to you?"

"We try to remember what he has already given," said

Earth Woman. "We thank him for the changing seasons, for the fruits of the earth, for the preservation of our lives. Then we ask that he continue his protecting care over his children. He knows what is good for us."

"Perhaps then, he will give you a son," said Molly, "in place of the one you lost."

"Come, Corn Tassel! Come out at once!" It was Turkey Feather back again, calling. Molly looked at Earth Woman.

"Go and see what he wants," said the Indian woman. "Blue Jay has fallen asleep on the bed. I will look after him. He makes me think of my son. If he wakes, I will give him this rattle of woven wood splints to play with."

Molly lifted the deerskin and ran out. With Turkey Feather, she ran swiftly to the river banks, where she heard loud, fierce shouts coming from across the water.

"What is it? Who are they?" she asked.

"The warriors have come!" cried Turkey Feather, shrilly. "The warriors have come! They have returned from a war mission against the Virginia settlements. They are shouting news of their victory."

On the banks across the river, below the Falling Waters, but within sound of their thundering roar, the returning warriors stopped. They uttered a series of yells to announce their arrival, they shouted the news of losses the party had suffered and the number of captives, scalps, horses and other plunder which they had taken. In loud tones they boasted of the success of their expedition.

As Molly stood with Turkey Feather, her heart began to pound heavily. The thought of more white people being scalped, plundered and taken captive was unendurable. Across the river, standing with the warriors, she saw a white man. His face shone out with glaring whiteness and called to her for help.

"Is it . . . a white man?" She grasped Turkey Feather tightly by the arm. "Tell me, do you see a white man over there?"

"Oh, yes!" cried Turkey Feather. "One, perhaps more. Victory means white captives—what else could it mean? Don't you understand? If they are men, they'll have to run the gauntlet!"

Molly's heart sank within her. He was right. What else could it mean?

Before the echoes of the warriors' shouts had died away, Turkey Feather ran to join the crowds. Out from the Indian lodges, men, women and children came pouring. Molly looked at them in horror. Armed with knives, clubs, tomahawks, stones, any sort of weapon, they formed themselves in two long, disorderly lines that reached from the council house almost to the river.

"If they are men, they'll have to run the gauntlet!" Turkey Feather's words kept ringing in her ears.

Again she looked across the river. There seemed to be a long delay. An Indian from the village was paddling across, to bid the new arrivals welcome. Beneath a tree Molly saw that the white man's head was being shaved and across his face, broad streaks of red were painted. She shivered with remembrance.

Then she saw Old Shagbark walking by himself, hastening toward the river. Shagbark, whom she had always thought of as a tall, straight tree in the forest—dependable, a friend to lean upon. Shagbark was her only hope.

The next moment she stood beside him. He bent his ear and listened. "The white man!" Breathless, she managed to speak, pointing with her finger. "You helped a white girl captive once. Oh, won't you help a white man now? You know so many English words, words that he could understand. . . ."

Shagbark frowned. "You know not what you ask," he answered gruffly. "No one can save him, not even Shagbark. Only by the gauntlet can a male captive be adopted into the tribe. Every male must run the gauntlet. If he is not strong enough to bear it, then he is not worthy of being a Seneca and he must die. He must look out for himself. Waste not your pity on him."

"What *is* the gauntlet?" begged Molly.

"Gauntlet!" Shagbark looked down at the girl before him. His hand reached out and rested for a moment on her pale yellow hair. "Oh, may you never know!" The words sprang out from lips unguarded.

"Go back! Go back to Red Bird's lodge at once! I command you!" His voice was angry now. It was the first time he had ever spoken to Corn Tassel in anger. "This is no place for a white girl. Go back to your lodge and stay!"

"Oh, be kind to him as once you were kind to me!" Molly's blue eyes did the pleading while her trembling lips formed the words.

She watched Old Shagbark advance more slowly toward the river. Then she ran back. She stopped at Earth Woman's lodge and picked up Blue Jay.

"It's the warriors!" she explained in haste. "They've returned with captives. Shagbark said I must go back to Red Bird's lodge."

"Shagbark knows best," said Earth Woman. The girl's white face frightened her. "Go! Make haste! Don't leave the lodge tonight."

Shining Star stood waiting at the door. Molly handed Blue Jay to her and watched her hurry off. Then she threw herself upon her bed. She found her corn-husk baby, her little white woman, and held it to her lips. She tried to drown out the shouting by covering up her ears.

In came Squirrel Woman, panting with haste.

"Come, Corn Tassel!" she cried. "The warriors have returned from battle. The day will be spent in feasting and rejoicing. It is the highest kind of frolic ever celebrated by the Senecas. Come, we must not be late."

Molly drew back into her corner, filled with fear. The shouting of the angry crowd gathered on the river bank swelled high above the woman's words.

"You are now an Indian, you are no longer a white girl!" cried Squirrel Woman. "You cannot remain forever a weakling. Come and see the white prisoner run the gauntlet! Your backbone of soft willow must be stiffened to oak."

"Oh, I don't want to go!" cried Molly. "Please don't make me go."

While her daughter spoke, Red Bird had been standing by, silent. Red Bird, whose voice was as gentle as the south wind, who was never known to raise it in anger. Red Bird spoke and her voice burned like fire.

"Daughter," she cried, "how can you be so cruel? Have you no heart of kindness in your breast? How can you think of going to the feast and watching the suffering of the unfortunate prisoner? How can you bear to listen to his cries and groans? Corn Tassel has lately been a prisoner herself. Torn away from her loving family, she has been brought from the light of freedom to the darkness of captivity. Like a flower transplanted to new soil, she wilted first and drooped. Now she has just begun to take heart again. Once more she lifts up her head to sunshine. You, Squirrel Woman, wish to open all her wounds and make them bleed afresh. You wish to speed her on her way to the happy fields of the blessed.

"I had thought that you, my daughter, were acquainted with better wisdom. But since it is not so, then I must plainly speak. With war, we women have nothing to do. It is the duty of our husbands and brothers to defend us. Their hearts beat with fierce pride when they overcome our enemies. Oh, stay then, my daughter! Learn the ways of wisdom. Let our warriors, not our women, carry out the customs of war."

But the words of fire did not touch the heart of Squirrel Woman. "They have brought a handsome young pale-face!" she cried, in excitement. "He is very handsome, but his pretty, proud face won't save him from the gauntlet. His face will not look pretty when he has finished his run." Squirrel Woman rushed to the door and was gone.

Gauntlet! The same threatening word again. What was it? How could it change a captive's face? If no one would tell her what it was, Molly must go out and see. Red Bird's back was turned. Busy with her cooking-pots beside the smoldering fire, she did not hear the girl creep out the door and go. Was Red Bird's the only kind heart in the village? Was Red Bird the only Indian woman who, on a day like this, stayed in her lodge because she had kindness in her heart?

Molly found a place in the thick bushes near Earth Woman's lodge, which stood not far from the log council house. There she could watch without being seen. She saw that the warriors had forded the river in a shallow place and brought their captive over. The Indians, restless with waiting, grew more angry and revengeful, thinking of all the wrongs done to them by the pale-faces. It was Shagbark, Molly saw, who held the white captive back. Then, when the crowd's zeal had begun to slacken, he bent forward as if to speak, and gave him a push.

Molly saw the white man give a startled look and go.

This was the gauntlet. He was running now, like the swiftness of the wind, like the swiftness of a hunted animal. The angry Indians, shrieking and yelling, waited for him to come, and when he came, they pelted him on all sides with cruel cuts and blows. But with apparent ease and bold indifference, he dodged from side to side. When a tomahawk grazed his ear, he merely bent his head and watched it fall and hit the ground. When Shagbark joined the others and threw pieces of rotten pumpkin, the white man laughed aloud with the Indians. No ordinary white captive was this—so said the Indians on all sides.

Molly saw him closer now. He was not a man at all, but a youth of about eighteen years. He was younger and stronger than Nicholas Porter and in his eyes there was no look of dulness, but a bright gleam of fighting courage. The Indians were right. He was no ordinary white captive—he who laughed aloud while running the gauntlet!

At the door of the council house, a group of savage Indians quickly gathered. No captive should have it too easy, they meant to see to that. With tomahawks uplifted they waited, but the white boy did not come to meet them. To the surprise of all he turned and dashed round the side of the council house. As swift as a running deer, he crashed through the thicket of bushes and ran straight into Earth Woman's lodge.

Molly reached the lodge almost as soon as the white boy did. It took her only a second to rush in from the sheltering bushes. Beside the fire stood two Indian women, Red Bird and Earth Woman—no, three, for behind them was Shining Star. Molly saw the women catch the white boy in their arms and, swift as flashing lightning, cover him with blankets and whisk him out of sight. Had the Great Spirit sent the terrified young man to their kind breasts for safety? It was all over in a moment. Then the women stood and looked at each other trembling and at the white girl who now stood there beside them.

Footsteps came and angry Indian voices shouted loudly at the door. Earth Woman found her voice and answered. Her quiet words sent the men away again.

The women waited calmly. After a long time they raised the white boy up, all bruised and bleeding, and concealing him from view with a covering of blankets, led him to the safety of the house of council.

For all the rest of the day and evening, Molly stayed with the women in Earth Woman's lodge. As night approached, great fires were kindled in the open space in front of the long houses and feasting, dancing and frolicking took place. The women of the village, headed by Panther Woman, secreted all the men's weapons, to prevent injury to themselves. Long into the night the frolic lasted, then the fires died away and the rioting Indians fell down asleep.

The white boy remained at the council house during the night and through the following day. A meeting of the council was held at which it was decided that he had endured the gauntlet with fortitude and was to be given to Earth Woman to replace her dead son. In a fitting ceremony he was adopted as a full-blooded Seneca of the Hawk clan of his mother and was given the name *Running Deer.* In the evening, weak and ill, suffering from the loss of blood, he was brought back to Earth Woman's lodge.

"The Great Spirit has given you a son," said Molly, "in place of the one you lost. Now you will have a man in your lodge again."

"The Great Spirit's kindness is so great, it cannot be measured," replied Earth Woman.

Molly came often to the lodge to inquire about the white boy, but a high fever had set in and he was too ill to see or speak to her. Each day she came, eager for the sight of his pale white face, for the exchange of English words, and each day, disappointed, went away.

The white boy's wounds were many, but not dangerous. In Earth Woman's lodge he was in good hands. The woman devoted all her energies to making her pale-faced son strong and well again. She bound his wounds with

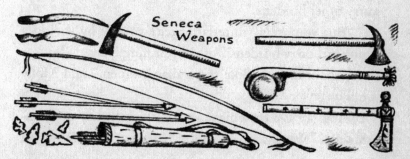

Seneca
Weapons

balsam and juniper bark. She brewed strengthening teas of sassafras and witch hazel. She kept him in bed for days. Her dark eyes glowed with happiness when she saw him begin to mend.

One day when the boy woke up from an afternoon sleep, he gave a start of surprise, for Molly Jemison sat on the ground by his bedside. Intently he watched her braiding strands of bark. Her head was bent, her eyes were fixed upon her work, but her long braids of yellow hair hanging down beside her cheeks told him what he wanted to know.

"Am I dreaming?" he asked, rubbing his eyes.

Her eyes found his at once. "No, you are awake," she said. "You have slept well."

"What are you doing?" he asked in a quiet voice.

"Braiding a bark rope," she replied. "Earth Woman showed me how." She glanced at the Indian woman. "And Earth Woman is making me a new burden-strap."

"A burden-strap?" asked the boy, puzzled. "What do you want with a burden-strap?"

"Now that Blue Jay walks," answered Molly, "I shall carry other burdens."

"But you are a white girl, aren't you? Why should a white girl carry burdens?" asked Running Deer.

"I have to work like the Indian women," said Molly simply.

"You do? Do they make you?" asked the boy in astonishment. "What are you doing here, anyhow? Who are you? Where did you come from?"

There was so much to tell, it was hard to begin. The happy English words flowed swiftly back and forth as Molly explained her situation. Then it was the white boy's turn. His name was Josiah Johnson and he talked a long time about his home in Virginia and told how he was taken.

"The Indians liked you," Molly said. "You showed no fear or sadness, no irritation when you ran the gauntlet. Not a muscle of your face betrayed what you were thinking. They decided you would make a good Indian."

"A good Indian?" cried Josiah, in amazement. "What do they think? I'll never be an Indian as long as I live!"

"I said that, too, at first," replied Molly, sadly, "but there's no other way. When once you are adopted into their tribe, there's nothing can be done about it."

"We'll see about that!" said Josiah, fiercely. "See here! Don't tell me you believe all they say about our white blood being washed away and there's nothing now to fear from them and how they're going to love us like one of their own people—all those things that old fellow, Shagbark, was saying. Don't tell me you believe that the cruel, revengeful Indians who can half kill a poor captive in the gauntlet, know what kindness is! You don't think they mean what they say, do you?"

Molly hated to disappoint her new friend, but she had to speak the truth. "I'm afraid I do." The words came softly. She looked over to Earth Woman and watched her brown fingers busily weaving delicate bark threads over and under. "I believe every word they say," she added. "I never knew what kindness meant until I came here—perhaps because I never needed it so much till then."

XII   *Porcupine Quills*

Y ou look as handsome as an Indian Chief!" exclaimed Molly.

"I'm not an Indian Chief!" protested Josiah. "And you must not tease me. I only put these clothes on to please Earth Woman."

"Your Indian mother worked so hard to make them for you," said Molly. "She must be very proud. . . ."

"She is a good woman and she is always very kind to me," said Josiah, interrupting, "but I can never call her Mother."

Molly looked up and down at the white boy's splendid new Indian clothes. His long shirt was held in at the waist with a wide belt. A broad red sash, strung across shoulder and chest, was tied with long-fringed ends on his left hip. His red broadcloth leggings, richly embroidered with beads, were held with garters below the knees. He wore a close-fitting cap with a hawk's feather emerging above a cluster of smaller feathers. He carried no tomahawk or weapons. Except for his face, he had all the outward appearance of a Seneca.

"I'm to have a new gown . . . too," said Molly, slowly, "after I finish the moccasins I'm making."

"You are?" asked Josiah. "Bright red leggings like mine? Broadcloth all trimmed up with fancy beads? It will look mighty pretty on a girl."

"No," said Molly, biting her lip. "Not cloth . . . only deerskin."

"Deerskin! Backwoodsman's deerskin would be good enough for me!" growled Josiah, savagely. "I feel like a fool, dressed up like this."

"How funny!" said Molly, laughing. "You have a handsome cloth outfit and all you want is deerskin. I have to wear deerskin—but what I want is cloth, embroidered with beads."

"I would trade with you, if I could!" answered Josiah. Then, changing the subject: "How do you like the way the Indian girls play football?"

"I don't like it," said Molly, emphatically. "Star Flower and Gray Mouse keep throwing me over in the snow banks. I could kick better, too, if my stomach wasn't so empty."

"What? Are you hungry too?" asked Josiah. "Earth Woman had no meat in her pot today and I'm half-starved." The two captives looked back where a group of Indian boys were throwing long sticks along an icy trough made by dragging a log through the snow. "That snow-snake game, as the boys play it, is great fun," added Josiah.

"Did you throw the *gawasa*, the snow-snake?" asked Molly.

"I did!" laughed Josiah. "I threw it farther than any of them. My side always won. That's why I stopped playing. They place a colored stick in the snow to show how far each snake goes, and then keep moving along. Those snow-snakes can travel fast—they are polished as smooth as rattlers."

"Come, let's go to Red Bird's lodge and get warm," suggested Molly, pulling her blanket more tightly about her. "The story-teller's coming tonight and maybe there will be something boiling in the pot. Squirrel Woman won't be there. She's gone to help Panther Woman today."

The village below the great Falling Waters looked bleak and cheerless now that the freezing moon had come and the ground was covered with snow. The trees in the forest with their bare branches stood out more plainly, silhouetted against dark evergreen pines and hemlocks. In the frozen fields, dried-up cornstalks shook and rattled in the wind. The thunder of the pouring water was stilled, for the river was partly frozen over and in the center of each of the falls, only a trickling stream kept running. All the canoes had been buried deep under mounds of sand on the river's bank. Except for the Indian children at play and the columns of smoke pouring from the roofs of the lodges, there were no signs of life.

The two captives walked slowly, making criss-cross patterns in the snow with their snow-shoes.

"Squirrel Woman doesn't hurt you, does she?" asked Josiah.

"She's never plunged me in water yet," laughed Molly. "Red Bird told her once that she must not use violence, but that she might plunge me in water till I promise to do better. She hasn't—yet!"

"She'd better not try!" muttered Josiah, fiercely. "It seems funny with the men away, doesn't it? Only Log-in-the-Water, ancient and lazy; Shagbark, laid up with a lame foot; and Running Deer, a good-for-nothing white captive."

"Running Deer is good for a great deal," said Molly, softly. "Earth Woman never lacks meat now that she has a man in her lodge."

"You mean she *did* have meat until the ground froze up and all the squirrels and small animals hibernated. Even then, what could I do with a miserable small boy's bow and arrow? They won't even give me flint arrowheads. If Running Deer isn't allowed to go out with the men, he will soon grow as lazy as Log-in-the-Water and as fat as Big Kettle. I tell you, I need something to do! This thing of sitting around all day doesn't appeal to me."

"Chief Burning Sky knows you would give them the slip and never come back here again," said Molly.

"I can understand why he doesn't want me to go with the warriors on any of the expeditions against the white people," said Josiah, "but he might give me a gun and let me go with the hunters down the Allegheny to the Ohio country. At least I can hunt. I'm as good a shot as any of the Indians."

"If they had taken you with them," said Molly, "I would have no one to talk to."

"I'd hate to start off anywhere," said Josiah, thoughtfully, "without taking you along."

"Oh, Josiah!" cried Molly, trembling. "Promise me if you ever try to go back home you'll take me with you."

"I'll try every way I can to take you," said Josiah, soberly. "I swear I will. But if I can't—then I must go without you."

"Oh, I couldn't bear it . . ." said Molly, "to be left behind."

"Well, don't worry now," said Josiah. "We can't try a thing till spring. With the streams frozen up and ice and snow everywhere, we can't take a step. We must just lie around and wait. If only I could have gone with the hunters, it would have been something to keep me busy."

"Do you know," said Molly, "the deer meat is gone in Red Bird's lodge, too. There's been none in the hominy for over a week. That's why my stomach feels empty all the time. Why don't you ask Log-in-the-Water for his gun and go out and take a deer?"

"He won't let me have it," said Josiah, crossly. "I've asked him already. He won't trust me."

"If only it were Shagbark . . ." ventured Molly.

"He's just as bad," said Josiah. "I asked him, too, and he said a male captive must not leave the village."

Leaving their snow-shoes leaning against the outside wall of the lodge, Molly lifted the bear-robe flap and the two entered. Turkey Feather and Earth Woman were inside. Earth Woman threw a proud glance at her adopted son, but did not speak as she followed Red Bird and Shining Star into the adjoining room.

"Where's that new gown you were talking about?" asked Josiah, grinning. "And those red broadcloth leggings with fancy beads?"

"Oh—it's not started yet," replied Molly, in a disappointed tone, "and it won't be cloth at all—only deerskin. Squirrel Woman and Shining Star bought fine cloth from Fallenash, the white trader. Perhaps they mean to make new costumes for themselves. I had hoped for broadcloth too, but Squirrel Woman says deerskin is good enough for me. But first, I'm making a new pair of moccasins—just to learn how."

Molly went to her bunk and came back with a finished moccasin in one hand, a large half-circular piece of deerskin and several smaller pieces in the other.

"Wouldn't you like a blue homespun gown better than either broadcloth or deerskin?" asked Josiah, softly.

Molly's eyes filled with tears. "Of course I would—if I could have it. But if I have to live with the Indians, I might as well dress like them. Beaver Girl and Star Flower have beautiful cloth gowns and I thought . . ." Molly fell into silence as she set a bowl filled with colored porcupine quills on the ground.

"Are these quills from my porcupine, Corn Tassel?" asked Turkey Feather eagerly.

"Yes, they are," answered Molly. She sat down on a mat, picked up a piece of deer sinew and started to work. "Moccasins are easier to make than I thought they would be," she went on. "They are cut in one piece and held in gathers over the toe. The flaps at the top are cut separately and so is the pointed patch in front. I'm working designs on these small pieces now."

"See!" cried Turkey Feather, happily. "In what beautiful colors you have dyed the quills!"

"I helped Grandmother Red Bird," said Molly. "We used blood-root and sumac for the orange and red ones, yellow-root for the yellow, and butternut hulls for the black. Before I embroider with them, I soak them in water

and flatten them with this bone. It's not much like sewing because I don't use a needle. I have to make holes in the deerskin with this awl and push the sinew through, fastening the quills at each end and bending them over to hide the fastening."

"The quills will make your moccasins and your new gown very beautiful, will they not?" asked Turkey Feather. "Porcupine quill embroidery is much more beautiful than bead-work, is it not? If your new gown were broadcloth, you could not use the quills, could you?"

"No, I couldn't," said Molly, thoughtfully. Then she looked up, smiling.

The Indian boy's enthusiasm was infectious. Suddenly she was ashamed that she had wanted a cloth gown so much. Deerskin *was* good enough and Turkey Feather's quills were more beautiful than any beads.

"Your quills will make my new gown beautiful," she said to the Indian boy. Then she explained to Josiah: "I'm glad it's to be deerskin, after all. It means so much to Turkey Feather—he brought me the porcupine. When I first came to live with the Indians, I hated the sight of deerskin—even the touch of it. But I'm used to it now. It's more practical than cloth, especially in the woods. It doesn't soil easily nor tear on sharp thorns and branches. I am sure Squirrel Woman knows best—a girl should learn how to embroider with porcupine quills before she tries beads."

"He was a fighter, this old porky was!" Turkey Feather exclaimed with delight. "Grandfather Shagbark said it would be easy. He told me just to go out and hit him with a club."

"An arrow wouldn't get a chance in his prickly hide, I suppose," said Molly.

"All you need is a stout club," said Turkey Feather. "Grandfather says a porky never throws its quills, but I can tell you he puts them in everything he touches. When I hit him on the snout he didn't even feel it. Then I hit him again and he switched his tail back and forth, filling everything in sight with quills—the club, tree trunks and everything he could reach with that tail. What a fighter he was!

Then all at once he rolled over dead, and I brought him to you."

Proudly Turkey Feather watched the design grow under Molly's busy fingers, as she fastened down one quill after another. "The moccasins will be beautiful," said the Indian boy. "May they make Corn Tassel's path an easier one."

Even Josiah looked on with a show of interest. "Do you like doing it?" he asked.

"Better than I ever liked sewing at home," confessed Molly. "I always left my seams for Betsey to finish and ran outdoors to be with Pa. Betsey was such a good sister." Molly was surprised to find that for the first time she could talk of her family calmly.

"Your Ma would be surprised if she could see you now, wouldn't she?" asked Josiah.

"Yes," said Molly, "but pleased too I think. I can sit still easier than I used to. The Indians have taught me that—and so many other things. I never thought I'd like to sit still and do embroidery, but I do. The Indian designs always mean something—whether quill work or bead work. Did you know that?" She pointed to the designs outlined on the deerskin.

"The half-circle resting upon two straight lines is the sky-dome resting upon the earth," she explained. "The little curly sprig on top is the celestial tree. Here are the sleeping sun and the sun awake. These lines that curl inward mean sleep or death. The Indians have so many ideas that never occur to the white people."

"How do you like your new comb and brush, Corn Tassel?" asked Turkey Feather.

Molly ran to her bed, lifted the top and took them out. "See, Josiah, Turkey Feather made them from the porcupine's tail," she explained. "I comb and brush my hair with them every day."

"I never knew that a porcupine was good for anything except gnawing hemlock trees," said Josiah, chuckling.

"Then you'll be surprised to hear that there is a woman sitting in the moon, embroidering with porcupine quills!" exclaimed Molly.

"Is there?" laughed Josiah. "What next? Who told you?"

"Earth Woman told me," replied Molly. "Near the woman there is a bright fire and over the fire hangs a clay pot with succotash boiling in it. By the woman's side sits a large dog that always keeps his eyes on her. Sometimes she gets up, lays aside her work and stirs the food in the pot. While she is doing this, the dog unravels her work."

"Then what happens?" asked Josiah, eagerly.

"The same thing happens over and over again," Molly went on. "As fast as the woman embroiders, the dog un-

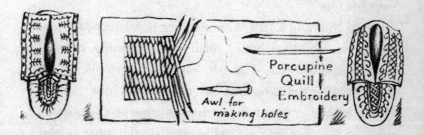

ravels. If she could finish her work, or if she ever does, the end of the world will come that instant."

"Good!" laughed Josiah. "Earth Woman has it all figured out, hasn't she?" Then he added in a low voice: "You don't seem to think about home as much as you did, Molly. I don't like to hear you repeating these Indian tales and talking about wanting red broadcloth leggings and a fancy gown with beads on it—so you will look like the Indian girls. You are not getting to like the Indians too well, are you?"

"Oh, no!" laughed Molly. "Of course when you know and understand them, you can't help liking the Indians. But it's not that. I shall never like them better than the white people. It's just that since you've come, Josiah, I've been much more contented living with them. Before, I had nobody to talk to and now I have you."

The bear-robe flap was lifted and Squirrel Woman entered.

"There she comes!" whispered Molly. "She doesn't like for me to talk English to a pale-face. She always suspects I am trying to get away." She closed her lips tightly and bent over her work.

Red Bird and Earth Woman came in from the adjoining room. Wooden bowls filled with steaming hominy were passed around. The two captives ate in silence, as Squirrel Woman crouched on the ground not far off. Molly looked at Josiah from time to time and wondered what he was thinking. As the women on the other side of the fire began to talk in low tones, she listened carefully. But she did not speak until Squirrel Woman went outdoors for firewood.

"Red Bird says the hunters are late," said Molly, interpreting. "They should have been back several weeks ago. All our meat supply is gone and so is Earth Woman's. They say the other families have none left. They are all eating hominy every day and if they keep on, the corn will be gone before it is time for the fresh crop to be ripe. Panther Woman is putting all the villagers on short allowance. We are to have our bowls only half full from now on. Earth Woman says she can find some good roots in the woods to help out."

"How can she dig them when the ground is frozen?" asked Josiah, gruffly.

"I don't know," replied Molly. "Shining Star says she had a dream last night. First she heard children crying, then she saw deer tracks in the snow. It's clear they are worried. They say that when the men return from the winter hunting-trip, there's to be a great feast—a nine-day celebration for everybody."

"But in the meantime we starve, eh?" burst out Josiah, bitterly. "That's the way the Indians manage. The white people do better than that."

"Perhaps we can get used to being hungry," said Molly, slowly. "If only I could be as cheerful as the Indians about it. They are accustomed to such things, I suppose."

As Squirrel Woman returned to her place, Josiah rose

abruptly and put on his cap.

"Oh, are you going?" cried Molly. "I thought you were staying for the evening."

"Why should I stay?" asked Josiah, crossly.

"The story-teller is coming," replied Molly, "and there will be a big crowd. Shining Star says his stories are wonderful to hear. The Indians have stories the white people never dream of. You would like them."

"I'm more interested in meat than in stories!" growled Josiah.

"The story-teller comes only in winter," Molly went on hastily. "As soon as the buds open on the trees the stories are hushed, because then the spirits of nature are awake. . . ."

But Josiah was not listening.

"*Where are you going?*" cried Molly. She rose suddenly, dropping her bowl and ladle upon the ground. Wild panic seized her. The look in Josiah's eyes was desperate. She watched him speak to Turkey Feather and she saw the two start for the door.

"Don't worry, Molly!" called Josiah. "Just trust me if you can. Once more I'm going to ask that lazy Log-in-the-Water for his gun."

"You're not . . ."

"Don't worry!" begged Josiah. He lifted the flap at the door and stepped outside.

"Whew! Molly!" he called back, poking his head in again. "The snow's coming down harder than ever. We will be buried alive here till spring, that's certain."

Molly's impulse was to rush out and follow him, but she stayed where she was. Left alone, all her happiness faded. What if he should start for Virginia without her? She knew that if he made up his mind to go, even the snow would not keep him. But how could *she* travel in the snow, in freezing weather like this?

* * * *

With the light gone from her eyes and her spirit she watched the people come into Red Bird's lodge. All the holes and open places in the bark walls had been tightly stuffed with moss, and the six fires along the middle of the central hallway were constantly fed by the women with fresh supplies of dry wood. Still it was cold. Each time the flap was lifted, a breath of icy air was admitted. She shivered and pulled a wool blanket close about her shoulders.

The crowd waited expectantly as night closed in. At last a shout was heard outside and all the children ran to the door.

"*Dajoh*, enter! Enter!" they cried, in great excitement. "Hosk-wi-sä-onh, the story-teller, has come!"

A tall, dark man entered and threw off his blanket. He was dressed in deerskin leggings and overshirt, embroidered with colored moose hair. His silver-banded cap was trimmed with the usual cluster of drooping feathers, topped by an eagle feather set in a socket to twirl. He carried two bags, one for pipe and tobacco and the other filled with mysterious lumps.

Red Bird stepped quietly forward and placed a bench by the fire. Other women spread corn-husk mats on the ground. The crowd gathered close at the man's feet.

The story-teller took his bear-bowled pipe from his pouch and filled it carefully with tobacco. A small boy ran up, took the pipe to the fire and placed a hot coal upon it, then returned it to the man's hand. He smoked peacefully. After a moment he threw a pinch of tobacco upon the fire and said a prayer to the unseen spirits.

"Hoh!" he exclaimed. "What story shall I tell you? Let us see."

He plunged his hand into his second bag, which was filled with an array of objects selected to remind him of his stories—shells, bear teeth, strings of wampum, feathers, bark dolls, bears' tusks and animals' claws. Slowly he drew forth a small, round, smooth stone.

"Hoh!" he cried. "The story-telling stone! This is a story about a stone. Listen, my children, while the fire burns red and the shadows come and go like mighty giants and I will tell you the story of the story-telling stone.

"Many hundred moons ago, an orphan boy went out to hunt, in order to bring home game to his foster mother. One day, the sinew which held the feathers to his arrow came loose and he sat down to tighten it. He sat down on a high, smooth, round stone in the woods. 'Shall I tell you stories?' asked a voice. 'What is that—stories?' asked the boy. 'It is telling what happened a long time ago,' replied the stone on which the boy was sitting. 'If you will give me your game, I will tell you stories.' The boy gave up his game and the stone began telling what happened long ago. Each day, in return for the boy's game, the stone told him another story. One day the boy brought a friend with him, and the day after, two men of the village came along to hear the stories. By and by all the people in the village came, first giving meat or bread to the stone.

"Afterwards some of them forgot all the stone's words, some remembered only a part, but a few of the people remembered every word. To them the stone said: 'You must keep these stories as long as the world lasts. Tell them to your children and grandchildren, generation after generation. To the person who remembers them best, ask for a story and take him a gift, bread or meat or whatever you have.' And so from the story-telling stone, came all the knowledge the Senecas have of the world of long, long ago!"

As the story-teller talked, the people listened with glistening eyes. Often someone cried, *"Un!* Good! Good!" to show his pleasure. Some smiled and others laughed aloud. "A story in the cold winter warms the heart," said Red Bird softly.

The story-teller drew a bird's feather from his mysterious bag. "The singing bird!" he cried, smiling broadly. "This is a story about a boy who learned the songs of the birds. Do you all now listen.

"Many moons ago, a boy was once sent to the woods to hunt for birds. Instead of shooting them, he hid behind a tree and listened to their songs. Then he put feathers in his hair and danced and sang the birds' songs. The boy's brother asked him why he had stopped hunting for birds. 'I listen to their songs,' said the boy. 'I have learned to sing their songs and I will teach them to you. What I do now will be for all the people who are to come. I will make it a rule that the people to come must wear feathers and dance and sing.'

"So the boy taught his brother to sing and dance. Then he taught all the people in the village. The boy said:

"'I sing what I have heard the birds sing.
I give thanks as I heard them do
when I was hunting.
I dance to my songs
because I hear the birds sing
and see them dance.

We must do as they do.
It will make us feel glad and happy.
The Great Spirit tells the birds
to teach us songs.'"

The story-teller paused for a moment. Then he added: "So now you know that from the birds come all the Indian songs and dances!"

"*Un! Un!* Good! Good!" cried the people, happily. The story of the singing bird was one of their favorites.

As story followed story Molly forgot her hunger as well as her anxiety over Josiah. The Indian stories gave her new strength and happiness. "Now I can understand their songs and dances better," she said to herself, "since I know they came from the birds. I can tell the stories to Josiah and he will love them, too."

The fires flickered low and the snow-laden wind whistled boisterously round the corners of Red Bird's lodge, as the story-teller closed his bag and tied it up carefully. He lifted his bear-bowled pipe to his mouth and began to smoke again, while the Indians filed past, dropping gifts into his open palm—a pinch of tobacco, a silver brooch, a strand of deer sinew or a skein of bark fiber. Molly went, too, dropping tobacco with which Shining Star had provided her. For all gifts, large and small, the story-teller nodded his thanks.

The next day, Molly heard from Shagbark that Running Deer was gone. The gun was gone, too, from Log-in-the-Water's bedside. Only the fact that Turkey Feather had accompanied him, saved Running Deer from serious suspicion.

Old Shagbark shook his head with disapproval. "Running Deer has been not only disobedient; he has shown lack of wisdom."

Days passed. Molly waited, with the others, for the return of her two missing friends, and for the return of the hunting party. The snowstorm abated and a mid-winter thaw set in, melting much of the ice in the river. On the fourth day, Panther Woman announced that there would be only one meal daily.

All the morning Molly worked busily at her porcupine embroidery, to try to forget her hunger. At last when she grew tired she laid the work aside and walked to the edge of the village. There to her surprise she saw two figures approaching on snow-shoes, carrying a deer trussed up by the legs to a pole swung between their shoulders. It was Turkey Feather and Running Deer.

"I killed it!" cried Turkey Feather, shrilly. "Running Deer gave me the gun to hold and just then the deer appeared and I fired."

Shagbark came out of his lodge, limping. He put his hand on Turkey Feather's head. The boy seemed to have grown half a head taller.

"My son," said the old man, solemnly, "I am proud of you. When a man has killed a deer, he is a great hunter." Then he turned to Running Deer. "My son," he said, "of you, too, I am proud and that justly."

All the people came running out of the lodges. Swiftly a fire was laid and while the story was being told, the deer

was skinned, dressed and divided according to the strictest rules of justice. That night, the smell of roasting venison filled every lodge in Genishau and all the villagers enjoyed the taste of good meat.

Two days later the hunting party returned. With the arrival of the men, the town became suddenly alive. The hunters brought large quantities of bear meat and oil, dried and fresh venison tied up with bark strings, and piles of fresh hides. When they reached the outskirts of the village they dropped their loads and went forward to notify the women that food awaited them. Out ran the women eagerly, making loud exclamations of delight, to return with backs heavily loaded.

The village became the scene of renewed activity, as the women pulled the fresh venison into strips, hung and dried it in the sun, over smoldering fires. Tanning operations began with the scraping, cleaning, and soaking of hides. Soon there was game in abundance hanging from the rafters of the bark lodges, and skins were piled high in the store-houses. The famine was over.

The return of the men from the winter hunt meant feasting and rejoicing. All had plenty and no one spared eating or giving. The Indians strolled from house to house, visiting and eating, always eating. The whole village celebrated the hunting frolic for nine days by singing and dancing to the beating of drums, eating, smoking and playing games.

Wearing her new deerskin moccasins, Molly stood

with Josiah in front of Red Bird's lodge. Together they watched a moccasin game played by a group of boys and young men. Four moccasins were placed upside-down upon a blanket before each side and the players, with long sticks, took turns guessing under which moccasin a hidden pebble lay concealed, while a flat drum was beat in time to their singing.

"I knew you had not run away," said Molly, softly. "When I heard the gun was gone, I knew you had gone after meat."

"I couldn't bear to see you so hungry and do nothing about it," said Josiah. "The Indians forbade me to go, but they were glad to get the meat when I brought it. And now—aren't they funny? When they have plenty, they eat everything up at once! Why don't they save some of it? Even the white people know better than that."

"It is quite a change," admitted Molly, "from one meal a day to twenty. Every time I go into the lodge, someone is eating. They have no regular meals at all. I'm getting as fat as a woodchuck. When they offer you food, it's bad manners to refuse and they're offended, so I have to eat!" Then she added, laughing: "They shouldn't be so wasteful, but they never think of that. It's the Indian way, I suppose!"

XIII   *Willing Sacrifice*

"Now is the time when the sap begins to flow," said Molly. "Spring will soon be here, so we are starting for the sugar camp. You're not going with us, Josiah?"

"No, only the women and girls make sugar, I understand," Josiah answered. "The men are going on the spring fur-hunt, but I can't go along. I'm to help the Indian boys make traps and tend them. Maybe we'll take some raccoon and a fox or two. . . . What is it, anyhow—maple sugar?"

"It's that sweet stuff they put in bear's oil," explained Molly, "to dip their meat in. It took me a long time to get used to sweet food instead of salty. They get it from the maple trees. It's the sap boiled down into sugar, Earth Woman told me."

"We never had it at home," said Josiah.

"Ma never did either," said Molly. "I wonder Pa didn't take some from our maple trees, too, if it's so easy to get.

The Indians know so many things . . . Is the canoe nearly done?"

"Yes," answered Josiah. "As soon as the seams are covered with spruce gum to make them water-tight. That's what Shagbark is doing now."

Molly looked at the new canoe—one long, perfect piece of red elm bark—which lay on the shore, framed in with small branches stuck into the ground to hold it in canoe shape. Within, along the bottom and sides, white-ash pieces and ribs had been inserted. The two ends were closed alike and sewed with bark strips, making sharp, vertical prows. Shagbark, bent over, was working busily.

"I wish you could go along to the sugar camp," begged Molly.

"If I go anywhere," burst out Josiah, gruffly, "it won't be to a sugar camp." Then he lowered his voice so Shagbark should not hear. "It won't be on any Indian trail. I'll make a trail of my own through the woods on which they can never find me. They are clever, but I can outwit them."

"You won't go till I get back from the sugar camp, will you?" asked Molly. "Promise me you won't."

"I can't promise that," said Josiah, firmly. "You don't know what you ask. If I get a chance to go, I must take it. Surely you want me to, don't you?"

"Yes . . ." said Molly, slowly and unhappily. "If you get a chance . . . I want you to take it."

"The canoe's been fun to make," said Josiah, changing the subject abruptly, "and Shagbark seemed to want my help. Besides, you know I like to keep busy."

Molly put her hand to her mouth and choked back the tears. She kept staring at the canoe while Shagbark removed the frame of branches. She saw him pick up the canoe and drop it lightly on the water, but she scarcely realized what was happening until she heard Shagbark speak.

"Step into the canoe, my son," said Shagbark to Running Deer. "The canoe is yours!"

"Mine?" cried Josiah, his eyes sparkling. "You don't mean that I can go where I like in it? I thought a male captive was not allowed to leave the village."

In answer, Shagbark silently handed the white boy a paddle.

"May your canoe carry you safely over rough waters and take you wherever the Great Spirit may lead you!" said the old man, solemnly.

"Oh, Josiah!" cried Molly, torn between happiness over this unexpected good fortune and uncertainty over its possibilities. "Then you're not going trapping with the little boys after all, to take raccoons and a fox or two?"

But Josiah did not answer.

With a smile on his face and a firmer set to his shoulders, Running Deer stepped into the canoe and shoved off. He lifted the paddle high over his head for a moment in farewell, then began paddling upstream.

Molly watched him go with a sinking heart. She wished that she understood him better. Would he be loyal to Shagbark's trust or would he run away now that spring was coming? Was there a new brightness in his eyes, a new glint of determination? Would he debase the beautiful gift of the canoe by using it to help him on his return to Virginia? Was Shagbark suspicious or innocent of Running Deer's intentions?

Molly took one last look at the straight figure in the canoe as it rounded a bend. Then she turned to Shagbark. She looked up at him, but she did not need to speak. The old man knew her thoughts.

Shagbark put his hand on her shoulder. "Do not fret," he said gently. "Running Deer may be trusted. He will return. He will be more apt to return if he is not confined too close. We have not done wisely to keep him close like an animal caught in a trap."

"Oh, are you sure?" begged Molly.

"I am very sure, little one," said Shagbark. "He will return."

Beaver Girl came running. "It is time to go, Corn Tassel," she announced. "Squirrel Woman is very angry because you are not ready."

Snow still covered the ground and except for the warmth of the midday sun, it might still have been winter. In front of her lodge, Red Bird was rolling up dried meat and packing it on sleds for the journey. The other women in the village were doing the same. Gradually they all assembled in front of Panther Woman's lodge and waited.

Panther Woman gave the signal and they started off in the direction of the maple forests, accompanied by a few men and boys. Some of the women pulled the loaded sleds, others carried the younger children in baby frames or pack-baskets. Storm Cloud, Star Flower, Woodchuck, Chipmunk and all the other children ran ahead, skipping and shouting happily.

With Blue Jay in a pack-basket on her back, Molly trudged slowly along behind the others. Despite Shagbark's reassuring words, her heart was very heavy. Each step was taking her away from Josiah. She knew she could not go on living with the Indians after Josiah went away. His coming had changed her life entirely and given her the first real happiness she had had since Marsh Creek Hollow.

Beaver Girl left the others and waited to walk beside Corn Tassel. Beaver Girl had her baby sister, Little Snail, in a baby frame on her back. She walked quietly and did not speak. She knew that when the white girl captive had tears in her eyes she was thinking of her white family far away, and Beaver Girl was sorry. From time to time she glanced at Corn Tassel hopefully, but the white girl did not look up or smile.

After a journey of several hours the women and children reached the sugar camp. In a clearing at the edge of a fine grove of maple trees stood a few bark lodges. The women and children crowded into them, first clearing out great piles of snow and dry leaves. Here they were to stay for the length of the sugar season.

The party set to work at once. Before nightfall maple trees had been felled and several logs hollowed out by the men, making troughs to hold the freshly gathered sap. The women washed and mended all the bark vessels left in the sap-houses from the year before.

The next morning the work was continued. With crooked sticks, broad and sharp at the end, the women stripped bark from a felled elm tree and made many new boat-shaped vessels, each holding about two gallons. The men notched the maple trees with their tomahawks, driving in long hardwood chips to carry the sap away from the trees. The children ran back and forth setting the bark vessels at the bases of the tree trunks to catch the flowing sap.

Each night the ground froze hard and fast; each day the sun was warm enough to melt it again, and so the sap flowed freely. Drop by drop it filled the vessels. Each day's run had to be carried to the camp.

Molly and Beaver Girl put wooden yokes on their shoulders and worked with the women, trudging over the hard frozen crust of the snow. They took empty vessels out and carried the heavy filled ones back, emptying the sap into the log canoe troughs by the fires.

Great clouds of white steam poured out from under the bark shelter where the hissing sap boiled furiously, filling the air with a delicious fragrance. Squirrel Woman and Red Bird kept the pots well filled, stirring to prevent their boiling over. Other women made frequent trips to the woods for firewood and kept feeding the fires. When the syrup was boiled down, the women tested it upon the snow, dipping it out with wooden paddles. When it was of correct thickness, they poured it, still warm, into a trough and pounded it with a wooden paddle until it turned into sugar. Part of it was poured into wooden molds and set aside to harden into small cakes.

As the days passed, one exactly like the other, Molly worked impatiently, for she wanted only one thing—to get back to the village to see Josiah. The work was hard and the yoke was heavy. Every day it seemed to cut more deeply into her shoulders. Would this endless sugar-making never be over? Her feet became so tired she could hardly lift them.

Once while passing the wood-pile she stumbled over a

loose branch and fell, spilling her vessels of sap on the ground.

Panther woman came running up and scolded her for carelessness and wastefulness.

"Corn Tassel has no eyes in her head!" the woman cried out, in hot anger. "She walks with the blindness of a bat!"

The words lingered in Molly's mind as she hastened out again to the forest. On her way, she noticed the foot tracks which the party had made in the snow upon arrival. No fresh snow had fallen to hide them.

"I will show her that I do have eyes in my head!" said Molly to herself. "I will show her that I care not how much sap I spill and that I can find my way back to the village alone."

Dropping her yoke and sap pails, she started off at once. She had gone but a short distance when she heard the sound of footsteps behind her. Looking back over her shoulder she saw with irritation that it was Beaver Girl. On she ran, faster and faster, but no matter how fast she ran, the Indian girl came closer and closer. At last, out of breath and tired, she sank exhausted to the ground. The next moment, Beaver Girl's arms were around her.

"Do not go, Corn Tassel," begged Beaver Girl. "If you go back to the white people, I shall never be happy again. I will have no one to talk to, no one to work with, no friend to love. Stay with me, Corn Tassel and be my friend."

Molly could not tell Beaver Girl what the trouble was,

but she was touched by the girl's friendship. It was true, they were just of an age, and there were no other girls their age in the whole village. Beaver Girl wiped the tears off Molly's cheeks with her sleeve, then helped her to her feet. Arm in arm the two girls walked back to the sugar camp. They came just in time to see Shining Star dropping thick ropes of hot syrup on the top of a clean bank of snow to harden. They joined the shouting children in the scramble to fill their brown fists with the delicious candy and to stuff their mouths full.

At last all the sugar was made and it was time to go back to the village. In three weeks' time, a supply large enough to last a year had been made and packed in bark cones for storage. The sleds were reloaded and they left the sugar camp.

The air was soft and sweet on the day when the party

returned to the village. Only a few patches of snow were left in shady spots in the forest. Robins and bluebirds were singing, hopping from limb to limb, but Molly had no eyes to see or ears to listen. She was thinking of only one thing—Josiah.

Immediately the village became the scene of turmoil and excitement, for the bringing of the maple sugar must be celebrated with a festival of thanks to the maple. The men had returned from the fur-hunt, so the women hurried to prepare an elaborate feast and soon had huge pots boiling. The people sat down in the open space in front of the lodges and listened to speeches given by the keeper of the faith and other important men. Then Chief Burning Sky scattered sacred tobacco on the great central camp-fire and gave a song of thanks to the Great Spirit. He said:

"We thank thee, Great Spirit,
For sending the soft winds and fair breezes
To melt the snow
And make sweet waters flow
From the heart of the Maple.

"We thank thee, O Maple,
For thy sweet gift
To thy children
Who roam in the forests—
We thank thee,
We thank thee, O Maple!"

During the dancing and feasting which followed, Molly looked for Josiah but could not find him. She ran to Earth Woman's lodge, but when she saw a sweetfern broom propped up to hold a bark slab over the door, she knew no one was there. Then she looked for Shagbark and wondered at his absence. With a feeling of uneasiness, she kept watch on all sides, but neither Shagbark nor Josiah appeared.

Not till the day after, did Molly learn what had happened. Before the fire was laid in the early morning Earth Woman ran into Red Bird's lodge in frantic haste. Molly

dropped the load of wood she carried on her back and ran to meet her.

"He is gone! My son, Running Deer, is gone!" cried Earth Woman, overcome with grief. "He has gone back to the pale-faces. I have hunted for him all through the night and I cannot find him."

Red Bird's family and all the others from the adjoining rooms crowded up to hear.

"Shagbark missed the canoe three suns ago," Earth Woman went on, "but Running Deer may have gone before that. When the boys returned from their trapping, they said he had never been with them at all. Oh, we should have kept closer watch; I should never have gone to the sugar camp . . . He knows the forest like an Indian, he runs as swiftly! He should not have been given a canoe to speed him on his journey . . ."

"Is it wise, then," cried Molly, indignantly, "to keep a captive bound too close? A strong animal caught in a trap will break it to pieces and flee!"

"Hush! Hold thy tongue!" said Red Bird, severely. "Corn Tassel has not been asked to speak. Even when all have spoken, she shall not be asked to speak."

"Now must I mourn the loss of my pale-faced son," sobbed Earth Woman, "as once I mourned my own flesh and blood."

"But have not the men taken action?" demanded Red Bird.

Earth Woman's head sunk low on her breast. "They

have been searching for him ever since they learned the canoe was gone. They did not tell me they knew he was missing and had gone to bring him back. They will bring him back to recapture and punishment. Oh, why could they not let him go free?"

"Go free?" snorted Squirrel Woman. "You would not have your son returned to you then?"

"I would let him go free," said Earth Woman, in a low voice, "rather than see him suffer. I would let him return to the pale-faces. If they had asked me, I would have said, 'Let him go. Do not bring him back to me!'"

"But he is now a full-blooded Seneca!" cried Squirrel Woman. "He has been adopted into our tribe. He cannot go."

"Hush! Hold thy tongue, daughter," cried Red Bird. "Can you not see how much she loves him? Can you not see that his suffering would kill his mother?"

"But what can we do?" cried Molly. "What can we do to help him?"

"Help him?" A man's voice spoke. A man had entered the lodge and heard what the women were saying. The man was Old Shagbark.

"Should, then, Running Deer be helped? We gave him more freedom than any captive ever had before. A man who breaks a trust should not be helped but punished. The rules of the tribe must be obeyed."

Shagbark's voice sounded like that of some other person—like that of a cruel, relentless man. Molly saw in his eyes how keen his disappointment had been.

"But, oh, what can we do?" she cried again.

No one answered. All the Indians looked at her with disapproval in their eyes. Shining Star stared coldly, and so did Turkey Feather and even Beaver Girl—all the Indians she had looked upon as friends.

Seeing they were all against her, Molly quickly left the lodge. If Josiah had run away, there was nothing for her to do but follow.

Outside the door, she almost bumped into Gray Wolf. "Where are you off to, little Pale-Face?" he called, drunkenly. "Running away again?" But Molly ducked out of his path and did not answer.

She ran through the corn-field and entered the forest. The little white dog ran at her heels, but she stopped long enough to scold and send him back. She remembered the route Josiah had said he would take. If she followed the River Genesee to the southward she could cross in a shallow place and branch off east toward the Susquehanna. The Susquehanna, Josiah had told her, would take her nearest to Marsh Creek Hollow.

She followed the trail along the river bank, passing the lower and middle falls. She came to the high cliff overlooking the upper falls, but she did not stop. The roar of the great Falling Waters grew fainter in her ears and then died away altogether, as up and down over the rugged hills she made her way. She looked behind once or twice, but saw no one coming—not even devoted Beaver Girl—to bring her back. They were thinking only of Running Deer at the village. They had no thoughts of her.

The trail grew more wild and tangled. Impatiently, she pushed her way through. Suddenly, on a running black-berry vine, she tripped and fell, twisting her ankle. Then she knew she could never go. She had tried it before. It was hard enough to go through the wilderness traveling with the Indians. It would be impossible alone, without food of any kind, without a tool or a weapon. The forest was hateful. She had always known it. She could never, never go.

She heard the crackling of branches and looked up. Was it Gray Wolf come to fetch her back again? No—the little white dog came bounding toward her, barking with delight. He ran to her lap and she held him close. She was not forgotten, after all. The little dog whined in sympathy as she cried, broken-hearted.

Then like a flash, a happy thought seized her. She was glad that Josiah had gone. She would only have been a heavy burden for him to carry. She was glad he had not waited for her.

As she sat on the ground, nursing her lame foot, she looked up and saw that the sun was shining brightly. The trees were budding and the birds were singing. It was really spring. It was the spring that she and Josiah had waited for so long. A feeling of relief and happiness spread over her. Spring had come and brought Josiah his chance to go, and even though he had been obliged to leave her behind, she was glad. She had meant it when she told him if he had a chance to go, he should take it. He would travel faster and with less risk alone. He would reach his home and family, and be happy again. He would not have to live a caged life with the Indians, caught in a trap like an animal. Whatever happened to her, she would always be glad she had let him go.

Then she knew he was beyond the fear of capture. With an undoubting assurance, she knew that he was safe. He could conceal his trail as well as any Indian, he would run no risks. If the Indians had not found him in three days, it meant he was out of danger and well on his way down the River Susquehanna. Molly knew he was safe. Then her eyes filled with tears, for she knew with equal surety that she would never see him again.

Slowly she rose to her feet. She broke a branch off a dead tree and, using it for a cane, made her way painfully back along the trail, while the little dog scampered joyously ahead. She came to the cliff overlooking the upper falls, to the very spot where she had stood that first November day and looked upon her double rainbow. It was spring now and the scene was changed, but still the same. The Falling Waters spoke to her in welcome, and again the tender beauty of the place brought solace to her aching heart.

On the edge of the cliff she sank down to rest. There she thought of Earth Woman, who loved Running Deer like a son. Why should the Great Spirit give her a son, only to take him away so soon? It seemed so needlessly cruel.

Molly remembered Squirrel Woman's threatening words—if a captive were returned, it meant all the torture of recapture and fresh punishment. Earth Woman had been willing to let him go free, to let him go back to the pale-faces, rather than see him suffer. By giving him up, Earth Woman showed how great was her love.

Molly made her way back slowly toward the Indian woman's lodge in the village. Putting aside her own sorrow in her loss of friend and companion, she thought tenderly of Earth Woman and wondered how she could comfort her. She came to the lodge. Black smoke was rising from the hole in the roof. The broom had fallen to the ground beside the door and the bark slab stood at one side, showing that the owner had returned.

Molly lifted the deerskin flap and put her lame foot over the threshold. Then she stepped inside and let the flap fall. The change from bright sunshine to the darkness of the interior blinded her for a moment. She stood still, then, hearing no sounds of grief or pain, wondered if the lodge was empty after all.

At length she saw Earth Woman sitting on Running Deer's bed. On the wall behind hung his clothing, and the weapons she had given him. Several pouches, belts and other possessions lay undisturbed, just as he had left them—as if he might return at any moment. On the woman's lap lay the small boy's bow and arrows which

Running Deer had used to bring meat to his Indian mother's lodge. The woman's eyes were dry, but she grasped the bow and arrows so tightly, her knuckles showed white beneath the skin. Limping, Molly ran to her arms.

Before any words were spoken, the flap was raised to admit a shining ray of light and Old Shagbark entered. He stared a moment at the blazing fire, then he saw the two figures on the couch and walked over to them.

"He is safe!" he said, in a low voice. "The Great Spirit has led him to safety."

"I knew it," said Molly. "I knew they could never find him."

"Good!" said the Indian woman, softly.

"I knew you would both be willing to lose him, if he could get away safely," said Shagbark. "You are not sorry he has gone?"

"Oh, no!" answered Molly.

"I am not sorry," said Earth Woman.

"Then you were not angry at him because he broke his trust?" asked Molly.

"No," said Shagbark, "for I understood. I speak words now which you must bury deep within your heart forever. I gave him the canoe so that he might go away. There was only one thing to do and one way to do it, and I take the responsibility. I saw from the first that we could never keep him. As time passed, I knew we must let him go. So I made it as easy for him as I could."

"He is free again!" said Earth Woman. A smile broke

across her grief-stricken face, the smile of willing sacrifice.

At that moment, Molly saw a bear cub, big, fat and roly-poly, go lumbering through the forest—a bear cub with no rope about its neck. She saw, too, a young deer—a buck with antlers like a growing tree upon its head—go crashing through the bushes. A bear cub, a deer, running with the fleetness of perfect freedom, and with them somehow, in her mind, she saw Josiah running free.

"Oh, Shagbark!" she cried. "My heart overflows with gratitude. You knew how miserable and unhappy he was. You helped him to get away. You are all kindness and goodness. Do you think Running Deer knew, too?"

"He knew!" said Shagbark.

XIV *A New Cooking Pot*

The days passed slowly after Josiah went away. The sun seemed to have lost its brilliance; the sky was no longer blue.

At planting-time, Molly knew that she had been with the Indians for a year. Once more she saw round, pale yellow grains of seed-corn fall from her hand to the rich, black soil. Once more she watched slim, grassy blades poke upward and grow taller, ever taller. Once more she hoed, pulled weeds, and waved her blanket from the platform shelter to frighten crows away.

One day she walked in the green shadows between the tall stalks pressing the ears gently with her hand.

"The green corn will soon be ripe for boiling," she said to herself. She pulled an ear off and tucked it under her arm.

Leaving the corn-field, she returned by way of Earth Woman's lodge. On the ground beside the bark building, a smoldering fire was burning. A group of clay pots had been placed upside down in a pile and covered with dry cedar wood, cedar bark and other fuel. Earth Woman had stacked them carefully so that the heat might circulate freely and affect all parts alike.

"I brought you an ear of ripe corn," called Molly.

Earth Woman came out of her lodge with a long stick in her hand. Molly stripped the ear down and handed it to her. The Indian woman put the corn to her mouth and began to munch it, while she poked at the fire with her stick.

"Are they done at last?" asked Molly.

"A good thing is never made in a hurry," said Earth Woman, solemnly. With her stick she uncovered the pots, pushing the smoldering logs aside.

"Oh, they are beautiful! Beaver Girl's pots are beautiful!" exclaimed Molly. "I must run and call her to come and see. And mine! My pot is the most beautiful of all, is it not?"

"A girl's first pot is always the most beautiful in the world," said Earth Woman, softly. "Pride in one's work is never harmful."

"May I take it to Red Bird at once?" asked Molly, eagerly.

"Yes, if you wish to burn your fingers to the bone!" replied Earth Woman, laughing. "The pots are very hot. They will not be cooled before the sun has run its course."

"Everything takes so long," sighed Molly. "It took so long till I grew strong enough to pound and beat the clay.

It took longer still to shape the coils evenly into a pot. So many small crooked ones I had to throw away before I could shape a large one. And now that it is shaped, it takes so long to fire and harden it."

"A good thing is never made in a hurry," said Earth Woman again. "When you have learned to work as slowly and thoroughly as an Indian woman, you may well be proud."

Molly ran to Beaver Girl's lodge and brought her back with her. In the late afternoon, while the Indian children and some of the women looked on, Earth Woman took the pots out of the cold ashes. Exclamations of delight greeted Beaver Girl's pots, then the crowd waited impatiently, for it was Corn Tassel's pot they most wanted to see.

It came out last. Earth Woman brushed the ashes off with care and held it up high. The pot was round and full at the bottom, with a narrow, graceful neck. It had a turned-over collar at the top, which was scalloped along the edge. The crowd waited in silence. Not a word was said.

"It is not cracked, is it?" asked Molly, breathless.

Earth Woman turned it slowly round in her hands. "I see no crack," she said, solemnly.

"It has no holes for leaking?" asked Molly, full of fear.

"I see no holes," said Earth Woman, peering inside.

"It looks a trifle crooked, does it not?" asked Molly, anxiously. "It bulges more on one side than the other, does it not? But when it is a girl's first pot, that is not a serious matter, is it?"

Earth Woman turned the pot around and looked at it from all sides. "I see no bulges," she said.

"Will it hold water for boiling corn?" asked Molly, eagerly.

"It will hold water," said Earth Woman. She put the pot in Molly's arms. "The pot is beautiful, Corn Tassel!" she said, with a broad smile. "Take it to Red Bird."

"Corn Tassel has made a cooking-pot!" sang Woodchuck, Star Flower and the other children. "Corn Tassel has made a fine cooking-pot! Oh, let us eat green corn boiled in Corn Tassel's cooking pot!"

Molly walked in triumph to Red Bird's lodge, followed by Earth Woman, Beaver Girl and the shouting, laughing children.

Red Bird and her two daughters came out to meet them.

"A cooking-pot for Grandmother Red Bird!" said Molly, holding out the pot. "May the green corn boiled in this pot always lie sweet on the tongue!"

"*Ohè!*" cried Red Bird, taking the pot in her hands and smiling broadly. "Corn Tassel has made as fine a pot as Beaver Girl of long experience! Come, we will fill it with green corn to boil. Shining Star has gathered the first ripe corn of the season. We will eat green corn to honor Corn Tassel's cooking-pot."

"Ugh!" grunted Squirrel Woman. "A brass kettle is more useful. Earthen pots are foolishness."

But Molly did not hear. Not since Josiah went away

had she felt so happy. Her excited thoughts tumbled over in her mind. Could there ever be any happiness greater than this—the joy of making a beautiful thing with one's own hands?

"The Great Spirit is happy, too," whispered Beaver Girl shyly, as if reading the white girl's thoughts. "He made the beautiful world with his hands and took pleasure in its beauty."

"Come, Corn Tassel," said Shining Star. "Come inside the lodge. I have a surprise for you."

Wondering, Molly and Beaver Girl followed the Indian woman into the lodge. The children waited impa-

tiently outside the door. "Corn Tassel has made a fine cooking-pot," they sang over and over.

"Hush! Hold thy noisy tongues!" cried Squirrel Woman, angrily.

She pointed across the meadow to the lodge of Chief Burning Sky. "Visitors have arrived. Strange men have come unannounced to the village. A dark cloud lies low on the horizon."

Red Bird and Squirrel Woman stared uneasily at the Chief's lodge.

"Pale-faces!" cried Squirrel Woman. "Pale-faces have come."

In silence, the women and children waited. Gray Wolf came running up, panting.

"Chief Burning Sky says that pale-faces, Englishmen, have come to have secret talk with the Chief and the sachems."

"Englishmen?" cried Red Bird. "Did he not say Frenchmen?"

Gray Wolf bent over and spoke whispered words in Red Bird's ear. Then he hurried away. Red Bird and Squirrel Woman talked together in low tones.

The flap was raised and Molly stepped out. The children stared to see her, then clapped their hands and cried out with joy. For she wore a fine new gown, made in Seneca fashion, not of deerskin, but of cloth. Her blue skirt and bright red broadcloth leggings were richly embroidered in bead designs. Her over-dress of flowered calico was fastened down the front with a row of silver brooches.

"Corn Tassel is a Seneca woman now!" cried the children. "Corn Tassel is dressed as fine as Beaver Girl!"

Molly looked down at her new finery with becoming modesty. How beautiful the clothes were! How lovely the bead designs! How kind of Shining Star to do all the work! Just when she had made up her mind to be content with deerskin . . .

Up came Squirrel Woman and took her roughly by

the arm. "Go within! Go within and take off the new gown quickly. Put on deerskin. Then come with me!"

Molly looked up bewildered.

"But the green corn!" cried the children, unhappily. "Corn Tassel was to eat green corn with us."

"There will be no corn to eat tonight," said Red Bird, sadly but sternly.

"My pot!" cried Molly, seeing it was no longer in Red Bird's arms. "What have you done with my pot? Is it cracked? Does it leak? Or is it that it bulges on one side more than the other, that you cook no corn tonight?"

"Come!" commanded Squirrel Woman, irritably. "This is no time for words. We must make haste. Go within. Take off those garments . . ."

"There is no time," interrupted Red Bird. "Take her as she is." She thrust a blanket into Squirrel Woman's arms. "Go quickly."

"Is something wrong with my pot that I know nothing about?" cried Molly tearfully. But no one listened.

Away from the lodge strode Squirrel Woman, pulling Molly along behind her. They entered the corn-field, hurrying through the rows. Soon they came to one of the pole platforms.

"But it grows dark!" cried Molly, indignantly. "Kahkah comes not to steal corn at night."

The woman tossed the blanket up and pointed to the ladder.

"Shall I search out the ripest corn for Red Bird and

bring it in?" asked Molly, hopefully. "The children are waiting to fill the new pot with corn and boil it for a feast. Shining Star said my new gown was in honor of the feast."

"Climb up!" ordered Squirrel Woman, and when the girl obeyed, she went on: "Stay here. Do not leave this platform until I send for you. Sleep here tonight. I will send food tomorrow. I will send for you when it is time for you to return to the lodge."

The woman stood still for a moment, without speaking. As Molly watched her, she noticed a strange expression on her face. She was not cross or angry—she was

troubled. Wondering, Molly watched her go.

The night was long and the pole floor hard, with only a blanket for softness. Molly stretched out, thinking of her fine, new cloth garments and of the pot she had made, but her pleasure in them had been spoiled. For several hours she tossed and turned, then, lulled by the rustling of the corn, she fell asleep. When she awoke, she was surprised to find that in spite of her discomfort, morning had come. Lame and sore, she climbed down from the platform.

The new pot must be sitting on the fire, filled now with fresh green corn. She could see the children crowding round. The thought of it made her very hungry, but she remembered Squirrel Woman's words and decided it would be wise to obey.

But why should she stay all alone in the corn-field? Why should she stay alone and starve? She pulled off an ear of corn, stripped it and nibbled the soft, milky grains. She remembered seeing strangers before Chief Burning Sky's lodge when she came outdoors wearing her new gown. Surely the strangers were gone by now. The sun rose higher and higher till she knew it was long past midday.

Why should she be hidden away from strangers? If they were pale-faces, she must see and talk to them. Yes, it was because they were pale-faces that Squirrel Woman had brought her here. Why hadn't she thought of it before? *What if someone had come to take her home? What if they came and she never knew it? What if the Indians kept her hidden and sent them away again?* These alarming thoughts spurred her onward, as she ran pell-mell back to the village. She must find the pale-faces and talk to them. Now, at last she knew why the women had rushed so to hide her.

Straight to the council house she ran, and there heard voices. No, she was not too late. They had not gone. Panting and breathless, she stood beside the building and listened. Then all her courage oozed away. She was afraid to talk to the pale-faces, but at least she would listen. Down she dropped on the grass and hugged her knees with her arms. A man was talking in Indian. She knew by the way he said his words that he was a pale-face.

"The expedition of three thousand British and Indians was organized by General Pridieux at Fort Ontario," the voice was saying, "but the General died before victory. Sir William Johnson, his second in command, stormed the enemy positions and captured the fort on July 25th. Fort Niagara, like Fort Duquesne, is now in the hands of the English. The French are finished. The French have gone forever. The English will take Quebec next."

The words brought back to Molly a sharp memory of Old Fallenash, the white trader. "When the English take Fort Niagara," he had said, "I'll have to run fast to save my hide."

Where was Fallenash now? Was he gone forever? Had he been killed by the English at his trading-post on Buffalo Creek? Molly put her hand on the string of glass beads about her neck, the beads which the kind trader had given her.

After a pause, Molly heard Chief Burning Sky speaking, slowly measuring each word: "Many moons ago, there was a time when there were no pale-faces in the land of the Iroquois. Then were the people happy and content. The first pale-faces who came were the French traders and hunters. We gave them our skins and furs and they gave us steel hatchets, tomahawks, paint and tobacco. We made them our friends, not knowing what friendship with the pale-faces would lead to. The Indians were happy until the pale-faces began to change their way of life. Now, the Indian wants cloth to wear in place of deerskin garments, blankets to take the place of fur robes, brass kettles in place of earthen pots and fire-arms for bows and arrows. Worst of all, the pale-face brings fire-water . . . Can he who pours down our throats water that burns like fire, be called friend?"

"Sir William Johnson wishes earnestly to make friends with the Iroquois," replied the Englishman. "Sir William has made a home in the forest with the Mohawks. He has married a Mohawk wife. He understands the Iroquois and looks to them for help. The Iroquois and the English together can accomplish great things. Will not the Senecas help?"

"The Senecas are not yet ready to speak," answered Burning Sky. "Since my sachems have decided that the matter is important enough for a Council of the People of the Long House, I have asked this runner to be ready. He will take this wampum message to the Cayugas, the

261

Onondagas, the Oneidas and the Mohawks. If the subject interests all and they are agreeable, a meeting of the League of the Iroquois will be held."

"They will decide to come over to us, of course," said Captain Morgan, in a casual tone.

"No man knows what they will decide," said Burning Sky. "The French are old friends of long standing, who are badly in need of help. The English are new friends, bringing sweet words and fair promises. Sachems, warriors and chiefs from each nation of the Iroquois will come and speak from the fulness of their hearts. After all sides of the question have been discussed, the council will decide whether we shall help the French or the English."

"Let the swift runner say to the Chiefs that the matter is urgent!" cried Captain Morgan.

"No matter is so important that it should be decided in haste," replied Chief Burning Sky. "The greater the matter, the more need for cool counsel, for slow and careful deliberation."

Molly saw the runner, bare except for a waist cloth and moccasins, with knife at his belt and wampum in hand, dash out of the door of the council house. His feet, like flying wings, seemed never to touch the ground as he started off on his long journey over hill, stream and valley.

There were no more words. Molly wondered if the talk was over. Still thinking of Old Fallenash, she walked to the front of the building. Perhaps the Englishman would know where he had gone. She would ask him as he went out the door.

The flap was up, the door was open wide. Holding tightly to the door-post, Molly leaned over and peeped inside.

"What!" the Englishman's voice cried out in surprise. "A blond Indian? An Indian with yellow hair?"

Hastily Molly turned and dashed off. But she was too late. The strong arm of a serving-man took her by the shoulder and marched her back into the council house. Then she forgot about old Fallenash.

She saw a white man, dressed not in blue like the man at Fort Duquesne, but in a bright red soldier's uniform. She had never seen a red so red before. She could not take her eyes off it. But at last she did.

She looked up into the face of the man who wore the suit and she saw him smiling at her like a friend. She looked down at her handsome cloth garments which so short a time ago had seemed so beautiful. Now they were hateful to her sight. She was ashamed of her bright red leggings, ashamed of her Indian moccasins and she tried to hide them beneath her skirt.

"Ah! A pale-face! So I thought!" said the man in English. "Don't be afraid, child. I only wish to talk to you."

Molly did not like the man's smile. His eyes were cold gray and his face looked hard. She turned away, frightened. She remembered the pole platform and Squirrel Woman's words, forbidding her to leave it. She was sorry now she had come. She could find no English words to say. Her tongue was sealed. She must hurry back to the corn-field. She twisted and pulled, trying to free herself from the man's tight grasp.

"Ah!" cried Captain Morgan, chuckling. "A little wild-cat already! An untamed savage, growing up like a wild beast in the forest! Does she bite and scratch, too?"

He turned to Chief Burning Sky. "She has lost her childhood's speech, no doubt. How long has she been here?"

"Twelve moons, more or less," answered Burning Sky, with a show of indifference.

"So short a time? But time enough, with so young a child, to blot out all memory of home and family. Time enough to cause her to forget her native tongue—the Indians would see to that." Captain Morgan turned again to the Chief. "The little white flower is drooping," he said, slowly. "The wilderness path is too rough for her tender feet. Will you not send her back to her native soil?"

"By the River Genesee, the soil is black and rich," said Burning Sky, with sternness in his voice. "A plant is nourished by the soil it feeds on, by the winds that blow, the rains that fall and the sun that shines. The little white flower has put her roots down deep. She takes nourishment and strength from the same sun, rain and wind that give life to the Senecas. If she were transplanted again, she would wither and die."

"I wonder how much she has forgotten," said the Englishman. Then he added, as if to himself: "If only I could make her speak . . ." He stared at the girl as he might have stared at a hard green bud waiting for it to unfold and open.

"*Our Father Which art in Heaven . . .*" he began, slowly, then he kept on to the end of the prayer which every English-speaking child could say by heart.

The words were enough. They were enough to unlock all the doors of memory. After the first sentence, Molly began to tremble. Then she looked up and followed each movement of the man's lips to the end. She ran to him swiftly and knelt at his knees.

"Ma used to say that over and over," she cried out in English. "Oh tell me, sir, what does it mean? I can't seem to remember any more. They make me talk always in Indian. I've had no one to talk to in English since Josiah went away . . ." Like a hard rainstorm pelting the dry earth the words came pouring, then as quickly died away.

In the back of the room, Molly saw the other white men and Burning Sky's sachems staring at her and she could not bear it.

"I thought so," said Captain Morgan. "I knew she was English." He pulled a handful of gold pieces from his pocket. He held them out to Chief Burning Sky.

"How much do you want for her?" he asked bluntly. "Any ransom that you may name I will gladly pay."

Not till then did Molly know that the Englishman wanted to take her away. In the back of the room Old

Shagbark was standing. She hated the Englishman's smile. She wanted to run to the safety of Shagbark's arms—Old Shagbark who could always be trusted.

"I'll take her to Fort Niagara," she heard the Englishman saying. "I shall give her a good home and every advantage. She will be happier among people of her own kind."

Chief Burning Sky rose up. Like a tall, strong oak tree, braced against the storm, he stood.

"The Senecas do not sell or exchange captives," he said in a hard, cold voice. "After adoption, the captive is a full-blooded Seneca. To surrender this child would be to give up an Iroquois to the English. It is indeed a noble privilege to be chosen an Iroquois by adoption. She is flesh of our flesh and blood of our blood. We will part with our hearts sooner than with this child."

"May I not speak to her family?" asked Captain Morgan.

"It would be of no use," replied Burning Sky. "They took her to replace their son who died on the Pennsylvania frontier. They love her as they loved him. They will never give her up."

Chief Burning Sky and Captain Morgan walked out of the council house, each followed by his men.

"I must go," cried Molly, trying to free herself from the man's hand.

Then Squirrel Woman appeared from nowhere. Squirrel Woman saw the white girl captive in the midst of the men who had met for secret counsel. With scowling looks, she descended upon Molly and pulled her to one side.

"She won't hurt you, will she?" demanded the Englishman.

The words were the same as those spoken by the man in blue at Fort Duquesne. Why did the pale-faces always doubt the Indians and suspect them of cruelty and unkindness? Didn't they know that a captive was treated the same as an Indian child? Didn't they know how kind the Indians were to their own people?

Molly looked from Squirrel Woman's scowling face into the Englishman's friendly one, but she could find no English words to say. And even if she could find the words, she wondered if she could make him understand.

With a feeling of happy relief, she walked away with the Indian woman, ready for whatever punishment might come.

XV   *The Rattlesnake*

Don't catch that little fish by mistake!" cried
Molly. "He wouldn't taste good for supper."

"I won't!" answered Turkey Feather.

Molly watched Blue Jay swim. He was a real boy already. How well he deserved his new name, Blue Trout,
for he slipped through the water as easily as a fish. From
the very first moment when Turkey Feather put him in
deep water, keeping his hand under his chest, Blue Trout
had begun to paddle with his hands and kick out with his
feet. Now he swam alone, for all the world like a little
trout.

"He'll soon be shooting fish like you," said Molly.

"It won't be long!" cried Turkey Feather.

A group of boys waded in the shallow waters at the
river side. Turkey Feather was shooting small fish with his
bow and arrow, while Chipmunk and Woodchuck
reached down under the stones to the places where the fish
lay hidden and pulled them out with their hands.

"Soon Blue Jay will be shooting with a boy's bow and arrow!" said Molly.

"But he'll have to wait many moons before he gets a man's," added Turkey Feather.

"And after that, in no time at all, he'll grow up to be a great hunter and a warrior!" cried Molly.

Two canoes came silently round the bend in the river. They were paddled by Shining Star and Squirrel Woman and were loaded with children.

"Where are you going?" called Turkey Feather.

"To the hills to pick huckleberries," answered Shining Star. "We want Corn Tassel. Do you boys want to go, too?"

Turkey Feather looked at the other boys, who shook their heads. "Let the girls pick berries," they shouted. "We like fishing and swimming and diving better." "Besides," added Turkey Feather, "we are to bring plenty of fish home for cooking."

"Wait until I catch Blue Trout," called Molly.

She walked into the shallow water, picked up the dripping baby, as squirmy and wiggly as an eel, and held him tight in her arms. Then she waded to Shining Star's canoe.

"I will pick berries, too!" cried Blue Trout, happily.

After going a short distance, the canoes turned into a smaller creek and wound about among cat-tails and rushes. Passing a marshy meadow, they soon came to higher land, where rough, broken hills covered with small trees and low brush, came down to meet the stream. Here the women beached their canoes on the shore and, with the children, stepped out.

Star Flower cried at once, "I will take Lazy Duck, Beaver Girl and Gray Mouse. We will fill our baskets more quickly than all the rest of you put together."

"Very well," answered Molly, looking at the little girls—Storm Cloud, Pine Bough and Red Leaf.

"Follow the creek," said Shining Star. "Do not wander away from the sound of flowing water. If you go too far into the hills and underbrush, you may not be able to find your way back again." She passed out baskets and the children quickly scattered.

Picking up her large splint basket and another smaller one, Molly started out. The little girls followed along behind with Blue Jay, chattering contentedly. They walked across the boggy shore, then up on the drier hillside, where clumps of barberry, hardhack, and sweet fern grew in a tangle of undergrowth. Here rose up huge huckleberry bushes, loaded with sun-ripened blue berries.

"All day we shall stay, Little Trout," said Molly happily.

As the burden strap fell loosely across her palm, she looked down at it. Its beauty never failed to please her. Diagonal stripes of yellow, red and blue in delicate moosehair covered the forehead portion. "Red for the falling leaves," she murmured to herself, "blue for the sky, and yellow for Corn Tassel's hair—all woven together with kindness." Molly looked at the burden strap's beautiful workmanship, and love for Earth Woman, Shagbark, and

Turkey Feather flooded her heart. She placed the big basket on her back and the strap across her forehead.

"Come, children!" she cried. "We must hurry and fill our baskets. We must not let Star Flower beat us."

Thick and full the berries grew in clusters. Molly held her basket under and with swift, careful movements, stripped them off the bushes and watched them fall. When the small splint basket was full she emptied it into the larger one on her back.

Faithfully, little Blue Trout followed at her heels. He picked berries, too, and brought them to Molly. One by one he dropped them from his chubby brown hand into the small basket, laughing and chuckling with glee. Storm Cloud, Pine Bough and Red Leaf ran back and forth picking busily. A short distance away, Molly could see the two women working and farther still, Star Flower and the other girls.

As the sun rose higher and the hot hillside grew hotter, the children's chatter grew fainter. Farther and farther off they wandered. Molly worked fast. Her thoughts were as busy as her hands, for whenever her hands had work to do, her thoughts could travel far away—back to Marsh Creek Hollow.

For a time she did not miss Blue Trout's bubbling words. She did not miss his help in the filling of her basket, or the sight of his chubby, bare body marching back and forth on two sturdy legs. There were berries like these on a hillside near Marsh Creek. Each year at mid-summer, she and Betsey went together to pick them. Would she ever pick berries with Betsey again?

"Corn Tassel! Corn Tassel!"

It was Storm Cloud calling, in a voice of sudden distress.

Swiftly Molly came back from dreaming and ran to the place where the small Indian girl, with a black frown on her face, was standing. But before Molly could ask a question, she saw Blue Jay and her heart leaped into her throat. He was still her baby, Blue Jay. No matter how old he grew and what splendid names he earned, to Molly he would always be Blue Jay.

A sharp, rattling sound pierced her ear and made her tremble from head to toe. She gasped, for she saw the small, straight, brown-backed baby walking straight into danger. There, not four feet away, ahead in his path, lay a deadly snake, its tail held erect in the circle of its coiled body. Its sharp eye gleamed with wicked ugliness in the head held low in front of the S-curved neck, as the angry reptile prepared to strike. The rattles vibrated again. Molly shivered with fear.

"So coils the forked-tongue, whose bite is like the sting of bad arrows . . ." Earth Woman's words came back to her clearly. "The heedless man will close his eyes in sleep, unless quickly he obtains help of our brother, the ash tree . . ." But he must not strike, he shall not strike, thought Molly.

On the ground at her feet lay a large stone. Quickly she picked it up. Overtaking Blue Jay in a few steps, she threw it, swift and sure, with all the force of her strength, with all the power of her love for the Indian baby. "His

eyes shall not close in sleep . . . his eyes shall not close . . .
he shall live to be a great warrior . . ."

As the snake began to twist and turn, Molly felt suddenly faint and sick inside. "To be sick is weakness,"
Turkey Feather had said. Then she knew that she had no
time to be sick, no time to faint.

She snatched up the Indian baby and clutched him
fiercely to her breast. She saw the snake wriggle off into the
brush and escape—the blow of the stone had merely
stunned it. With a tremendous relief she was glad she had
not killed it. She turned and ran down the hillside. She saw

Storm Cloud running, too, still frowning, dragging her basket behind her, spilling half the berries. At the bottom of the hill the women and the rest of the children came running and crowded close around her. When she caught her breath, she heard what Storm Cloud was saying:

"Blue Jay wanted to pick up the pretty snake, but Corn Tassel threw a stone and made it go away."

Then they all began talking at once, and above the loud babble, she heard Beaver Girl's words. "You are not hurt?" cried Beaver Girl. "Oh, I should have stayed with you. You are not hurt?"

"It was a rattlesnake," said Squirrel Woman, briefly. "When you hear a warning rattle, you must run the other way. You must call at once for help. Blue Jay is old enough to learn . . ."

"But he's only a baby . . ." cried Molly, indignant. "How could he know?"

"A boy of two is old enough to know that the snake's rattle means danger!" replied Squirrel Woman, crossly.

"We've picked the most berries," announced Star Flower, but nobody heard her. The number of berries picked seemed somehow no longer a matter of importance.

"Come, we will go home," said Shining Star.

"But Panther Woman will scold!" protested Star Flower. "She wants the baskets full, so she can dry them all for winter!"

Molly did not speak. But she saw Shining Star, with sparkling eyes, pick up her boy and all the way back in the canoe hold him close. Though Shining Star spoke no word, Molly knew she had her thanks.

Molly took the paddle of Shining Star's canoe herself. It was the first time the women had allowed her to take it, the first time she had ever paddled a loaded canoe. Smiling to herself she reached out with the paddle, and the canoe seemed to be taking her into unknown waters, but oh how glad she was to go! New strength and sureness were hers to make her path easier no matter where it led.

When they returned to the village, even Star Flower forgot to boast of the berries picked. Little Storm Cloud told her story over and over: "Blue Jay wanted to pick up the pretty snake, but Corn Tassel threw a stone and made it go away."

"But I thought it made you sick to see an animal killed or injured," said Turkey Feather astonished.

"I forgot about that," said Molly smiling a little. "I thought of only one thing—that Blue Jay was in danger and I must not let the snake strike."

"You were in danger, too!" said Turkey Feather, softly.

"I?" repeated Molly. "Oh, no, I was behind Blue Jay."

"I wish now I'd gone to pick berries," said Turkey Feather. "I'd like to have seen you do that. You showed more courage than an Indian girl—an Indian girl would have run away."

"I'm glad the snake didn't strike *you!*" cried Beaver Girl.

"When someone we love is in danger," said Old Shagbark, "the Great Spirit makes us strong and gives us courage."

Molly could almost hear her mother speaking and the

words were much like Shagbark's: "It don't matter what happens, if you're only strong and have great courage."

"You went straight into danger . . ." now it was Shining Star speaking, "you thought not once of yourself . . . and you saved my son's life. No member of Blue Jay's family can ever forget. As long as you live, you will have our gratitude and his!"

Molly looked from one face to the other in surprise. Was there once a time when she had distrusted these, her dear friends? If there had ever been such a time, from this day on, it was wiped out and forever gone. The tears came now, long after the danger was over.

"Why, this don't sound like a white gal at all! Don't tell me a white gal's won praise from the Senecas for bravery and courage. 'Tain't possible, is it?"

It was a white man speaking in English. Molly forgot her tears and looked up in surprise. All the Indians, men, women and children, were gathered close about her, but through the crowd, a white man came pushing. Over Turkey Feather's and Beaver Girl's heads she saw a raccoon skin cap, with its striped tail waving in the air. Above a fringed deerskin hunting-shirt, she saw a man's weather-beaten face all wreathed in smiles. But even before he caught her in his arms and she looked up into his eyes, she knew that it was Old Fallenash, the white trader.

"But I thought you were dead!" she cried. "I thought you'd never be able to come again."

"They ain't scalped me yet," said Fallenash, with a twinkle in his eye, "and even after they put me under the ground, like as not I'll be popping up again. Yes, I made out to come. I had to come to see you, Molly. I came a long way round just to see you. Laws-a-massy, seems like I been most halfway round the world!"

"Have you brought news?" asked Molly, breathless.

"No news I might have brought could please me like the news the Indians have just been tellin'," cried Fallenash, heartily. "When they praise you for courage, Molly, it means you've got the real thing."

"But I didn't do anything . . ."

"Oh, come now, I heard it all," laughed Fallenash, "so you needn't try to be modest. They've took ye to their hearts now. They've bound ye to themselves tighter today than any adoption ceremony could do it. They've made ye one of themselves. You can do no better from now on than to make your home with them."

"You've not come then to take me back?" asked Molly. Her heart stood still while she waited for his answer.

"No, child, and I'll tell you why," said Fallenash quickly. "'Cause you ain't got no home to go to—your home's right here."

"No home?" cried Molly, lifting her hand to her trembling lips.

The Indians wandered off to their lodges and left the two alone. The trader took Molly by the hand and together, in silence, they walked to the river bank. There Molly listened to his words:

"Yes, Molly Jemison, child, it's sad news for ye I've brought. I'm glad to hear from the Indians that you're a gal of courage, for you'll need all the strength and courage you can fetch. I wouldn't tell ye a word, if I thought you couldn't bear it, but I know you're strong both in body and in heart. You've lived with the Senecas goin' on two years now and it's made you strong and well-hardened. I could see it in your eyes, even if they hadn't told me."

"Has anything happened?" cried Molly. Her throat was dry and the words came low. "Have you had bad news? Have you been there—to Marsh Creek Hollow?"

"Yes, I have news and it ain't good, Molly, but hold up your chin and I'll tell ye." He fumbled nervously with his powder horn, then held it up.

"Take a look here, will ye? I've scratched out a map upon it. Here's Marsh Creek Holler and there's Conewago Creek and Sharp's Run. Here's the mountain ranges they took ye over and there's where Fort Duquesne used to be but ain't no more. Now, foller the River Susquehanna up north here, then skip over west and there's Genesee Town by the great Falling Waters, where ye be standin' this minute."

"Yes," said Molly, "and . . ."

"I've been back there," said Fallenash, bluntly, "back to Marsh Creek Holler, since I saw ye last." His words came fast now, as if their fleetness could balance the pain they would bring. "I met Neighbor Dixon and he took me over. Your Pa's house and barn was burned the minute you got out of sight, with everything in 'em . . ."

"The beds and Ma's two spinning-wheels and the loom and . . . ?"

"Everything!" Fallenash continued. "Dixon told me how your two older brothers came and roused him, sayin' the whole two families was took, your Pa's and Mrs. Wheelock's. He got the neighbors together and they started hot on your trail . . ."

"I knew they were following," said Molly, trembling.

"They follered too close," said Fallenash, sadly. "It would have been better for your folks if the neighbors had stayed to home. They follered too close for the Indians' comfort. That's why the Indians took you and the Wheelock boy and left the others behind . . . and killed them . . ."

"Killed them?" gasped Molly. "All this time . . . they've never been alive at all?"

"They've never been alive since the day after you left them," said Fallenash, in a low voice. "You see, the Indians couldn't get away fast enough with so many prisoners. They were afraid the pale-faces might catch up. You're lucky to be alive, gal, and still in your skin."

Molly hid her face in her two hands. She cried out, in a muffled tone: "Then I'll never see them again . . . Pa and Ma and Betsey and the boys and the little ones?"

"Your two older brothers might be alive somewhere," said Fallenash, with sorrow in his voice. "Nobody knows. They ran off to the southward, so Dixon thought. But, for the others, their troubles are well over. They didn't suffer the half of what you did, gal!"

"You can't take me then . . ." said Molly, slowly. She looked up and in her eyes there were no tears. "Because I've no home or family to go to . . ."

"You're right, I can't!" said Fallenash. Then in a relieved tone, he added laughing: "Oh, Molly, I most forgot to tell you. My Indian woman's got a baby—an Indian baby as brown as any in this village. Won't it be funny for him to call Old Fallenash Pa?"

"An Indian baby of your own?" asked Molly, with a crooked smile.

"Yes," said Fallenash. Then he began to boast: "I'll teach him to shoot with bow and arrows. I'll teach him to dance and beat a drum. I'll make a great warrior out o' him. By the way, I won't be seein' you again . . ."

"Oh, Fallenash, where are you going?" cried Molly.

"Them English—they keep me on the run," said Fallenash, his sharp eyes flashing. "Wherever I go, the French and the English foller me and start their fightin'. I only come back this way to bring ye the news, 'cause I figgered ye ought to know and not go on hopin' and makin' yourself miserable to the end of your days."

"Yes, it is better to know," said Molly, "and not go on hoping."

"Now I've got to move on," said Fallenash. "I always had a hankerin' to try the climate of Quebec so we're takin' a little canoe ride, me and my family. When them English take Quebec, only the Lord knows what'll become of Old Fallenash."

"Then where will you go?" asked Molly.

"I'll find a little corner somewhere, where there ain't no French or English to bother—me and my Indian woman and my little warrior! We can look out for ourselves. Don't worry none 'bout us."

"Thank you for coming such a long way just to tell me," said Molly. "I'd have liked to see your Indian baby . . ."

"Try to be happy!" said Fallenash, kindly. "You ain't so bad off, after all."

"This is the only home I have now," said Molly. She watched the trader start off. "I hope you'll find some place to go to, after they take Quebec . . ."

She waved her hand till he was out of sight. "How good he is!" she said to herself. Then, like a young thin sapling, broken by cruel winds, she sank to the ground.

XVI *Born of a Long Ripening*

Several days later, at noon, Molly walked slowly to the spring, carrying her water vessel. She wore the new cloth garments which Shining Star had made for her. She studied the embroidered tree pattern on her skirt as she walked along. At the spring, she was surprised to see Gray Wolf waiting.

"The English Captain has come," he announced.

"Who? What?" asked Molly.

"Captain Morgan has come with a message from Sir William Johnson to Chief Burning Sky. Sir William Johnson is glad to know that he can count on the help of the People of the Long House. He sends word that Quebec has been taken by the English and all the French soldiers have been withdrawn. Soon he will be raiding the frontier settlements and sending out war parties."

"What is that to me?" said Molly, with scorn in her voice. "With war I have nothing to do. That is the affair of the Chief and the sachems. Go, speak to them." She shivered, then bent over to fill her vessel, so that she might hurry back.

Gray Wolf jumped up and took her roughly by the arm. "Come, little Pale-Face!" he commanded. "I will take you to him."

Molly dropped her vessel of water. In a flood it poured over her feet.

"What?" she cried out. "Where will you take me?"

"To the fine English Captain, whose name is Morgan, *you* know!" said Gray Wolf sneering. "He *says* he comes with a message from Sir William Johnson, but we all know

283

that he comes to take back the pretty captive, whose hair shines like gold in the sun and who has found great favor in the Captain's eyes. He will take her back with him to Fort Niagara and give her a home. You wish to return to the pale-faces, do you not?"

Not once since bidding Fallenash farewell had Molly thought of leaving the Indians. Not once since the Englishman in red went away, had she given him a single thought. Now that he was back, she was surprised and startled.

"You wish to go back to the pale-faces, do you not?" asked Gray Wolf again.

"No! Oh, no!" cried Molly, backing up. "I don't want to go with the Englishman."

"Come, little Pale-Face!" commanded Gray Wolf. "You shall go whether you wish to or not. Ever since you were first adopted, you have been trying to go back to the pale-faces. Squirrel Woman has caught you talking to them time and again. You've tried to run away more than once and I know it. Now that the Englishman will pay gold . . . I mean, now that the Englishman wants to take you . . ."

"But I don't want to go!" cried Molly. "I want to stay here!"

Seeing Gray Wolf advancing toward her, she stumbled over her water vessel, turned and ran.

"You can't run away from me, little Pale-Face!"

She heard the man's angry words and heavy breathing

behind her. Through the meadow to the corn-field, like a chased rabbit she ran. Then into the corn-field, the friendly corn-field, darting about among the corn-hills as fast as she could go. The sharp edges of the green leaves lashed her in the face, but after she passed, they concealed her. Gradually she slackened her pace, when she saw that she was not being followed. Gray Wolf had found difficulty ducking through and under the leafy corn-stalks. Gray Wolf's feet were clumsy and tottery. He went back to the village without his pale-face, doubtless thinking up some other plan.

Trembling, Molly returned to Red Bird's lodge. There she found Shining Star alone and poured out her story.

"Yes, I know!" cried Shining Star, in anger. "Gray Wolf says he will sell you for gold pieces. He wishes to take you to Captain Morgan himself. I will tell you why. He wishes to get his hands on the gold pieces, go to Fort Niagara and fit himself out in a white man's suit. He will go to Fort Niagara and buy fire-water which lies sweet on the tongue.

"Oh, that we had never seen the face of an Englishman . . . Oh, that we had never promised to fight with them . . ." Shining Star walked back and forth, overcome with anger. Molly looked at her in surprise. She had never seen her angry before.

"But Corn Tassel," the Indian woman stopped and spoke gently, "I have good news for you. The Chief and sachems have met in council and have given orders that you are not to be sold without your own consent. You may stay here quietly and undisturbed, if you choose."

"Will he soon be back?" asked Molly, full of fear. "Will Gray Wolf soon be back?"

"He will look for you everywhere," replied Shining Star, quickly. "So you must hide."

"Shall I go and sleep on the pole platform in the cornfield?"

"No, Corn Tassel, that would not be safe," said Shining Star. "He saw you go into the corn. He will look for you there. No—go down to the creek. Go down where the rushes grow and hide there till evening. After dark, come back to the lodge. I will bake a small cake and put it here, outside the door, if there is danger. If you see no cake, you may come in and sleep in your bed. If the cake is there, take it with you and go back to the creek. Wait there till by some means you hear from me again."

Molly ran fast to the water's edge and hid in the weeds and rushes. She found a dry stone to sit upon and rest, but the pounding in her heart would not be stilled. It seemed to shout and tell the world where she was hiding. She pressed her hand upon her breast, but could not stop the beating.

When darkness fell, she crept back to the lodge, where all was silent. There on the threshold, she saw a little cake lying. The cake told her that Gray Wolf was near, waiting for her, waiting to take her to the Englishman. Seizing the cake, she ran back to the creek to her hiding-place.

The night was worse than the night on the pole platform. Then the rustling, whispering corn had spoken to her in comfort. Now, on the hard stone, she could only crouch in weariness. Queer sounds on all sides came to haunt her—the sounds of night breezes among the rushes, night movements of flying birds and creeping animals. Mosquitoes buzzed and bit incessantly, making sleep impossible. But worse than discomfort was her own fear. Would Gray Wolf manage to find her and sell her to the Englishman?

Dawn came up red over the marshy creek and Molly ate her little cake. Still she waited, as the sun rose higher and higher. Sometime after midday, her hope returned, for, hurrying through the tall grasses came Beaver Girl, carrying bread in a small basket.

"Chief Burning Sky has sent for you!" said Beaver Girl, sadly. "Shining Star says you are to come at once."

"Chief Burning Sky!" cried Molly. "What does he want with me? Is Gray Wolf there?"

"I know nothing of Gray Wolf," said Beaver Girl, sobbing. "All I know is that the Chief has sent for you, because the Englishman in red is there. Turkey Feather says he has come to take you away and I won't have my white sister any more."

"But must I go?" demanded Molly. "Must I go away with the Englishman?"

"Don't you want to go, then?" cried Beaver Girl, in astonishment. "Turkey Feather says that for many moons you have cried to go back to the pale-faces and it is right you should go . . ."

"Yes, it is right that I should go," said Molly, thoughtfully. "The Englishman said he would take me to Fort Niagara to live with people of my own kind."

"Oh, how can I live without you?" cried Beaver Girl, sobbing afresh.

"Weeping is weakness," said Molly, sternly. "An Indian girl should be strong and well-hardened. Turkey Feather said so."

"But how can I be strong and hard," cried Beaver Girl, "when I love you so much?"

Molly hadn't gone far into the village, when Turkey Feather came running to meet her.

"I spoke to Chief Burning Sky," he said, solemnly, "about the trouble which lies so heavily on your heart. He listened and said it would all be arranged. I'm *glad* you're going back to the pale-faces, where there will be no need to drown your sorrow in tears. I'm glad you will always be happy, even if you won't see me go off with the men . . ."

"Go off with the men?" asked Molly. "What do you mean?"

"The Chief says I'm to go with the men on their autumn hunt down the River Allegheny!" Turkey Feather's chest puffed out with pride.

"You are!" cried Molly, in excitement. "You're to go just like a man?"

"'When a man has killed a deer, then he is a great hunter!' You heard Grandfather Shagbark say that," replied Turkey Feather. "But I only wanted to prove to *you* what a great hunter I am, and now you will not be here to see me go—or return with the game . . ."

Then, suddenly, Shining Star was standing by Molly's side.

"Gray Wolf—where is he?" cried Molly, fearfully.

"He came last night, just after you left," said Shining Star, calmly. "He searched for you through the lodge and the village. He was very angry when he could not find you. Since the rising of the sun he has been searching in the corn-field. We will go now to the Chief. He will settle the matter—before Gray Wolf returns."

On the way to the council house, all the children came running up—Star Flower, Storm Cloud, Gray Mouse, Lazy Duck, Chipmunk, Woodchuck and the two smallest, Little Snail and Blue Trout. They hung on Molly's arms and clung to her skirts.

"Oh, Corn Tassel," they cried. "Do not go away and leave us." "We love you, Corn Tassel. You are our gentle, sympathetic sister." "We shall never be happy again if you go away and leave us . . ."

Impatiently, Molly tried to shake them off. She wanted to be free of their clinging arms and bodies. She wanted to be free of all their claims upon her, free of their loving devotion, so she could think. Now, at last, her time had come—the time she had waited for so long, her chance to go. Josiah had had his chance and, without hesitation, he had taken it. Now hers had come. What should she do?

"Are you going to leave us, Corn Tassel?" cried the children.

"I don't know . . . oh, I don't know . . ." she said, slowly.

"Don't leave us! Don't leave us! Don't leave us!" The children's cries kept ringing in her ears as she left them beside the door and entered the council house. She took one fleeting glance round the room. The Chief was there, the sachems and warriors, but not only these—the women were there, too—Panther Woman, Red Bird, Earth Woman, and all the others. The council house was filled with faces and all of them were staring at her.

Then she saw the white man, dressed in red—a red so red it almost hurt her eyes. She saw gold lace and shining buttons of brass, and then above, his smiling face.

"Captain Morgan has come to us from Sir William Johnson." Molly turned her eyes away from the shining red to hear what the Chief was saying. "He brings a message of thanks for our offer to join forces with the English."

Chief Burning Sky paused, then went on: "It has not been our policy, heretofore, to sell or exchange captives, as you know, for we consider our adopted captives our own flesh and blood. But now that we fight with the English, our policy has altered. Sir William Johnson says that as soon as the French are subdued, all white captives in the hands of the Iroquois will be given up by treaty agreement. Since this is undoubtedly true, it would seem the better part of wisdom to listen to Captain Morgan's offer. Because the treaty has not yet been drawn, Captain Morgan has generously offered to ransom you himself.

"The sachems and I have decided in council to give you your freedom, if you desire it. If you do not desire it, you may stay quietly and undisturbed with us for the rest of your life. You are not to be sold without your own consent."

Sold! The word hit Molly like the sharp sting of an arrow from a tightened bow. Looking up, she saw Gray Wolf's face against the bark wall, leering down at her. When had he come? Was he waiting to get the money? Was he already holding out his greedy hand to the Englishman?

Sold! A white girl sold—to buy Gray Wolf a white man's suit at Fort Niagara, to buy Gray Wolf fire-water to turn him into a worse beast than he was! Molly's breast heaved up and down with righteous anger. Her eyes flashed as she stared at the man's wicked face against the bark wall.

But the Chief was speaking again. She turned to him and looked up into his face. There she saw real sorrow, which moved her deeply, as she drank in his words:

"My daughter, these are men of the same color as yourself, who speak the language you spoke in childhood. Soon a treaty will be signed which says you must go free. But you need not wait for that. Captain Morgan offers you a home and every comfort of the pale-faces, if you wish to go.

"My daughter, for many moons you have lived with us. I call upon you to say if Red Bird has not been a mother to you; if she has not treated you as a mother would a daughter of her own? I call on you to say if Shining Star and Squirrel Woman have not treated you as sisters?"

"Red Bird has been a mother to me," said Molly, in a low voice. "Shining Star and Squirrel Woman have been like my own sisters."

A murmuring sound ran through the crowd of waiting Indians like the hum of a rising storm, then died away, as the Chief spoke:

"My heart rejoices to hear you say so, my daughter. The women have taught you many things. They have taught you to grow corn, to prepare food, to care for the younger children, to tan skins and make clothing. Earth Woman, who has no daughter, has taught you an old, old art—how to make fine pots of grace and beauty. You mean as much to Earth Woman as if you were her daughter. She is growing old—you will be a support to her in her old age. She will lean on you as upon a staff. If you are going to leave us, we have no right to say a word, but we are broken-hearted. I speak for the women. I speak for the children. I speak for the men and boys, and for myself."

A vision of Earth Woman's kind face rose up before Molly's eyes. She remembered the look of pain upon it when Running Deer went away, never to return. Could she, who loved her so much, bring her still more sorrow?

"With us for many moons you have made your

home," continued the Chief. "With us you have eaten bread and meat. When we have had plenty, you have shared in it. When we have had nothing, you, too, have known the pinch of hunger. You have learned what giving is, without thought of return. You have learned what truth and courage are. By the hardships which you have suffered with us, you have learned bravely to live and, because of that, when your time comes, you will the more bravely die.

"If, my daughter, you choose to take the hand of this man of your own color and follow the path where he leads, I have no right to say a word. But if you choose to stay with the Senecas, then the pale-faces have no right to speak. Whatever you choose, no pale-face, no Seneca, shall change your decision. Now reflect upon it and take your choice and tell us. It shall be as you decide. I have spoken."

The room was very still. It was still with all the silence of complete emptiness, as if no man breathed or moved or stirred. It was still with the silence of mingled hope and fear, for hope and fear, with desperate strength, struggled against each other in the breasts of the waiting Indians.

Molly thought of everything, and yet it seemed as if the turmoil in her mind was so great, she could not think at all. She thought of the children she had just left crying at the door. She thought of her special friends—Turkey Feather, Beaver Girl, Shining Star and Earth Woman. She thought of her home and family, her parents, brothers and sisters—all gone, never to be recovered. She thought of the Englishman in red and his smiling face. She looked at him and he was speaking—speaking to her only, in English, so that the Indians might not understand.

"My child, you were torn away from home and family by the ruthless Indians," he said, speaking fast.

"Don't let their fine words blind you to the crime which they committed against you, in destroying your family, in stealing you away from your home, from white people. Don't fool yourself, or let them fool you into thinking that you can forgive them. You may at the moment, but later you will come to hatred. You will never stop hating till you have had your revenge.

"These Indians, who profess to be so friendly, have caused you to suffer every hardship—hunger, sickness, pain and distress. They are a cruel, relentless, wicked and savage people. They are revengeful and cannot be trusted. They are letting you grow up, an untamed savage, like a wild animal in the forest. They will marry you to an Indian whom you cannot love; your children will be Indian children, who will be hated by the white people.

"From this, my child, I will take you away. I shall give you a good home, send you to a school to acquire education and a polish of good manners. I shall give you all the benefits of civilized life. I shall make a lady out of you. Surely you would prefer to be a cultivated lady rather than a savage! Surely there is only one choice you can make!"

His words brought back to Molly a picture of the woman in shining silk at Fort Duquesne. What if she had stayed there as she had so much wanted to do? She wondered what life with the white people would be like—rich people, who wore not homespun, but silk in glistening, bright colors.

Then she remembered the Englishman's words. He was right. It was true. She was an untamed savage, growing up like a wild beast in the forest. She looked for a moment at the open palm of her hand and saw how hard and calloused it was—from work. It would never lie soft and idle on shining silk. She was not meant to grace a rich man's home—to be an elegant lady. An inner conviction told her so.

At that moment she saw Old Shagbark looking at her, his brown eyes overflowing with kindness and understanding. He knew how hard it was for her to decide. She did not need to say a word—he knew what was going on in her mind. She saw the Englishman, too. His lips were smiling, but his eyes of cold gray were hard. Even if she were able to put all her thoughts into words, she knew he would never, never understand. Better to live with those who understood her because they loved her so much, than with one who could never think with her, in sympathy, about anything. Better to stay where she belonged, with the Indians who loved and understood her, and whom she could always love and understand in return. Squirrel Woman's scowling face and even Gray Wolf's wicked one no longer held any terrors, because she understood them.

Perhaps the Englishman was right—she ought to hate the Indians for the crime which they had committed against her—but in her heart there was no feeling of revenge, no hate. It was only war that she hated—war which set nation against nation; the French against the English, and the poor Indians between them both. It was war which had deprived her of her family. As she had suffered once in losing her family, so did the Indians suffer like losses, over and over. Her loss was no greater than theirs.

No, by coming to the Indians, she was the richer. She had learned much that she might not otherwise have learned. No matter what lay in store for her, she was willing now to go out to meet it. All that she had suffered in coming to the Indians would make the rest of her life easy by comparison. No pain, no sorrow which the future held, would be too great to bear. She was sister to the animals, to all growing things; she was sister to the Indians, because she had suffered pain with them. Because her pain had been so great, she would be sister to the suffering as long as she lived. Washed clean by pain, she faced the future unafraid.

Molly turned and faced the assembled people. She held out her arms.

"I cannot go!" she said, in a clear, steady voice. "I wish to stay. The Senecas are my people. I will live and die with the Senecas."

There was no hesitation. The words came with deliberate calm. Her decision was made. It was a decision born of a long ripening and so there was no faltering, no regret.

A hubbub of excitement filled the council house. Cries

and exclamations were heard on all sides. The Englishman stalked out without ceremony, followed by his men and Gray Wolf.

Shining Star whispered in Molly's ear: "Gray Wolf did not earn his gold pieces, after all. But he goes to Fort Niagara with Captain Morgan just the same. The Englishman has promised him a white man's suit and all the fire-water he can drink. We are well rid of them both." Outside, Molly heard little Blue Trout cry out: "Corn Tassel is going to stay!" The other children took up the chorus: "Corn Tassel is going to stay—Corn Tassel is going to stay with us!"

As Chief Burning Sky raised his hand, the people quieted down. "Your name, Corn Tassel," said he, "was given to you by the women on the day when your two sisters brought you to us, because your hair is the color of the tassel on the corn. But now you have earned your real name.

"By the sympathy, perseverance and courage which you have shown since you came among us, by your willingness to give up the life of a white woman cheerfully to become an Indian Woman, you have earned the name, *Little-Woman-of-Great Courage*. Cherish this name and do not tarnish it. Like this piece of silver, cut in delicate design, which I bestow upon you, keep it shining bright."

He placed a delicately wrought silver bracelet upon her slender wrist. "You are now a woman, and the women of our tribe will welcome you as one of themselves. Welcome to the Senecas, Little-Woman-of-Great-Courage."

Again Molly heard her mother's voice speaking and the words sounded like an echo of Chief Burning Sky's: "It don't matter what happens, if you're only strong and have great courage."

Molly went out of the council house, surrounded by her happy, smiling friends. The children came running joyously to meet her. Swiftly she caught up little Blue Trout and held him to her breast.

Inside, her heart was singing: "Oh, Ma! You are pleased, too, I know—with your Little-Woman-of-Great-Courage!"

Silver Bracelet

BIBLIOGRAPHY

Canfield, W. W.—*Legends of the Iroquois*, 1902.

Curtin, Jeremiah—*Seneca Indian Myths*, 1922.

Howe, Henry—*Historical Collections of Ohio*, 1902.

Hubbard, J. Niles, and Minard, J. S.—*Sketches of Border Adventures in the Life and Times of Major Moses Van Campen*, 1893.

Morgan, Lewis H.—*The League of the Iroquois*, Vols. I and II, 1851.

Parker, Arthur C.—*Analytical Study of Seneca Indians*, 1926.

——— —*Life of Ely S. Parker*, 1919.

——— —*Seneca Myths and Folk-Tales*, 1923.

Phelps, Martha Bennett—*Frances Slocum, The Lost Sister of Wyoming*, 1916.

Quaife, Milo Milton (Editor)—*The Indian Captivity of O. M. Spencer*, 1917.

Seaver, James Everett, M.D.—*Life of Mary Jemison*, 22nd edition, American Scenic & Historic Preservation Society, N. Y., 1925.

Severance, F.H.—*Gilbert Captivities*, 1904.

Tome, Philip—*Thirty Years a Hunter*, 1854.

N. Y. State Hist. Ass'n. Pub.—*History of the State of New York, N. Y.*, 1933.

Vol. I., Chap. III. *The Iroquois.* By A. C. Parker.

——— Chap. IV. *The Civilization of the Red Man*, By A.. C.Parker.

Buffalo Hist. Soc. Pub. Vol. VI.—*The Life of Horatio Jones.* By Geo. H. Harris. Buffalo, N. Y., 1903.

Standard works on American Indian life; publications of Buffalo Historical Society; Rochester Historical Society; New York State Museum Bulletins.

Captivity stories of New England and the Middle West.